LOST 🐾
UNDER A
🐾 LADDER

D1264658

OTHER BOOKS BY LINDA O. JOHNSTON

A SUPERSTITION MYSTERY

LOST  UNDER A LADDER

LINDA O. JOHNSTON

MIDNIGHT INK
WOODBURY, MINNESOTA

Lost Under a Ladder: A Superstition Mystery © 2015 by Linda O. Johnston. All rights reserved. No part of this book may be used or reproduced in any manner whatsoever, including Internet usage, without written permission from Midnight Ink, except in the case of brief quotations embodied in critical articles and reviews.

FIRST EDITION
First Printing, 2014

Book design by Donna Burch-Brown
Cover design by Kevin R. Brown
Cover Illustration: Mary Ann Lasher Dodge
Editing by Connie Hill

Midnight Ink, an imprint of Llewellyn Worldwide Ltd.

Library of Congress Cataloging-in-Publication Data
Johnston, Linda O.
  Lost under a ladder : a superstition mystery / Linda O. Johnston. —First edition.
       p.   cm.
  ISBN 978-0-7387-4077-5
1. Fiancés—Fiction. 2. Dog owners—Fiction. 3. Human-animal relationships—Fiction. 4. Superstition—Fiction. 5. City and town life—Fiction. 6. Murder—Investigation—Fiction. 7. California—Fiction. I. Title. II. Title: Superstition mystery.
  PS3610.O387L67   2014
  813'.6—dc23   2014019584

This is a work of fiction. Names, characters, places, and incidents are either the product of the author's imagination or are used fictitiously, and any resemblance to actual persons living or dead, business establishments, events, or locales is entirely coincidental.

Midnight Ink
Llewellyn Worldwide Ltd.
2143 Wooddale Drive
Woodbury, MN 55125-2989
www.midnightinkbooks.com

Printed in the United States of America

To you, my readers.
And as ever and ever, to my dear husband Fred.
My fingers are crossed that all the good luck in the universe
heads your way, every one of you!

ACKNOWLEDGMENTS

I'm really delighted to be starting this special new Superstition Mystery series! My ongoing thanks to my fantastic agent Paige Wheeler and my wonderful editor Terri Bischoff. Thanks, also, to the members of my long-time, much cherished and currently inactive critique group, Janie Emaus, Heidi Shannon, Marilyn Dennis, and most especially Ann Finnin, who gave me lots to think about while editing my *Lost Under a Ladder* manuscript.

ONE

So this was Destiny.

I'd anticipated that the town I now cruised in my car would look like this, but even so, the pictures I'd seen hadn't done it justice. It was a quaint locale, filled with a myriad of people who appeared to be tourists. They strolled along sidewalks in front of rows of stores, most of which were built in the ornate styles of California Gold Rush days.

Stores with names like Knock-on-Wood Furniture and the Falling Star Gallery would have shouted this town's theme to me if I hadn't already known it.

But did I, Rory Chasen, actually believe in superstitions? Not really. I was here on a personal research mission.

Right now, I drove slowly along the main street, Destiny Boulevard, just looking around. I took my time—not that I had much choice, with all the traffic. I kept my eyes open for the Broken Mirror Bookstore, probably the town's most famous shop. That was where I'd find my answers. I hoped.

"What do you think of this place? Nothing like L.A., is it?" I glanced over at the passenger seat of my car where my dog Pluckie sat. She was just that—plucky. Nimble. Friendly, but sure of herself. She was more than just an adorable little spaniel-terrier mix. She was my closest family.

A rescue dog, she was my model for keeping on going in life, despite adversity.

Naturally, I had fastened Pluckie to the seat using a special front-seat dog carrier with a safety harness—one of the best-selling items in the MegaPets store where I work.

Pluckie barked in what sounded like a positive response to my questions. Or maybe she was just responding to the many dogs outside on the street, walking on leashes at the heels of some of the meandering tourists, letting them know she was there and eager to meet them.

"Okay," I said. "As soon as we find the bookstore, we'll go check into our room, then we'll take a walk, too."

As if mentioning the shop had conjured it, there it was. Of course, that wasn't much of a surprise. I'd already looked up the address and knew which block it was on.

What I hadn't known, though, was that there was a pet store right next door. The sign for the Lucky Dog Boutique materialized just on the other side of the Broken Mirror Bookstore's sign.

"Looks as if we have more than one reason to head back to this area," I told Pluckie, who looked at me with her huge dark eyes and wagged her white-tipped black tail. "Our B&B is supposed to be only a few blocks from here. We'll—"

Before I finished, my cell phone rang and I pressed the button to answer with my Bluetooth setup.

"Hello?"

"Hi, Rory," said Gemma, my closest friend. It was thanks to her that I was here. "Where are you?"

"In Destiny. I just spotted the bookstore."

"Good." She paused. "Are you okay?"

Tears rushed to my eyes at her question—reminding me why I had come. I blinked them away. "Sure. How about you?"

"Fine, of course." Again she seemed to hesitate. "Maybe this wasn't such a good idea."

"Of course it is. Like I told you before, Gemma, I really appreciate all you've done to help me through this, including suggesting that I visit Destiny. I'll be able to put all that silliness behind me once and for all when I learn the truth about superstitions here."

I heard the bravado in my own voice. But, heck, that was in fact why I was here—to learn the truth.

Gemma Grayfield was not only my friend—she was a librarian. She had borrowed the book *The Destiny of Superstitions* for me when I needed more information about the origin—and reality—of superstitions.

That was why I had ended up in this town, on this afternoon. Closer, I hoped, to the answers I needed—able, at last, to get on with my life.

"You'll keep in touch with me, won't you?" she asked. "Let me know what you're up to, what you find out?"

"I told you before I left that I would. Don't worry about me. I needed a break, a vacation, and this is a great getaway."

We chatted for only a minute more before I spotted the Rainbow Bed & Breakfast, the place where I'd reserved a room for several nights for Pluckie and me. "Gotta run now," I told Gemma. "Time to check into our hotel. But I'll be in touch. I promise."

Which I would—when I had something to tell her, not just to hear how she fretted over me.

After pressing the button to end the call, I parked in the lot in the front of the B&B and attached Pluckie's leash. Then, walking under a horseshoe above the door, we entered the ornate, three-story building.

Unsurprisingly in the B&B called Rainbow, there was a pot of gold in the lobby near the small registration desk. It didn't appear to be real gold, of course, but in this town each locale evoked a related superstition. Maybe everyone was entitled to find a pot of gold at the end of the rainbow, as the town's founders were reputed to have done.

Sure they did. Call me a cynic, but that kind of stuff just doesn't make sense to me.

The woman behind the registration desk had a nametag introducing her as Serina Frye, the establishment's owner. I guessed she was about ten years older than my age of thirty-four years. She was dressed in a frilly skirt and blouse that seemed to fit with this town's theme.

Not me, though. I wore a denim shirt tucked into snug jeans. Nor was my hairdo old-fashioned like Serina's soft brown upsweep. Looking at her, I brushed my bangs out of my eyes. They were getting a little long, but I'd had my straight blond hair highlighted and cut recently enough not to need another styling.

"Welcome," she said with a huge smile. We went through all the formalities, I handed her my credit card, and she soon showed Pluckie and me to our room on the second floor. A teenage bellboy followed with my suitcase.

Nice room, but I didn't intend to stay to check it out. Instead, Pluckie and I headed back downstairs almost immediately.

The sun was bright outside, so I put on my sunglasses. We headed toward Destiny's main street. The sidewalks were less crowded than before, but we still couldn't exactly run. I was careful, though, in guiding Pluckie, who pranced beside me. As I'd already noticed, other tourists who were out and about also had leashed canines along, of all breeds and sizes.

That wasn't surprising. Dogs were the subject of a number of superstitions, or so I understood from my reading of *The Destiny of Superstitions* and the other research I'd begun.

Research that included the superstition that had become my focus. My obsession. One I intended to dispel as fast as possible.

But it still wasn't time to think about that. Instead, I started listening. Eavesdropping. Maybe paying attention to the amiable chatter around me would help.

I noticed that some of the gabbing folks kept looking down at the sidewalk. I wondered if the townsfolk purposely made sure there were plenty of cracks in and between the thick paving blocks. Believers here were trying to avoid stepping on them. Maybe even nonbelievers, like me. Which was especially silly on my part. "Step on a crack, break your mother's back" would have no effect in my life. My poor mom had passed away several years ago.

Even so … I didn't want to stand out in this crowd or call attention to myself so, like the others, I stepped over those ridiculous cracks.

I watched Pluckie put her nose in the air to inhale whatever smells doggies could absorb, then against the nose of another pup, a French bulldog, that had stopped to say hi.

I found myself listening, but discussions about which tours on superstitions would be best to take the next day, or which restaurant was the best place for dinner—really, which restaurant name evoked the luck of the best superstition, the Apple-a-Day Café or the Shamrock Steakhouse—weren't especially useful. Even so, I found them interesting.

Eventually, Pluckie and I reached the shop that was our destination.

Our Destiny? Hah!

But before I could lead Pluckie into the bookstore, she instead pulled me toward its next-door neighbor, the pet boutique. In fact, my dog seemed quite insistent about it.

I figured the bookstore could wait.

The Lucky Dog Boutique was especially attractive—a three-story wood frame building, the shop had lots of small paneled windows on each floor. A couple of people exited through the door, walking a large boxer. Or maybe he was walking them. I saw no bags in their hands so they might just have been looky-loos.

I didn't get too many of them in that huge pet supply chain store where I was an assistant manager. Usually people came into Mega-Pets with a purpose: food, toys, accessories, or a combo of them. A boutique was different. It probably showcased clothes and upscale training equipment and more—things expensive and gifty enough that people might have to consider first whether to buy them.

Which of course most would, for their pets. Their beloved family members. Their fur kids.

Before opening the shop door, I took a deep breath. I've worked in retail since getting my undergraduate degree in business administration. I've considered going back for an MBA but haven't gotten around to it. Instead, I've settled myself as an assistant manager in a retail chain store. For now. But I have higher aspirations.

I'm obsessed with pet stores. Intend to own one myself someday, not just run someone else's—no matter how wonderful and revered MegaPets stores are, even by me. I really do like the store where I work, and the way the whole chain caters to animals. Mine is a really nice, large MegaPets store in a great area of Los Angeles, near Beverly Hills. Working there always made me curious about competition and what I could learn to improve our store.

Blinking my eyes at the sudden glare as I tucked my sunglasses back into my shoulder bag, I grabbed the door handle and pulled. Pluckie darted in first, and I followed her.

And stopped. The place took my breath away. It wasn't very large, but the displays showed a copious amount of upscale and adorable clothing for dogs and cats. Toys to keep them occupied and amused, some that even talked to them. Rhinestone-studded collars and leashes. And those were only the things nearest the door.

I stood there for a moment, drinking it all in. Oh, yes, I liked the look of this place. And the scent. Catnip, or something similar that would appeal more to pet owners to get them to purchase things? I might even buy something for Pluckie here, just to show how much I love my pup.

I looked around. This place could have been anywhere, not just Destiny—even though there was a plethora of evidence of superstitions. In the center of the store was a huge display of black plush toy cats. Then there was the glass counter filled with amulets that could be attached to collars—or human necklaces—that had smiling animal faces and symbols of good luck.

I didn't see a clerk, which I thought was brave in such a busy town. People could "borrow" things so easily and get away with it, with no one around to see them.

I looked up at the walls. They were mostly painted in textured beige, but one held wallpaper in a design overflowing with cute faces of kittens and puppies. Made me want to hug the surface. And I, being in the business, was probably less vulnerable to such things than the average customer.

I thought about calling out, asking for someone's help. But when I looked down at Pluckie, who'd insisted on coming in here, she wasn't lunging on her leash toward food or toys or anything else. Instead, standing beside me, she issued a low growl from deep in her throat.

She never did that.

"What's wrong, girl?" I started to kneel beside her. Her response was to dart toward the back of the store, so fast and unexpectedly that I nearly let go of her leash.

I rose and kept hold, following her. She reached a door hidden in a corner behind a flowing mesh drape adorned with shapes of dog bones.

The door was closed. Pluckie began scratching at it with one of her fluffy white paws, whimpering at the same time.

I knocked once, knowing how much we didn't like customers barging into our stockrooms at MegaPets. I heard nothing but Pluckie's shrill cries, so I made an executive decision.

I turned the knob and opened the door.

It was, indeed, a stockroom. In its center sat a card table with a couple of chairs around it. No computer, though. It probably wasn't where the manager kept track of stock or communicated by email with suppliers, but—

That was when Pluckie darted forward yet again, toward a pile of material lying on the floor.

No. Not material. A person.

A woman in jeans and a flowing, gauzy top. An older, gray-haired woman, who wasn't moving.

Hadn't any customers heard her fall? Apparently not—or surely someone would have gotten help for her. But Pluckie had obviously heard, or otherwise sensed, something.

"Hey," I cried, hurrying over to the woman. "Are you all right?"

Dumb question. She clearly wasn't.

Pluckie stood near her face now, nuzzling it as I bent to check the woman's neck for a pulse. That was what you were supposed to do, wasn't it?

Did I remember enough to do CPR? I thought I did, just from seeing it on TV.

Fortunately, though, there was a pulse and she was breathing. Not only that, but the woman stirred. Opened her eyes.

"Are you okay?" I asked again.

She gasped for breath as she tried to respond.

"No, you don't need to talk. I'll call for help." I reached into my jeans pocket for my phone.

"I'll be fine," the woman managed to say in a low, gaspy voice. "Don't you see?" She slowly turned onto her side and reached out her upper arm. She stroked Pluckie with a wizened, pale hand. "I was about to have a business meeting." I had to bend down a little to hear her. "And here is this wonderful black and white dog. That means good fortune." She smiled faintly and repeated in a stronger voice, "I'm going to be fine."

TWO

I HOPED SHE WAS right, but I knew she needed help to make her statement true. I used my cell phone to call 911.

I explained the nature of the emergency to the person who answered but was somewhat stymied when she asked for the address. I knew the street name and general location but hadn't noticed the number. "It's the Lucky Dog—"

"—Boutique on the 1300 block of Destiny Boulevard," the dispatcher finished for me. Clearly, this was a small enough town that just part of the name of a store was enough.

"That sounds right," I said in relief, even as the woman on the floor turned even farther toward me and glared.

"You didn't have to do that," she sputtered, each word an individual gasp that belied what she said. She'd lifted her head a little, but her hair still splayed on the floor beneath her. She squinted eyes sunken into her ashy, aged face—in pain, or because she couldn't see?

"Maybe not," I fibbed, "but I'm sure my dog Pluckie will feel a lot better if I act as overprotective of you as I do with her."

That either satisfied the woman or she'd run out of her microscopic supply of energy, since she said nothing more, just blinked and let her head loll sideways. I looked around for something to use as a pillow. Dog or cat beds? I saw nothing immediately, and the paramedics arrived so quickly, heralded by blasts from a siren, that it felt as if they must have been waiting a block away for me to call. Another good thing about this small a town, I supposed.

I heard them enter the store and stood, running to the doorway from where I'd entered this back room. "In here," I called, pushing the dog-bone drapery to one side and gesturing to the man and woman in white jackets who carried medical bags. I had to duck out of the way to avoid being stomped on during their enthusiastic entry.

I'd let go of Pluckie's leash, but she came over to stand by me, confusion making her cock her sweet head as she watched the activity, her fluffy tail wagging slightly, back and forth.

"It's okay, girl." I stooped to pet her as I watched. "You did good."

The woman on the floor remained alert enough to talk a bit. The EMTs did what they usually do, I supposed, from what I'd seen their fictional counterparts do on TV.

I hadn't been there for my fiancé, Warren, when emergency help had arrived for him. It had been too late anyway.

"Hey, Martha," said the female EMT as she fastened a cuff to check blood pressure around the woman's arm. "Can you tell us what happened?"

I didn't hear what she said, since it was drowned out by another siren outside. More help arriving?

In a minute, two uniformed cops ran inside. I was standing in the store by then with Pluckie, wanting to stay out of the way. "Are you the person who called for help?" asked one of them, a lanky kid with a ruddy face and overbite beneath his buzz-cut hair. His counterpart rushed into the back room.

"Yes," I said.

He whipped a small notebook from his pocket, along with an electronic thing that was probably a recorder. "Give me your name, please."

"Rory Chasen." I also responded to the rest of his questions more or less honestly. Yes, I was here as a tourist. I could say that with a straight face, even if I had an agenda that most tourists didn't have.

Or did they? Many probably came looking for answers. Just not the kind I was after.

"Okay, ma'am. Tell me the reason for your call, what you saw."

Ma'am? I supposed that was just normal courtesy, but I sure hoped I didn't look ancient in my mid-thirties. But no matter how young this cop looked, he had to be beyond high school age to have received police training and a job with the local department.

And did he think a crime had been committed here, or was this standard operating procedure? I hadn't seen anything but an apparently ill woman, but maybe there was more than I'd perceived.

I told the cop all I could remember from the time I entered the store till he arrived with the other police officer. Almost everything, at least. I didn't know the ill woman, whom the EMTs had called Martha—and I didn't repeat what she had said about a black and white dog, and how obvious it was, therefore, that she would be fine.

Why? I wasn't sure, but it sounded so hokey to me.

On the other hand, in a town that survived because of superstitions, maybe that was exactly what this guy needed for his notes: a supposed omen of some kind.

I couldn't help it. I ended with, "Do you think she was the victim of a crime, officer?"

"No, ma'am. At least I don't have any reason to think so. Not yet at least. We just needed to check—" His last couple of words fell from his mouth as if he'd forgotten what he was saying. He was looking over my shoulder, suddenly frozen.

I turned to see what he was looking at and just caught his shaky salute out of the corner of my eye.

A man had stepped inside the shop behind me, so I hadn't noticed. Pluckie had, though. She was standing up, facing him and wagging her tail.

"What's wrong with Martha?" the guy demanded, hurrying toward us. "Is she okay?"

He was tall, with the broadest shoulders I'd ever seen expanding the top of his button-down blue shirt. I assumed, from the way his sleeves bulged, that he was also muscular, but he had a tapered waist and slim-fitting black pants. He brushed past me and looked at the note-taking cop with what appeared to be pain in his brilliant blue eyes.

"Don't know, sir. I was just—"

"Interviewing a potential witness? Fine. I'll check on her." He was already inside the back room by the time he finished speaking.

"Witness?" I asked the cop who remained with me. "Then you do think a crime was committed?"

He shrugged a shoulder—a much slighter one than those on the guy who'd just disappeared. "We don't know one wasn't, and this is

14

Martha's place," he said, as if that explained everything. "Just a few more questions." He looked at me pleadingly.

I wondered what he would do if I said no. I considered it. I really wanted to see what was happening with Martha. But I gave a brief nod.

No, no one else appeared to be in the shop when I entered, although I'd seen some people and a dog leaving. No, I saw no indication of what had caused the woman's problem.

Then—"Was there any sign of superstitions at work here? I mean, I realize you might not know, since you're not from around here, but any broken mirrors? Birds flying inside? Anything like that?"

What would he say if I told him about the woman's comments on how she knew she'd be fine, thanks to seeing a black and white dog? Would he subject Pluckie to a doggy interrogation?

"Um…no."

He looked relieved. "Good. I'm not officially supposed to ask that, but around here, well…we always do."

"I get it," I said. And I did. This was the unique town of Destiny. "Anything else?" I made sure my icy stare suggested that there'd better not be anything else. And there wasn't.

Signaling to Pluckie to join me by a soft tug on her leash, I sidled around the cop, who was just finishing his notes, and reentered the back room.

Martha lay on a gurney now. It hadn't been wheeled in through the shop and past me, but a rear door was open at the far side of the storeroom. Beyond appeared to be an alley. I could see another building's concrete block wall across a wide gap of space.

Martha's face was obscured by a plastic mask, and an oxygen tank was strapped to a narrow pole on the gurney. One EMT was fussing with how the thing was connected, and the other EMT must have gone outside since I didn't see her. The cop who'd rushed in here seemed to be perusing the shelving and boxes that lined the room, and the one who'd talked to me followed me in and started doing the same.

I figured they were looking for evidence of a crime, no matter what the cop who'd interviewed me had said. Would they find any? I still assumed that the woman had just had some kind of medical emergency, but what did I know?

The man who'd rushed past me stood beside her now, holding her hand. "You're going to be fine, Martha," he said softly. The glaze in her eyes lifted a little, and she nodded. She aimed a glance toward me, then downward, as if she expected me to confirm what he said—and the reason for it.

Pluckie just sat down beside me. Martha couldn't possibly see her, but she must have figured my dog was there.

The man apparently realized what she was attempting to convey, since he looked down and smiled. "A strange dog," he said, then smiled at me. "That's good luck, especially around here. That's why this is the Lucky Dog Boutique. Lots of strange dogs come into this place, and Martha's home is upstairs."

Somehow, I felt comfortable relaying to him what I'd been reluctant to say to the young cop interviewing me. "A black and white dog this time, while she was on her way to a business meeting, she said. She knew she'd be all right."

"A business meeting?" He looked at me inquisitively, as if I had further answers for him.

I shrugged. "That's what she said."

16

He glanced at her, but she obviously wasn't going to explain. He looked back at me. That was when the two paramedics joined up again near the gurney.

"We need to take her to the hospital now, Chief," they said to the man. "Okay?"

"Absolutely." He looked down at her as they started wheeling her out. "I'll come visit you in a little while, Martha," he said. "Feel better fast."

Which she possibly would, in a hospital.

I was curious now, though. Chief?

"Anything interesting?" he asked the two uniformed cops who seemed to be slowing down in their scrutiny of the room.

"No, sir," said the one who'd come in here first.

"Good. I appreciate your taking special care here, though."

"Any time, sir," said the kid who'd questioned me.

I sometimes jump to conclusions, like it or not. My assumptions now were that this guy was the others' superior officer. Martha was his mother, or he had some kind of close relationship with her. As a result, no one was taking any chances on a major issue not getting addressed if Martha was the subject of a 911 call.

No one wanted to displease the chief, which concerned me a little when I suddenly was alone with him in this back room, after the cops followed the EMTs relocating Martha.

At first he, like his apparent subordinates, scanned the room as if looking for answers, possibly evidence of some nasty person coming in and waving a superstition wand, or whatever they did here in Destiny, and making Martha ill.

What was I doing here? I suddenly had an urge to flee, to return to the B&B, retrieve all my stuff, and drive south fast—home to L.A.

I didn't believe in any of this. People who did—well, to me, they might be a few slices short of a loaf. Fixated on unreality.

On the other hand, there was that ladder that Warren had walked under before . . . I shook my head.

"Thanks for being here," the man said, looking at me. "I've only lived in Destiny for a couple of years, but Martha has treated me like a son. If anything really bad happened to her—" He broke off, his troubled look segueing suddenly into a smile that made his unusual blue eyes sparkle. "I'm Justin Halbertson, by the way. Police Chief of Destiny—and that's quite a responsibility, as I'm sure you can imagine." He looked at me expectantly.

"I'm Rory Chasen, Destiny tourist. And imagine? Yes, around here people apparently imagine a lot."

His deep bark of laughter made me smile. "Guess I'd better lock up." He looked outside, then closed the back door and turned the latch. "They're still out there getting Martha situated. They'd be gone a lot faster if they thought she needed immediate treatment, so that's a good sign. Anyway, let's go out the front."

I nodded, and he gallantly waved Pluckie and me through the door from the storeroom into the boutique before following and closing it.

"Cute, lucky dog there," he said, and stooped briefly to give Pluckie a pat on her head. That active tail of hers started waving again. She's a real people-lover and attention sponge. She was now buddies with the chief for life.

"That's Pluckie," I told him. "She's been lucky for me, but I didn't know till now that that's her destiny."

He grinned. "Definitely, around here. My own dog, Killer, is a Doberman. Sweet guy but not the subject of any superstitions I know about." Standing, he patrolled the shop as if looking for people hiding behind displays, then motioned toward the front entry to the store. "Shall we?"

I was fine with leaving—only when I opened the door I saw that a large crowd overflowed the sidewalk and onto the street.

"What's going on with Martha?" asked a senior citizen wearing a "Destiny, Home of Superstitions" T-shirt and jeans, probably a local. A lot of those around him echoed the question until it turned into a roar.

Justin raised his hands as if he were a conductor leading an orchestra, and when he lowered them the sound abated.

"The paramedics took her out the back door. I think the ambulance is still there, but they're about to leave. It's not clear yet what's wrong with her, but it's a medical issue."

"How can we find out more?" asked a lady about half the first inquisitor's age. She was wearing a bright red T-shirt with a black cat grinning evilly on it.

Chief Halbertson seemed right at home in managing the crowd. He made suggestions, then asked them all to disperse for now. "I'll have the Department's IT guys put something on the town's website as we get more information about her condition," he promised them.

Another nice thing about a small town, I supposed. I doubted that would happen in Los Angeles about a mere shopkeeper, at least not on an official website.

A siren started up again. It sounded as if it came from behind us. In a moment, the ambulance drove surprisingly slowly from the street to the right, then turned left onto Destiny Boulevard behind the crowd.

"Everyone hold your breath," called the old guy in the Destiny shirt. "At least till you look over there." He seemed to point toward Pluckie. A lot of people in the crowd nodded, appeared to visibly suck in their breath, then smiled in our direction. After that, people start walking away as the ambulance disappeared in the distance.

"What's that all about?" I asked.

Justin smiled and shook his head. "You won't be surprised to hear it's another superstition. This town is full of them."

"Explain this one," I said. "Or is it made up?"

"That does happen around here," Justin acknowledged. "People create their own, sometimes to fill whatever need they have at any time, especially to impress tourists. But I've heard this one before, as odd as it seems. If you see an ambulance, you need to hold your breath until you see a dog. Otherwise, the person inside the ambulance may die. And most of the people who were here are townsfolk. Martha's friends."

"I see." Sort of. People around here believed enough to follow what superstitions told them. At least some did. Others might have been concerned about not looking like they conformed to the group mentality around here.

"You sound dubious," he said. "Do you believe in superstitions? If not, what brought you here?"

I wasn't about to blurt out the truth to him, or to anybody. At least not yet. Even if my quest for answers made me just one of the gang here, I didn't want to admit to having even the slightest belief in superstitions.

Instead, I chose an easier route. "Curiosity, mainly. I read a book about superstitions and Destiny. It was written by one of your local citizens, I think. It's called—"

"*The Destiny of Superstitions*, of course. And you know what? The author is one of the co-owners of that store there." He pointed to the shop nearest the Lucky Dog Boutique in the direction where the ambulance had gone. The bookstore had a red brick façade and upstairs dormer windows.

"I noticed the store," I told him, not admitting it had been my primary reason for being here. "It looks interesting. I thought I'd stop in there while I'm in town and check it out."

"Now's a good time," Justin said. "I see one of the owners near the door, probably trying to find out what happened here. I'd be glad to introduce you. Interested?"

"Sure," I said, wondering if I'd soon be sorry. "I'd be delighted."

THREE

Kenneth Tarzal was one of the tallest men I'd ever seen.

I wondered if there were any superstitions about tall men. If so, he'd probably know them. But I wasn't about to ask him.

Nor would I ask him—right now, at least—about the superstition I'd come to Destiny to learn more about so I could finally cast it to the deepest depths of my mind, never to think of it again. I hoped.

He had included that superstition—walking under a ladder— in his book, of course. Anyone who'd ever heard of superstitions knew of that one. But was there more to it? Anything to give it a hint of reality?

Anything to show how absurd it was?

"How do you do, Rory?" Tarzal said in a deep, inquiring voice. My distraction must have been obvious.

"I'm fine, Kenneth," I responded jovially, holding out my hand, which he shook once determinedly, then released.

"He'd rather be called Tarzal," Justin informed me, and the man nodded and smiled.

"Sorry. I'm fine, Tarzal," I said. I understood nicknames. My real name is Aurora, but I prefer Rory.

Justin and I stood just inside the door to a shop that definitely answered to the label of "bookstore." There were dark wooden shelves brimming with books everywhere, lining all four walls while framing windows and doors. More tall bookcases, also filled with books, took up most of the space in between. They couldn't all be about superstitions, could they?

The display nearest to the door consisted of a table with stacks of copies of *The Destiny of Superstitions* laid out artistically with books leaning against one another. Not surprising. Tarzal's name was prominent on the covers, which also displayed rabbits' feet and shamrocks.

What appeared to be a small enclosed office with windows jutted into the room. And of course mirrors hung on the few spaces along the wall not covered by bookshelves. This was, after all, the Broken Mirror Bookstore—although these mirrors had only what appeared to be painted-on cracks down their centers and were otherwise intact. Picture frames holding five-dollar bills had been hung on either side of them. I wondered about their significance.

Tarzal had remained in front of us, which initially blocked us from proceeding very far into the shop. Now he became our host, bowing us in.

He was clad in khaki trousers and a soft plaid sports coat with a beige shirt beneath, a laid-back scholarly outfit. I gauged him to be in his forties, with bifocals and light brown hair that coordinated with his outfit. He had so many deep grooves and planes in his face that it looked nearly like a skull.

"I saw you next door at Martha's, didn't I? Were you shopping for stuff for this little fellow?" He bowed briefly to touch Pluckie's head.

My little *girl* cringed away a little. She's great at assessing who likes dogs and who doesn't. Tarzal had to be in the latter category. He might be an expert in superstitions, but Pluckie's opinion dropped him way down on my admiration list.

"Well, we started out just looking around," I began.

"She found Martha in the back room, ill," Justin cut in. "That's why there was an ambulance here and the crowd and all."

"Was everyone told to hold their breath?" Tarzal's tone conveyed concern. "I assume, if there was an ambulance, that Martha was okay—at least until she got into it."

"Yes, someone mentioned that," I said dryly. "Good thing there was already a dog for everyone to see so they didn't have to hold their breath long to make sure Martha survived the trip. Otherwise, they might all have had to pile into the ambulance with her."

"You sound skeptical, Miss—Rory, was it?" That was someone else talking. Another man had been sitting behind a desk that held the cash register, and he'd risen as we'd talked. He looked sixtyish, with a whole plume of silver hair. He was dressed similarly to Tarzal, although his color-coordinated outfit was in shades of charcoal. He even had leather elbow pads sewn onto his jacket. His gray hair went well with his couture. The wrinkles in the corners of his eyes also matched the lines in his forehead.

"A bit," I admitted, holding out my hand to him. "I'm Rory Chasen."

"This is my partner, Preston Kunningham," Tarzal said.

"I was eavesdropping," Preston said. "I saw the crowd, too, and watched the ambulance take off with Martha. I'd just been heading over there to see her and hope she'll be okay. Any idea what was wrong with her?"

He looked at Justin, not me. Not surprising. As police chief, Justin was probably considered the go-to guy for answers to all questions. Except maybe those relating to superstitions.

"Not really," I said before Justin could respond. "My dog Pluckie acted like she sensed something even before we walked into the store. We found Martha on the floor in the back room. She seemed unconscious at first but woke up somewhat before the EMTs arrived."

"Thank heavens for your being there—and your sweet little dog, too." When Preston knelt to hug her, Pluckie's tail began waving in ecstasy. This was a dog lover. I immediately liked him, at least more than I liked his partner.

"Will you be in town long?" Tarzal asked. "We'd love to have you come back to the store, but unfortunately we're closing early today."

Another reason not to love that guy. He was kicking us out.

"Not sure how long I'll be here," I said. "But I will come back. I want to hear more about your book, Tarzal." I waved in the direction of the table display. If I could get him to talk in generalities about it, I might be able to nudge the conversation to what I wanted to know without making it obvious. But that wouldn't happen this afternoon.

"And I'd love to talk about it." A smile lit his long face and made its grooves seem less cadaverous. "Anytime during store hours, usually."

We said our goodbyes, and then Pluckie and I walked outside with Justin.

"Glad I got an invitation to come back," I said. "That store looks delightful."

"You're a reader?" Justin asked.

"Voracious—especially about things involving animals. That's my business, after all. I don't know whether they had any books on animals there, though."

"What do you do?" the police chief asked. I'd noticed his shoulders before, but I hadn't paid much attention to how good-looking he was. His hair was jet black, just long enough to tousle sexily over his forehead. The darkness of his hair was reflected in the hint of five o'clock shadow, which was actually good timing since it was around five-fifteen now. That shadow emphasized the planes of his face and the prominence of his cheekbones. Then there were his memorably blue eyes.

His handsome self-confidence seemed nothing like Warren's demeanor had been.

My poor, lost, lovable geek Warren.

I didn't want to notice the chief any more.

"Oh, I'm the assistant manager of a MegaPets store in Los Angeles," I said airily. "That's why I was interested in the Lucky Dog Boutique. I think it's time for Pluckie and me to head back to our B&B now. Glad I met you, and I really hope Martha recuperates fast."

"So do I," Justin said. "Have a good evening."

———

I was surprised, an hour later, when my rather bland evening with Pluckie suddenly picked up in interest.

We'd been at the Rainbow Bed & Breakfast since we left the Lucky Dog. The owner, Serina, was behind the desk when we returned.

She'd immediately come out and began stroking a happily wiggling Pluckie. "I heard what good luck this dog brings." She looked up. "Rumor has it that she found and saved poor Martha after she fell ill."

"Guess so," I said. I wasn't buying into it, but if some people in this town wanted to treat Pluckie like a hero, that was fine with me. "How did you hear about that?" I suspected I knew the answer. This was a fairly small town and its inhabitants probably kept in close touch about how each group of tourists reacted to superstitions so each business owner could respond in a way to make the most money.

"A little bird told me," she said with a giggle that might have been more appropriate coming from a young kid, but it did fit with her clothing style.

"A little bird of superstition," I suggested.

She nodded. "One of our tours even takes people out bird-watching while describing superstitions relating to birds—crows and the like."

That figured. "Sounds interesting," I said. "I'll keep it in mind."

And that had been all until around six-fifteen. Pluckie and I had stayed in our quaint, chintzy little second-floor room, complete with a fluffy canopy over the bed. Its decor reminded me of Serina's clothing style. I was studying the Destiny guidebook to plan the next day—including a tour, as well as a visit to Tarzal in which I planned to offhandedly ask about the ladder superstition. I had just begun thinking about what to do for dinner when the room's phone rang.

"Rory?" said a deep male voice when I answered. "This is Justin Halbertson. I was wondering if you'd join me for dinner."

Good timing. But did I want to have dinner with him?

Maybe. I wouldn't mind the company. Plus, I'd sound him out more about Destiny and what its residents really thought about superstitions, not just the fronts they put on to garner money from tourists.

"If Pluckie can come too," I told him.

"Of course. There are a lot of places that welcome dogs, especially black and white hero dogs like yours."

"Do you get many black and white hero dogs around here?" I asked.

"No, but I'll be glad to have the first join me—us—for dinner."

―――――

Justin came by about twenty minutes later. We met him in the lobby, and I ignored Serina's delighted grin and wave as we left.

This wasn't a date. I hadn't dated since I lost Warren. I certainly had no romantic interest in this man. I just wanted to learn all I could from him.

And surely the town's police chief would know a lot.

We exited the B&B's lobby beneath that horseshoe hanging over the outside of the door. We walked a couple of blocks in the waning light of day, among another crowd of tourists that seemed more directed and less meandering than those I'd seen earlier that day. Maybe everyone was hungry now.

A lot of these people also had dogs on leashes—white, black, brown, and golden colors, from little Yorkies up through a shepherd or two. I'd already determined that Pluckie was welcome, and that she wasn't the only visiting dog. Even more seemed to be out at this hour.

Too bad the Lucky Dog Boutique might not be able to keep regular hours now—although I didn't know the situation. Hopefully, Martha had staff who could take over in her absence.

"Are the sidewalks ever empty in this town?" I asked Justin. I noticed that he didn't avoid stepping on cracks. I nevertheless stayed away from them—at least as much as possible.

"Not if we can help it," he responded with a smile.

The Shamrock Steakhouse was about three blocks from the B&B.

The B&B! I suddenly stopped and looked at Justin, my hand that wasn't holding Pluckie's leash on my hip. "How did you know where to find me?" I'd mentioned a B&B, but I hadn't said which one of the several establishments in town.

He shrugged one of those wide shoulders and grinned. "I'm the chief of police," he said. "I know everything."

"Right." As I turned to start walking again, I hid my smile. But there was undoubtedly truth to what he said. People around here would respond to his questions about visitors, especially locals who managed lodgings. Although I didn't really see him taking the time to call all the B&Bs, or even having a subordinate do it.

"It helps that you gave some info about yourself to the first officers on the scene at the Lucky Dog," he said.

Had I told the person interviewing me where I was staying? I didn't think so—but I may have mentioned I'd planned to return to my B&B after stopping at the store and that it wasn't too far. That would have narrowed down the possibilities.

I hadn't trod on a superstition that broadcast my location to the world. Thank heavens.

We passed the Black Cat Inn on the way to the restaurant. B&Bs weren't the only lodgings around here.

We soon reached our destination. The steakhouse was crowded, but we were seated in the patio area right away. I wasn't sure whether my companion had made a reservation, or if he got preferential treatment because of who he was.

It didn't matter. I was glad not to wait.

The collection of small round tables allowed for a choice between those under heat lamps and those without. I felt fine and opted for no lamp when Justin asked my preference.

Pluckie's nose didn't stop from the time we entered the area. She exchanged sniffs with a couple of Chihuahua mixes and a bulldog as we took our seats. Then her scent sense seemed enthralled by the smells of cooking food, since she kept her nose straight up for a while. "I'll give you a taste, girl," I promised in a whisper, patting her head.

"You need to meet my dog, Killer," Justin said.

"Why didn't you bring him?"

"I didn't have a chance to get him from home before joining you. But I'd like for you to meet him while you're in town."

Not likely. I wouldn't be here long. Nevertheless, I said, "I'd like that."

After asking my preference, Justin ordered a carafe of wine for us to split, then recommended one of the place's steak specials. Like all the servers, our waiter had on a green Irish-type hat, as if he were a large, overweight leprechaun. His apron, and the menus and table-cloths, were all decorated with—what else?—shamrocks.

Justin asked more about my life in Los Angeles as we waited for our wine. I didn't want to get into that, so I asked him instead how long he'd been the police chief.

"About two years," he said. "I'd been a deputy chief in a smaller town north of here, and I applied to become chief when I heard of the opening. Fortunately, I got the job."

"Did you wish on a star or knock on wood?" I asked.

He laughed. "Both, of course. I wouldn't have been chosen if I hadn't."

The wine was finally served, and the rest of our meal was quite pleasant. Other diners came and went, keeping Pluckie's nose and attention occupied. I enjoyed the company, even though Justin dissembled most of the time when I asked how superstitious the people living here really were.

"Some superstitions are definitely real," he said as he cut a bite of his rare steak, "or at least people want them to be. But how many, and which superstitions—well, I learn more all the time, but I think people have to decide themselves how much to buy into."

"Literally," I said.

"Pardon?"

"'Buy into.' Your residents want visitors like me to 'buy into' the superstitions a lot, so they can make money."

"Of course," he said with a grin. "That's good for me, too. It pays my salary."

I did as promised and gave Pluckie a few small bites of my own medium-rare steak. I found it delicious, and I was sure she did, too.

As we were finishing, Justin said, "I went to see Martha at the hospital after you left for your B&B this afternoon."

I looked at him in surprise. His face seemed a bit grave, which made me feel bad for him. "Really? How's she doing?"

"She'll be okay. The initial diagnosis is that she had a mild heart attack precipitated by self-overmedication with some prescription drugs she was already on. She says she didn't, and I didn't think she . . . well, that's the current thinking." Then I saw an expression I couldn't read pass over his face. "She'd like for you to visit her in the hospital when we're done here."

"Me?" I knew surprise radiated both from my question and my expression, since he graced me with another of those nice-looking grins of his. But only for a second.

"Yeah. She wants to thank you." Once more, his look was unreadable.

That should have told me to back off and not go see her. But curiosity swirled through me.

"No need," I said with a shrug. "I'm just glad she's okay."

"But she wants to. Please."

Okay, there was something I didn't get here. Something I might not want to get. But my darned curiosity took control. "All right," I said. "I'll want to take Pluckie back to the B&B, though. I doubt she's welcome in the hospital."

When we were finished and the server brought our bill, I took out my wallet to pay my share.

"I've got it," Justin said. When I started to protest—especially since I refused to consider this a date—he said, "You can get it next time."

As if there would be a next time. Unless we decided to grab dinner again together during one of the next two evenings, I'd be gone before I had a chance to pay. And if we had dinner together again before I left town—well, that would feel too much like we were dating, even for this short period of time.

Even so, I stopped arguing. In a way, I would be doing him a favor by going to the hospital to see Martha. He'd already said she was like a mother to him, and I'd agreed, somewhat against my better judgment, to visit her. If she'd asked him to bring me, maybe he would get some kind of brownie points with his pseudo-mom by my showing up. Worth the price of my dinner? That was for him to decide.

But what happened was not what I'd anticipated. Not in the least.

I felt sure Justin knew about it, though.

First, we took Pluckie back to the B&B. Soon thereafter, we were with Martha, who was lying in her hospital bed in a blue and white printed gown looking bright eyed, yet fragile.

"It's so good to see you again, Rory." Her voice was soft as she held out her hands for me to come close and clasp them. She was in a private room, hooked up to an IV and some monitors.

"I'm glad you're okay," I told her.

"Too bad they don't let dogs in here," she grumbled. "I want to thank Pluckie, too."

She knew my name and Pluckie's. Justin must have told her.

I found out a minute later that wasn't all he'd told her about me. I also learned why he stood at the door to the room, as if primed to flee—or maybe to keep me from fleeing.

"Rory," Martha said, still holding my hands. She had an iron grip for a senior lady still sick enough to be a hospital patient. "I know you're just visiting Destiny, but ... well, I need to ask you a favor. A big one."

She paused, as if waiting for me to inquire what it was. I doubted that I wanted to know. My own heart started thumping so hard that I felt glad I wasn't hooked up to one of those monitors. Otherwise, some nurse might show up to deal with me, stat.

I definitely had a bad feeling about this. I glanced toward Justin, but he was no help. He appeared to plant himself even more firmly in the doorway.

I gently started pulling my hands away from Martha. "Er—I'm not really good about doing favors," I said.

"Oh, but you'll like this one," she said, then coughed a little, turning her head to the side so her mouth faced her gown-clad shoulder—as if to remind me of her fragility. She picked up a water bottle from the table beside the bed, took a drink, then looked at me.

I inhaled, waiting for what she had to say.

"They tell me I'll need some rest to fully recuperate," she continued, "hopefully at home. I've got some part-time clerks at my store, but none has much experience or knowledge about running a store with pet products."

Uh-oh. I suddenly knew where this was heading. "Well, I'm sure they—"

"Justin told me you're an assistant manager—*manager*," she said for emphasis, "at one of those wonderful MegaPets stores." She smiled, opening her rheumy brown eyes wide in apparent hope. "I would be ever so grateful if you'd manage the Lucky Dog Boutique for me while I get better."

FOUR

I FELT MY EYES widen. My heart rate quickened even more, if that was possible.

Stay here? Run Martha's shop?

But I had a life in L.A. A job that I loved.

A need to stop obsessing about superstitions, then putting Destiny far behind me. Soon.

But I didn't have the answers I'd come for. Not yet. I might never get them, but the likelihood could be even less if I stayed here for only the few days that I had planned.

My hands were still Martha's captives. So was my gaze, since I couldn't quite tear it away from the pleading expression on her tired, aged face.

I liked her little boutique. I liked *her*, even though I had just met her, and under especially difficult circumstances.

And if I said no, what were her alternatives?

All that swept through my mind in seconds. I waffled, and that wasn't like me at all.

"I—I'll think about it," I finally said. Even that was enough to turn her expression from fear to relief. "But I need a day or so. Do you have anyone who can manage the store for you tomorrow?"

"My part-time employees don't know how to really manage the place," she said, "but they could keep it going for a short while. And oh, my dear, I'm sure that if you just give it a try you'll love it. It's such a delightful store, and we're usually quite busy. Maybe not as busy as a MegaPets, but a lot of townsfolk have pets, and you've seen that quite a few tourists, like you, bring their dogs along, too."

"But I don't know your systems—inventory control, accounting, anything else—"

"My staff knows the basics, and I can keep an eye on it to make sure it's all working. My computer system reaches upstairs—that's where I live. They'll surely be releasing me from here in the next day or two. If there's anything I need help with then, I'll be able to give you whatever information my helpers don't have so you can take care of it for now. And I'll pay you, of course." She named a weekly amount which, though not lush, was certainly adequate.

I tore my glance away. I had to, or I was liable to say yes right then and there. And that would be a mistake.

I had to think this through.

I looked toward Justin. Was that sympathy I saw in his gaze? It couldn't be. He'd brought me here so I could get put into this quandary.

I should feel furious at him. But I didn't.

He'd clearly thought he was doing the right thing.

"Tell you what," I said. "Please have some of your regular employees come in tomorrow. I'll meet them there. What time do you usually open the store?"

36

"Ten o'clock."

My gaze was on her once more. She looked so hopeful that I nearly accepted her challenge—er, invitation—right then.

"Can you call at least one of them tonight, tell him or her to get there at nine-thirty? I'll come in then and at least see that the store opens on time. I may not stay since I have other things to do tomorrow, but I'll at least drop in now and then. That'll give me time to get those other things out of the way—and to decide whether I can stay longer. Okay?"

Martha rose to a slight sitting position, squeezing my hands even more. "You are so wonderful, Rory. I can't tell you how much I appreciate this. And if you decide to stay, you'll be the absolute kindest person on earth."

"Is there a superstition for that?" I couldn't help asking. Doing this should at least get me some kind of pat on the head from the cosmos, or whatever's out there if superstitions were real, for me to stay for a short while to help this ill lady, right?

"I'll find one," Martha said.

———

A few minutes later, Justin and I left the hospital to walk back to my B&B.

I said nothing till we reached the end of the first block. Then, before we crossed the street, I turned to him. "You set me up," I accused.

"In a way," he said, "although I only suspected that was why she wanted to see you." He didn't look at all abashed, which didn't surprise me.

"But what if I do say yes? You don't know me. How can you—and she—trust me? What if I did something to Martha to injure her to set this all up so I could take over her shop if I want?"

He laughed, and I wanted to kick him. "Did you?" he said, his dark, arched eyebrows raised skeptically over his blue eyes.

"Of course not."

"That's what I figured. And I also intend to keep close watch on you if you do decide to help Martha. So don't you forget that I'm the chief of police around here." The big, gorgeous smile on his handsome face told me he was joking—at least somewhat. But I had no doubt that if I pinched even a penny from Martha's cash register he'd hunt me down and have me prosecuted to the full extent of the law.

Or maybe that look was because he knew of some superstition that would ensure that bad luck would rain down upon me forever if I dared to steal from an injured woman who'd received good luck thanks to visits from strange dogs—or whatever.

I asked him.

"Of course there is," he responded without even blinking. "But it would be bad luck for me to tell you about it."

The hospital was about six blocks from my B&B. The area we walked through beneath the adequate yet disappointingly regular-looking streetlights wasn't part of the town's downtown retail area. It had an atmosphere of more normality than where I'd walked before, where the stores and restaurants were located. Several of the closest modern, multi-storied buildings had signs indicating they contained doctors' offices—not surprising. A little farther away, there were some apartment buildings with almost normal names like Destiny Residences and Welcome Home Apartments.

What, no superstition themes?

On the other hand, this might be where some unbelieving residents lived who were only into superstitions to the extent they could make a profit from them.

Justin was wise enough to discuss neutral topics as we walked along the sidewalks. We talked about dogs—the ones we were currently owned by, mostly, but no hints about canine superstitions. Where he had grown up, which turned out to be near L.A., in Santa Monica. Where I had grown up, also near L.A., in Pasadena.

And soon, there we were, past my car in the parking lot and at the doorstep of the Rainbow Bed & Breakfast.

"I know you'll get breakfast here," Justin said. "The name tells me so. But how about if I meet you at the Lucky Dog at about ten tomorrow morning, after you've checked it out and talked to one of Martha's employees? We can go for coffee and discuss where your thoughts are heading then about staying or not."

"And if the answer is 'not'?" I aimed a wry smile toward his nice-looking face that was illuminated by the lights mounted on the building on either side of the horseshoe over the door.

He was smiling, too. "Then I'll have to convince you, won't I?"

"I guess you'll have to *try*," I riposted. "Goodnight, Chief. See you at ten tomorrow." At his suggestion, we exchanged phone numbers. I doubted I'd ever use his, but if it made him feel better to call me tomorrow to let me know he wasn't coming, that was fine.

I turned to head inside but stopped abruptly as he gently took hold of my upper arms and turned me back toward him.

Oh, no. The heated expression in his eyes suggested that he intended to give me a goodnight kiss. My thoughts immediately flashed guiltily on Warren and why I had come to Destiny. I wasn't ready for this.

But instead of anything hot and steamy, Justin planted a completely chaste kiss on my forehead.

A surprising whoosh of disappointment rushed through me as he released me and said, "Goodnight, Rory. Sleep well. Oh, and keep track of your dreams here in Destiny. They're often harbingers of things to come."

———

I used my key to open the locked front door. The lobby area was empty as I walked through and headed upstairs.

I felt utterly exhausted, while at the same time edgy. I doubted I'd fall asleep for a while, so it was a good thing that I needed to take Pluckie for her last walk of the night.

Unsurprisingly, she was waiting for me right inside the door to my room, wriggling her butt eagerly as she wagged her tail and gave a little leap of greeting.

I knelt to hug her. "You know what you did, little girl? You've discombobulated my whole life again, this time because you did such a good deed and saved Martha's life. What do you think I should do?"

Her quiet woof and dash toward the chair over which I'd hung her leash told me her immediate, if not long-term, answer. It was time to take her for that walk.

Maybe afterward she'd do something to let me know her opinion of my staying here with her to run a local pet boutique instead of heading home within the next few days.

"Okay, girl." I snapped her leash on her collar and reached into a totebag to pull out a biodegradable plastic bag to deal with any cleanup during our walk.

I didn't see anyone else in the hallway or downstairs lobby this time, either. No one was rooting around in the pot of gold, just in case—but I wondered how often patrons did that at night, thinking no one would see them.

Not that our hostess Serina was likely to be foolish enough to use real gold to illustrate the end-of-the-rainbow superstition theme of this B&B.

Pluckie and I headed out the front door. I decided not to go back in the neutral and not-so-Destiny direction of the hospital but toward the much more interesting downtown area, which was only a couple of blocks away, down the street on which we were staying.

We didn't run into any other people—or dogs—until we reached the closest block of Destiny Boulevard. There, despite it being close to ten o'clock at night, quite a few people remained out and about. And, yes, some had dogs with them, too.

As we reached the end of the block, I noticed that the nearest store, on the corner, was called Wish-on-a-Star Children's Shop. Its display window wasn't lit up, but the streetlights along the boule-vard—these in the shape of old lanterns, presumably from Gold Rush times—illuminated enough for me to see there were toys and clothes laid out in ways that would undoubtedly entice shoppers to enter when the store was open.

Above them all was a large star-shaped light that zoomed across the top of the window like a shooting star.

I wondered whether the idea was that kids—or adults, too, for that matter—could make a wish on it and have that wish come true. Or at least believe it did.

Logically, that wouldn't work. First, shooting stars aren't stars at all but meteors. They aren't shaped like stars, as this one supposedly was—although real stars also aren't in the five or six-pronged shapes that humans tend to depict them in.

But I was over-thinking this. "What do you say, Pluckie?" I said softly to my dog, who was sniffing the closest wall of the shop. I assumed there'd been guy dogs who'd left some interesting smells there that distracted her, so I pulled a little on her leash. She looked up at me with her sad brown eyes as if chiding me for interrupting her. But I went on, "Should I make a wish on this star that I make the right decision?"

She seemed to understand that, whatever I was saying, it was a meaningful question to me. She came over, stood on her hind legs, and put her front paws up on me. She gave a decisive snort before stepping back down.

"I take it that's a yes," I said.

I walked with her straight to the sidewalk abutting Destiny Boulevard, looked in the window, and waited until the mock shooting star began its descent again.

"I wish," I muttered to myself, "that I knew what decision to make about staying in Destiny, and that something tomorrow will make it come clear to me."

By then, the supposed star had reached the end of its trail and disappeared.

Yet somehow I had a sense that I had done something positive, and that the answer I needed would, in fact, come to me...somehow. In my dreams tonight, as Justin had said?

I needed to go to bed to find out.

FIVE

I slept reasonably well, and my thoughts were on superstitions and their validity when I awoke.

Was that because Pluckie stood up at the side of the bed and pawed at me? I knew she was a lucky dog, and she seemed to be guiding me to get out of bed on the same side I'd gotten into it. Wasn't there a superstition to that effect? And did I care?

Whatever I'd dreamed, it must have included something about superstitions, but I still had no harbingers of things to come as Justin had suggested. Would my wish on a falling star help me find out answers today?

I showered and dressed quickly in a navy button-down shirt and nice jeans, then leashed Pluckie to go downstairs for our morning walk.

Voices emanated from a room off the lobby where breakfast was being served. I didn't see Serina at her front desk, so I assumed she was with her guests.

I peeked into that room. It was fairly large and populated by people filling plates at a food bar or sitting at tables. The scents emanating from there suggested cinnamon rolls and good, strong coffee, maybe more.

No one paid attention to me, which was fine. I turned and walked outside with Pluckie.

We didn't go far. I wanted to feed her in our room, then grab some of that human breakfast to take with me on the walk to the Lucky Dog Boutique.

When Pluckie and I got back, Serina was at the registration desk on the phone. She waved as we went up the stairs.

I fed Pluckie her high-end kibble as I got ready for the day, placing everything I thought I'd need—like a sweater and some of her favorite toys—in a yellow MegaPets totebag. There were plenty of toys at the boutique, of course, but none were hers . . . yet.

When we returned back downstairs, Serina was off the phone. "Question for you," I said to her. "There's a possibility I'll be in town longer than originally anticipated. Would you have room for me to stay here for a while?"

"How long?" She was once again wearing a frilly, old-fashioned outfit that looked quite good on her.

"I don't know yet, but it could be indefinitely."

Her grin grew broader, adding wrinkles to the sides of her pale brown eyes. "That's great! And, yes, though I'm fairly full for the next few months, I'm sure we can work something out at a weekly rate. Just keep me informed about your schedule." She leaned toward me. "This town's superstitions are getting to you, aren't they?"

"In a way." I didn't want to go into how superstitions might not only have helped to save Martha but also convince her I could help her till she got well. "I'll have a better idea later today or tomorrow."

Her apparent pleasure pumped mine up, too. She helped me collect a cinnamon roll and fruit in a bag as well as a tall cup of coffee to take along. Then Pluckie and I were on our way.

I headed up the street till we reached the Wish-on-a-Star Children's Shop. We crossed the street, then turned right on Destiny Boulevard. The Lucky Dog Boutique was one store down.

On our way, I spotted a heads-up penny on the sidewalk and picked it up. Would it bring me good luck? And was its being there an accident or just another quirk of Destiny?

I had fun watching all the other people who were up and about early, many with dogs on leashes beside them. A few tour vans passed by even this early, undoubtedly pointing out some of the shops to visitors.

I enjoyed my breakfast-to-go, mostly ignoring Pluckie's begging expression. "You ate already," I told her. "And there'll be water for you once we reach the shop."

We were there in a minute. I maneuvered the bag and coffee cup so I had a free hand, then pushed the door. It was locked. I pulled my phone from my pocket and checked the time. Nine thirty-five.

Though it was still earlier than the store opened, I was five minutes later than the time I'd told Martha. Had she gotten one of her usual employees to take care of the shop today? The possibility that she hadn't tugged at my insides. I might wind up feeling I didn't have a choice whether to stay.

"Oh, Pluckie, what am I going to—" I didn't finish, since I saw a movement inside. A young lady, looking barely out of her teens, appeared from around a tall display and approached the glass-paned door. She looked worried as she unlocked the inside latch.

"Hi." She studied me with light blue eyes beneath dark, arched brows. "Are you Rory?"

"That's right. Are you one of Martha's employees?"

"Yes, I'm Millie Weedin. Please come in."

Pluckie and I obeyed, and she latched the door shut again behind us.

"What a wonderful, cute dog," Millie gushed, kneeling to give Pluckie a hug. "I talked to Martha on the phone, and she told me that your dog's very lucky and saved her life."

I gave a slight shrug. "Maybe, but I'd imagine someone else would have found Martha in time if Pluckie hadn't."

"*Maybe*'s the key word. Anyway, she saw this amazing, strange black and white dog and all came out well. She said she'll be released from the hospital tomorrow and will be coming home. At first, she'll be upstairs in her apartment and won't be able to run the shop, but she told me about your background and said you might take over for a while."

"Possibly," I said. "For now I'd appreciate your showing me around, letting me know how things are run. That'll help in the decision about how long I'll be here." That waffled enough for her to assume I was staying ... or not.

"Sure. Even though Jeri, the other part-time assistant, knows a lot more than I do, I'll show you some computer stuff now since we have a few minutes before we open. Once we're open, I'll show you what I know about our stock and inventory and whatever else you'd like to see—including how Martha taught me to wait on customers, assuming anyone comes in."

"To a place called Lucky Dog Boutique?" I said. "I'll bet we'll be swamped today." I hoped so for Martha's sake ... but maybe not so much for my own.

The computer was a laptop, locked in a drawer beneath the cash register until needed. The system looked logical, though different from what I was used to.

When the doors opened at ten, half a dozen people and two small dogs strolled through them nearly immediately. I'd walked to the front with Millie to watch what she did, and as the customers filed in she looked at me and smiled.

"Martha was right," she murmured. "Pluckie and you are good luck." She hurried toward the nearest group—a young couple plus their shih tzu mix. "May I help you find anything?" she asked.

I listened as they described wanting a special superstition-related collar and toys for their pup. Millie led them to some items I'd noticed before and began hand-selling them.

Good employee, I thought. I decided to act as if I really was the temporary manager and approached another group, two women who seemed interested in the amulets and other items inside the glass counter near the cash register. "May I help you?"

"Oh, yes," said the older woman. I assumed they were a mother and daughter. "Sally's eighteenth birthday is in a couple of weeks, and we've started visiting shelters near our home. We're going to get her a dog."

Sally gave a huge smile. "Coming to Destiny is part of my celebration. I want to make sure my family and I all have good luck forever. My new dog, too, when we get her. So we're collecting things to make sure that happens."

I wound up selling them two matching dog-faced amulets. Sally said she'd wear one as a necklace and make sure her new pet wore the other. I borrowed Millie from her customers long enough for her to show me how to use the store's credit card reader and cash register.

The other two people, a middle-aged couple, treated the Yorkie in the woman's arms as if he was their kid. I saw a lot of that at my MegaPets store and identified with it with my own Pluckie, who stayed at my side. After taking some time to pick out a superstition-decorated collar, the customers paid cash and I took their money, made an appropriate record, and printed a receipt.

When I next glanced toward the door, Justin stood there. I'd thought he'd intended to arrive here to get me when the store opened, but it was actually a good thing he was late since it had given me a chance to see the place in action.

And even to act as if I worked here.

As I drew closer, he smiled. "I was watching you. You looked right at home."

"Is that supposed to convince me to stay?"

"Does it?" he countered.

I shook my head, not in negativity but amusement. "Are we going out for coffee?"

"Do you want to?"

"Yes," I said. "As long as it staves off more questions."

He laughed. I turned and hurried around the store's displays toward Millie, who was just finishing up with the last of the initial shoppers. No more had come in, but it was still early. I told her I'd be gone for a while.

"But you will be back?" She turned from her customers to regard me seriously. "Our other part-timer Jeri is coming in a little later to help out, but Martha promised that someone would act as manager in her absence, and she seemed sure it would be you."

"Could be," I waffled. "But it's not definite yet."

"Please make it definite as soon as possible," Millie's youthful face looked almost panicked. "I saw how well you did with those people, and we really need someone like you."

Instead of convincing me, though, Millie's pushiness, combined with knowing I faced something similar over coffee with Justin, nearly made me run screaming out of there.

But I really did have to make up my mind fairly soon. And so far I still hadn't accomplished what I'd intended by coming to Destiny.

Justin, Pluckie, and I walked a few doors down to the Beware-of-Bubbles coffee shop. Outside it, I noticed a stand containing a few copies of the *Destiny Star*, a weekly ad-supported local paper I'd seen online while researching the town. Sometime while I was here I'd have to grab a free copy to actually read.

"Beware of Bubbles?" I asked Justin as we walked inside and I picked Pluckie up.

"There are a bunch of superstitions involving bubbles in coffee," Justin said. "Some are good, but others involve bad luck." At my urging he told me that big bubbles in coffee could mean you were about to get bad news, but other people thought they just meant someone you were meeting would be late. Smaller bubbles moving toward you could mean good fortune, but if they moved away the opposite was true.

"I never really paid attention to bubbles in my coffee," I said as we stepped up to the barista to order.

When I was handed my ordinary black coffee, I saw no bubbles at all. Just as well.

I enjoyed the additional time with Justin despite how, as I'd anticipated, he spent it trying in a nice way to continue the guilt trip he'd begun laying on me if I chose to leave before Martha resumed management of her boutique. Was being with him good luck or bad? Though I appreciated how he tried to help his senior friend, I wasn't sure how I felt about it.

We soon left, each carrying our cups to go. I also held Pluckie's leash, and she stayed right beside me.

Justin walked us back to the block where the Lucky Dog Boutique was, then said, "I'll be in touch later. In fact, I'll stop in and see how you're doing at the shop."

"And if I've decided to leave and I'm not there?"

He smiled. "Then I'll definitely make sure that someone finds a superstition that says leaving town when your help is desperately needed for someone who's ill brings bad luck."

"You don't believe that," I countered. "From the way you've been talking, I suspect you're like me and don't really believe in superstitions."

"Sssh." He put his finger in front of his nicely-shaped masculine lips. "Don't let anyone in this town hear you say that about me. I've settled here permanently." He paused, reached out and touched me gently on the cheek. "And, Rory?"

"Yes?" I responded cautiously.

"Something in me, superstitious or not, tells me you might do the same thing."

———

Me? Live here permanently? I said goodbye to Justin as fast as I could after that and he headed west, toward where he said the police station was.

Instead of hurrying to the Lucky Dog Boutique, I stopped just short of it and entered the Broken Mirror Bookstore.

I'd been contemplating doing that all day and was delighted to see Kenneth Tarzal behind the counter at the far end of several shelves of books, talking with someone.

Maybe it was rude, but I caught his eye, planted a frantic expression on my face, and gestured to him pleadingly to join me.

He excused himself and approached. "Everything all right, Rory?"

"That depends," I said. "Would you have a few minutes to talk with me? I really need you to convince me about the reality of superstitions."

SIX

THE TALL GUY'S GREENISH-HAZEL eyes behind his bifocals blinked in apparent incredulity as he looked down at me. His sudden nearness was enough to get Pluckie to assume a defensive standing position. Knowing she was about to growl, I bent down and stroked her back. "It's okay, girl."

"Surely you don't need convincing, or why would you be here?" That wasn't Tarzal but the man he'd been talking to. He was shorter than Tarzal—as were most people—and heavier, with a thick silver beard emphasizing his chin and his jovial smile. On the lapel of his suit jacket was a pin depicting a leprechaun.

In fact, had this guy been a lot shorter and wearing green instead of gray, he could have been mistaken for a leprechaun, even more than the servers I'd seen at the Shamrock Steakhouse.

"That's exactly why I am here." Did the man assume everyone who visited Destiny believed that superstitions were real?

Maybe he did, considering who he was.

"Rory," said Tarzal, "this is Destiny's mayor, Bevin Dermot. Bevin, Rory's the one who discovered Martha ill in her storeroom."

"Actually," I corrected, "it was Pluckie." I gestured toward my sweet dog, now sitting and watching both men. I knew she'd try to protect me if there was anything to protect me from, and I didn't want anyone angry with her, especially someone in authority like the mayor.

"Welcome to both of you." Bevin's smile revealed white but uneven teeth. "And believe me, Rory, superstitions are very real." He turned toward Tarzal. "You know that better than anyone, Kenneth. And I don't want to hear anyone else say you were teasing about whether or not superstitions come true. You're our town's greatest authority on them. You wrote the book. Don't make the mistake of trying to cause controversy about what we do here. It won't help you sell any more of your books, I promise you."

Interesting. I had the impression that I'd interrupted an intense and not particularly friendly conversation.

One in which Kenneth Tarzal, of all people, was being chastised for saying that those who believed in superstitions could be wrong?

"I hear you, Bevin. But you're wrong about controversy. It can be a good thing, both for my book and for Destiny. More people will talk about us if we get that kind of publicity."

"We do not want that kind of publicity." Bevin's face looked even more leprechaun-like as it grew ruddier. He shut his eyes for a split second, opening them to look at me. "Don't you worry about any of this, Rory. You may have some questions, but you already know that superstitions come true. You and your little black and white dog saved a life already, and I'm sure you know that dogs like yours are definitely good luck." He smiled, then said, "See you again soon, Kenneth. Hope to see you again, Rory." He turned and left the store.

"Were you pulling our mayor's chain again, partner?" Preston Kunningham had just emerged through a door from the back of the bookshop. The smile on his face that he leveled on Tarzal didn't appear particularly humorous.

"He makes it so easy." Tarzal's return smile also looked annoyed.

My turn to butt in. "But what he had to say…Gentlemen, can I buy you lunch later so we can talk about superstitions? I came here because of a…well, situation, that some people said was because a superstition came true. I didn't believe in superstitions before, but now I'm not so sure. I'd love to discuss the possibilities with experts like you."

"Of course, my dear," Tarzal said. "We'd be delighted."

But judging from the unreadable expression on Preston's face, I wasn't certain he agreed.

Since it was only mid-morning, we planned for me to come back in a couple of hours and we'd go someplace nearby to eat and talk. I looked forward to it.

Surely I'd get the best explanation of superstitions, where they came from, and how much validity they actually had—if any—from the man who'd written a definitive book on them. His business partner might have thoughts of his own about them, too.

Would they be honest with someone like me, a visitor, one of those Destiny relied on for purchases and profits? I'd just have to weigh what they said by their attitudes as they said it.

Pluckie and I returned to the Lucky Dog next door. Millie was busy with some male customers with a pit bull on a leash—a well-behaved one who sat there and ignored my dog.

I gathered that another employee had also come in. A twenty-something woman wearing a bright red Lucky Dog Boutique T-shirt stood behind the glass showcase that held the superstition-related amulets, pointing some items out to an older couple who seemed fascinated.

I waved at Millie, and with Pluckie still leashed beside me I approached the clerk and her customers.

"Now if I were you," that clerk was saying, "I'd start a special superstition animal charm bracelet. See there?" She pointed at an area where rows of animal-related enameled charms were tucked into velvet display boxes. "You can take a whole lot of good luck home with you: a rabbit's foot, a white horse, a black and white dog."

"Can I see them more closely?" the woman said.

"Of course." The clerk noticed me then. "Cute dog." She looked down at Pluckie. "I'll be with both of you in a minute."

Millie edged over. "This is Rory," she said to the other clerk, her tone sounding as if she was introducing a movie star. "Rory, this is Jeri Mardeer. She works part-time like me. When she's not here, she's helping to run her family's store down the street, Heads-Up Penny Gifts."

"Oh, you're Rory." Jeri sounded somewhat awed. I had a feeling that, in this town of superstitions, a story with a happy ending would be told and retold so often, with embellishments, that it could wind up sounding like more than even good luck had occurred—miracles, maybe?

"Good to meet you, Jeri." And in some ways it was. She obviously knew the retail business since her family also owned a store. If I decided not to stay, maybe she could devote more time to the Lucky Dog.

"'Scuse me," Millie said and returned to her customers.

Jeri's customers, meanwhile, were still making up their minds about which charms to buy. "I've heard so many great things about you," Jeri said to me. "About how your dog—what's her name?"

"Pluckie," I supplied.

"How Pluckie not only saved but brought good luck to Martha —by bringing you here. I mean, just like that, Martha needed someone to run this shop, and there you were, with all your pet store experience."

"But I'm not sure—" I began but was interrupted by Jeri's customers calling her over.

Millie finished her sale and approached me. "I hope it's okay with you, but Martha always lets us have a half-hour break every morning when we're here together, which isn't very often, maybe one or two days a week. Right now, well, I hope it'll be okay. Jeri and I are going out for lattes, but we'll be back soon."

I agreed, although I wasn't sure I had a choice. And just like that I was there alone, in charge of the store.

As I'd said to Justin before, for all those young ladies, or even Martha, knew, I was a miserable, dishonest jerk who'd take all the money and expensive goods I could find here and run.

But of course I wasn't.

Pluckie helped me wait on a woman with a Chihuahua who wanted something nice and superstitious and expensive for her beloved little pet.

Then there was a family who wanted to know if we had any special superstition food for sale. I showed them to the shelves at the back of the store where some bags and cans among more standard, yet good quality, brands were labeled Good Luck Dog Food and

Good Luck Cat Food. Was that for real, or just relabeled for sale here? I didn't know.

The time went fast. I was almost surprised when Millie and Jeri returned. I smiled as both greeted me, asked how things had gone, and seemed pleased I'd had no issues working here alone.

They weren't half as pleased as I was.

The time on the cash register's digital display told me it was time for me to meet Tarzal and Preston for lunch.

"I need to go out for a while," I told the two staff members. "Would you mind keeping an eye on Pluckie for me?"

Worrywart that I am about my closest family member, I gave them explicit instructions, including keeping Pluckie on her leash and looping the other end over a hook I'd seen on the counter near the cash register.

"Don't worry, she'll be fine," Jeri assured me.

Only then did I leave for my luncheon engagement.

———

The Apple-a-Day Café was on Destiny Boulevard, a block from the Broken Mirror Bookstore and the Lucky Dog Boutique on the other side of the Beware-of-Bubbles Coffee Shop. The men closed their bookstore when we left and said they usually shut down for lunch anyway.

Preston talked nonstop, pointing out other stores and landmarks that had to do with Destiny's superstition theme. He even gave a brief rundown on the origin of the town, some of which I'd read online before heading here. Destiny had been founded by two Forty-Niners from California Gold Rush days. While panning for gold, they had spotted a rainbow, hurried to what they'd considered its end, and discovered a fortune in gold at the riverbank where they wound up. Subsequently devoting their wealthy lives to teaching the value of following superstitions like the one that led to their success, they had created a town a distance from the goldfields to honor their beliefs.

An interesting tale. Superstitions—at least one—had apparently worked for those guys.

And the Rainbow B&B where I was staying was patterned at least somewhat on Destiny's beginnings.

Nothing Preston said indicated whether he bought into the idea of superstitions. Not that it mattered. I figured I'd get more information from Tarzal.

Both men ordered drinks with their meals—hard liquor. Gin and tonics. Me? I needed to stay awake and keep my wits about me so I stuck with water.

The Apple-a-Day was large and crowded. The wait staff all looked like normal people. No leprechauns here, not even the mayor, although paintings obviously intended to represent various superstitions hung on the wall—with discreet price tags stuck into their corners. Apparently they'd been created by local artists who also wanted to capitalize on the superstition theme.

There was a lot of healthy stuff on the menu. I ordered a walnut-apple salad. The guys ordered sandwiches, but ones with lean meat and small salads on the side.

Once our orders were taken by a pretty young lady, I decided to jump right in. "So tell me, please," I said to Tarzal. "With all the research you must have done to write your book, why do people believe in superstitions... and are they real?"

Sitting across from me, he bent his head to regard me over the top of his bifocals, even as he guffawed aloud. "Real? Well, let's start with your first question."

He glanced toward Preston, who regarded him sternly, as if trying to tell his business partner what to say.

Tarzal's smile didn't waver. "Here's the thing, Rory. Superstitions have been around as long as mankind. I won't go into a lot of detail. You can read my book, where I talk about origins as well as superstitions. In general, they arose because someone would see or experience something unusual, like seeing a rainbow or a four-leaf clover, and then something wonderful would happen to them. Or something bad. Were they related? Probably not, but early men assumed they were and passed a description of the exciting event along to friends and family. Some of it evolved from religion, too. I can't swear that any superstition is real, that if you knock on wood or cross your fingers or whatever that you'll have good luck. But if someone does either of those things intentionally and his luck is good, his mind will relate them as cause and effect. If he doesn't do them and nothing happens, then is that bad luck? That depends."

"Then you're actually a skeptic, too." Our server had brought some delicious looking cheese rolls and I grabbed one, though my appetite had disappeared. Because I hadn't knocked on wood perhaps?

"'Too'? Then you're not a believer? Why are you here?" That was Preston. He had also taken a roll and looked at me with apparent interest as he slathered butter on it.

Should I tell them? Why not? Maybe Tarzal, the superstition expert, would have an explanation, or at least an opinion that could help me find my own closure.

"Because I want to know the reality of superstitions." Not wanting to meet either man's gaze, I took a sip of water and gazed at one of the paintings on the wall—the one depicting a ladder and a man staring at it, as if daring himself to walk under it.

Feeling my eyes moisten, I drew in my breath, then told them my story, about how my fiancé Warren had walked under a ladder, then died. Not because the ladder fell on him or anything logical.

"He was a CPA who worked at an accounting firm in an office building in downtown Los Angeles. He went outside at lunchtime one day. A nearby shop was having repair work done on its exterior. I'm not sure whether he was even aware that he had walked under that ladder since it leaned over the sidewalk. Some construction equipment fell, and although Warren wasn't struck by it, a car swerved to avoid it and hit him. Killed him." I realized I'd been holding my breath as I said this and made myself exhale.

For the first time during this meal, I wished that I, too, had ordered an alcoholic beverage.

I was surprised when Preston reached over and gently took hold of my arm. "I'm so sorry for your loss, my dear."

"Me, too," Tarzal said. I glanced up at him and did see sympathy in his expression. And was that a gleam in his eye, too? Was he going to use this in his next version of his book or something else, proof that superstitions did come true?

"So what do you think," I asked him confrontationally. "Is that a sign of the reality of superstitions?"

"What matters is what *you* think, Rory, not me. Even after all the work I've put into studying superstitions, I can't give you a definitive answer. Are superstitions real? Maybe. Maybe not. Was your fiancé's death the result of one? Again—"

"Maybe, maybe not," I parroted. "That's my problem. I don't know. I want to know."

"All I can tell you," Tarzal said, "is that, in my studies and experience, I've never come up with an absolute answer. But here's the lowdown, as I understand it."

I sat up straighter, eager to hear.

"People long to control their lives, their destinies. Their luck. They don't want to believe that most things in life occur randomly. They want to be in charge. And so, at least some of them buy into superstitions. You want good luck, you want to avoid bad luck, then follow whatever superstitions you think will give you what you want. And then you can interpret what happens in whatever way you want, too."

He'd sort of said that in his book, but in a much more positive way: If you follow those superstitions, then you will be able to control your destiny. Experience of others had proven it over time.

Maybe.

"I understand," I said. "But the fact that my fiancé happened to have walked under a ladder, probably without even thinking about it ... does that mean—"

"That means ... who knows? Is that particular superstition real? What do you think?"

"Ah, our meals are here," Preston interrupted. "Let's eat, then we'll tell you about some superstitions that appear to have come true ... like yours."

What was that about? The expert on superstitions was a skeptic and his business partner believed? Or was there something else going on that I didn't follow?

I felt utterly frustrated that, during the rest of lunch, I couldn't return the topic to Warren's death. I had spilled my insides and neither of these men gave a damn.

Well, why should they? I was a stranger asking questions about the world in which they made their living.

I wanted to know more about the randomness, and the control, that Tarzal had spoken of—and their reality. But if these men thought they really had the answers, they weren't sharing them.

Even though they did share examples of both positive and negative superstitions.

I finished eating quickly and paid the check—despite their token attempts to treat me instead—and felt relieved when we finally walked back toward their store and the one where I was apparently, thanks to superstition, the temporary manager.

I considered that some of Preston's examples, a rainbow and crossed fingers and knocking on wood, were illustrations of the best known good luck superstitions.

There seemed to be an equal number—maybe even more—of those that supposedly brought bad luck, like spilling salt without tossing some over your shoulder, breaking a mirror, opening an umbrella inside a house, and having a black cat cross your path.

Not to mention walking under a ladder.

People wanted to control their worlds? Well, so did I. I'd only scratched the surface so far. These men hadn't convinced me either way.

Maybe Tarzal was right, and if you believed, they came true — because, rightly or wrongly, you accepted that they did.

But what if you didn't believe, or didn't know? My dear Warren had never struck me as superstitious, and yet he had died after his own ladder incident. That wasn't because I believed, either, since although I said "bless you" sometimes after people sneezed and knocked on wood, it was habit, not because I genuinely bought into superstitions' reality.

But what if they truly were real? What if I could have controlled my fate and Warren's by keeping him far away from that damned ladder—as I'd been wondering ever since?

Answers? No. Only more questions circled my mind, maybe like a murder of flying crows.

At this moment, I had an urge to ignore Martha's request and flee my doubts and insecurity and everything else gnawing at me.

And that meant fleeing Destiny.

SEVEN

I LEFT TARZAL AND Preston at their shop a short while later. As I started to walk next door to the Lucky Dog, I thought about calling Gemma since I'd promised I would, but, as luck would have it, she called me first.

It wasn't the first time this had happened. I didn't believe in psychic connections any more than I was certain of the reality of superstitions, yet over the years of our close friendship Gemma had called me more than once at a time when I'd just thought about her.

Especially while she helped me in my grief over Warren.

"How are you, Rory?" Her usual caring and curiosity emanated from the tone of her voice. "Is Destiny what you thought it would be? Is it helping you at all?"

I stopped on the busy sidewalk between the two shops. I figured it was better to have this conversation here than in the Lucky Dog where Millie and Jeri could hear it. Strangers kept on the move and were unlikely to listen in.

"I don't know." I kept myself from wailing, but only just. "I met Kenneth Tarzal, author of that superstition book. In fact, I just had lunch with him and his co-owner of the Broken Mirror Bookstore. But rather than convincing me that superstitions are real and one did cause Warren's death, he only stirred up my confusion even more."

A pause. Then Gemma said, "I'm so sorry, Rory. Maybe it wasn't a good idea to encourage you to go there. Have you learned about other superstitions and their possible validity?"

There I was, standing on the sidewalk talking on my phone, watching people walk by through the tears that suddenly formed in my eyes. I glanced across the street at the Bouquets of Roses flower shop and saw a bench outside with a sign overhead that indicated a tour van stopped there.

I didn't need a tour van, but I did need someplace to sit. I headed over there. The times on the nearby sign indicated that no van was due for the next fifteen minutes, at least.

Keeping my voice low as I sat there, I recounted all that had happened since I'd reached Destiny, ending with, "Now I have to decide whether to help that poor unwell lady Martha and run her pet boutique while I do more research on superstitions, or come home and try to put all of this behind me. What do you think, Gemma? Before you called, I was about to call you and ask your advice."

"My advice is to listen to your own mind, Rory. And I know what it's telling you."

"Fine," I said. "Please interpret my own mind to me and let me know what it says." But despite my sarcastic tone, I knew Gemma was right—as the bright, intuitive librarian usually was.

"You're going to stay there till you're convinced one way or the other about superstitions," she said. "It's fantastic luck that you have an additional reason to stay, to manage the Lucky Dog Boutique. What a great name—and with your background it's a perfect place for you to center yourself."

"I won't stay here forever," I mused aloud. "I'll want to head back home and to my own job as soon as Martha can return to her store. So . . . I'll call Beverly right away." She was the manager at the Mega-Pets where I worked as assistant manager. "If she says okay, I'll stay. For now."

"Good choice." Hearing the smile in Gemma's voice I felt my own lips form a tiny grin, too. "I'll assume that's what's happening unless you call back to tell me otherwise. And Rory?"

"Yes?"

"Be sure to check in with me more often. I really want to know what you learn about superstitions. It's all so . . . well, a matter of luck, isn't it? Good and bad. I want to believe . . . I think. And I definitely want to know how things go with you."

I promised I'd keep in closer touch, then I hung up.

Good timing. A family with a child of about six joined me on the bench. As I stood to leave, I called my boss, Beverly. While I waited for traffic to pass so I could cross the street, I quickly related the gist of what was going on.

"Your Pluckie helped to save this woman, brought her good luck and all that?" Beverly, usually one of the most down-to-earth people I knew, sounded awed. She knew about my loss of Warren and the oddity of his having walked under a ladder first, but she had never commented on the related superstition. Now, she said, "Of course,

Rory. Stay as long as you want. You can always return to your position here. Just let me know as things progress when you think you'll be back."

"I appreciate this, Bev." Or so I told myself. If she'd said no, I'd have had a good excuse to return to my old life.

Without answers, though.

Then Beverly added, "Oh, you're welcome, Rory. But it's not like I have a choice. I'd no doubt receive a run of bad luck if I don't cooperate. So let's cross our fingers and hope that we both have lots of good luck, and the lady you're helping gets well fast—and you find all the answers you're looking for."

I felt my fingers cross as if she had somehow talked them into it over the phone. "Talk to you soon, Bev." As I hung up, I finally got a break in traffic and crossed the street.

Had those two phone calls been the sign I'd wished for yesterday on a fake falling star? I didn't know, but if I'd truly been superstitious I could interpret them that way.

Unlike my conversation with Tarzal and Preston.

When I entered the Lucky Dog, both clerks were busy with customers. Pluckie's leash was in Millie's hand. When she saw me, she waved, smiled, and let go. My dog dashed over and jumped up to put her front paws onto my legs, her whole body wiggling like her tail as if she hadn't seen me in weeks. "It's okay, girl." I bent and grinned as she licked my face. When I stood up, the loop of her leash was in my hand.

A young couple with a Shetland sheepdog on a leash held two collars from a rack, apparently weighing which to buy. Pluckie and I headed toward them, but a man in a bright red knit shirt who'd been near the cash register counter got there first. "Can I help you?" he asked.

Was he another employee? I watched him as he pointed out the stamped-on decorations on the collars, explaining that the depicted head of the greyhound with a white spot on it was said to be lucky. So, on the other one, was the horseshoe. "Either can ensure your little angel will have good luck." He bent to pat the dog on the head.

"Let's get both, honey," said the woman. The man reached into his pocket for his wallet.

The guy who'd waited on them motioned for Jeri to come to the register. She complied and ran the credit card.

After the people and their Sheltie left, Pluckie and I hurried to where Jeri stood talking to the man. She looked frazzled.

I notice that the man's shirt had a logo on it that said "Destiny's Luckiest Tours." "Are you another employee?" I asked.

"Well, no. Not yet. But—"

"Rory, this is Arlen Jallopia, Martha's nephew. He heard about her illness and came here to … help."

I noticed the hesitation and wondered how unhelpful Arlen might really be. He appeared in his mid-twenties, with spiky dark brown hair, a lopsided smile, and a face that vaguely resembled a sitcom star whose name I couldn't recall.

"That's nice of you." I was unsure of what else to say until I settled on, "Have you gone to the hospital to see your aunt?"

"Yeah, before. I'm a local tour guide and had to wait till I was between tours, like now. I told her I'd be glad to take some vacation days and manage the store for her, but she said she already had someone lined up. You?" His expression suggested doubts that I could even count to ten, let alone run a store.

Considering his attitude and the fact that his own aunt hadn't thought of him first to help her out, I wondered the same about him.

"Yes," I said. "That's me."

From the corner of my eye I noticed that Jeri's face had gone from seriously concerned to a huge grin. "Did your aunt tell you about Rory's background?" she said to Arlen. "She's the assistant manager of one of the best MegaPets in Los Angeles, near Beverly Hills. She's got lots of knowledge and skill to run a pet supplies store." *Unlike you* seemed to be her silent message.

"Yes," I said again. "I'm not sure how long Martha will need me here, but I've worked things out so I can stay and manage the store in her absence."

"Really? Glad to hear that," said Millie, who'd joined us.

"I'm really glad, too, Rory," Jeri said.

The only one who appeared less than pleased was Arlen. I considered inviting him to stop in anytime to make sure things looked okay, but that was up to his aunt. Besides, I didn't really want him scrutinizing me.

"Well, I'm sure I'll be seeing you again, Rory. I'll be visiting my aunt upstairs, too, once she's back." The glare in his dark eyes suggested he'd see me a lot more than I wanted.

"Fine," I said untruthfully. "Oh, where do your tours go? Maybe we can work things out so you can officially show me around town one of these days." What I didn't say was that he could do his own job while I did mine, but I hoped he understood the underlying message.

"All over town. See ya." And he was gone.

More customers walked in as he left. Before Millie and Jeri went to help the newcomers they both joined me.

"Then you really are staying, Rory?" Jeri asked.

"For now."

Jeri gave me a hug. Millie looked a little less thrilled but shot me a quick smile, then bent to give Pluckie the hug she hadn't given me.

———

Pluckie and I remained at the shop till seven o'clock, when it closed. Jeri stayed to show me how to lock up.

Martha had called earlier and said she was being released from the hospital later this afternoon, in time to go to the Destiny Welcome event that night. I wasn't sure what that was, but Jeri explained it was a weekly gala held for visitors and locals in the Break-a-Leg Theater next to City Hall. I was curious, but I was also tired after this long day. Even so, when Pluckie and I returned to the Rainbow B&B, Serina kicked me out again with the promise she'd watch Pluckie for me.

"You really need to go to the Destiny Welcome tonight," she told me. "It's good luck for visitors to go there for the first performance while they're here." She said she'd given the same orders to all the B&B's newly arrived guests.

How could I tempt fate by not seeking that good luck with a show she'd said no one should miss?

Besides, I thought I should go to see how Martha was doing.

I dressed up a bit, putting on the nicest blouse I'd brought over the only skirt I had along, both silvery gray, plus open-toed shoes with heels.

Like almost everything in town, Break-a-Leg Theater was within walking distance of the B&B. I was charmed by its golden art deco facade with rounded arches and a large glass doorway. I realized how popular the welcome show must be even before I reached the block housing the theater, since the sidewalks were even more crowded than I'd seen before. At least the line, though long, kept moving.

There was a modest charge for entry. Most of the chattering people came in parties of two or more, including some I recognized as other guests at the B&B. Then there was me.

When I finally got inside, I figured the theater must have been remodeled recently, since the seats didn't look as old as the exterior and there were even places for the handicapped. Songs like "Superstition" and "Knock on Wood" played in the background.

I saw a wheelchair near the front with a woman seated in it with familiar gray hair. But the show was about to start so I took the nearest seat—in the middle of a row near the back, after excusing my way there. If that was Martha, I'd say hi later.

The lights were dimmed and the silky red and gold stage curtain opened. Unsurprisingly, Mayor Bevin Dermot walked out. What was surprising to me was that he actually wore a green sport jacket over his plaid pants. Did he know how much he resembled the leprechaun pin I'd seen him wearing and exploit it? Probably.

"Hello, everyone," he said into the microphone he held as he strutted along the stage in front of a platform raised behind him. "Welcome to the very special town of Destiny, California. As you all know, Destiny is the capital of all superstitions."

He proceeded to tell the history. Then he said, "I'd like to introduce you to the world's foremost expert on superstitions, Mr. Kenneth Tarzal. He even wrote the best book ever published on the subject that is so near and dear to our hearts. Tarzal?"

Tarzal entered from stage left. He wore a black suit with a white shirt. From here he looked serious and carried nothing until the mayor handed him the microphone. "It's all yours," he said. "And may all your luck be good."

Tarzal smiled, then made a gesture as if knocking on his own head—knocking on wood? "Hello, everyone." He gestured grandly to include the entire audience. "Welcome to Destiny, California, which could be the luckiest place on earth ... if you obey our superstitions, of course." He pivoted to stare down toward the front of the audience on one side, then the other. He must have seen Martha since he tipped an imaginary hat in that direction. "But do *you* believe in superstitions? I mean—well, let's check. Please raise your hand if you have ever knocked on wood the way I just did to increase your luck."

Almost everyone in the audience raised their hands.

He nodded, then asked similar questions about crossing fingers, picking up found pennies, and other common superstitions.

"Okay, then. If you've ever forgotten to do any of the things I just mentioned, did your luck turn bad? I mean, did you get hit by a car or lose your job or anything else that upset you? Some of you are nodding, but most are shaking your heads." I'd looked around, and he was right. "Now, Destiny is my favorite place on earth, mostly because I want you all to have heard of me and come to my bookstore. Buy my book. Maybe I should curse any of you who don't to have seven years of bad luck. My bookstore is called the Broken Mirror, so that would be appropriate, don't you think?"

Before anyone could say anything, he turned and climbed the steps on the stage to the top of the platform that was raised about two feet.

"Some superstitions started out as attempts to cause bad luck to other people, like the 'evil eye' way back when. So let me see how else I can curse you." He named a few other omens of bad luck, including the standard black cat crossing a person's path.

This seemed like a strange kind of talk, and I had a sense it wasn't his usual one since the mayor kept edging out onto the side of the stage where he'd exited. But Tarzal kept going—until the mayor walked up the steps onto the platform.

Tarzal didn't relinquish the microphone to him, though. Instead, he walked toward the opposite set of stairs from the platform and onto the rest of the stage.

Only, after he'd gone down only two of the three steps, he fell. He landed on the stage, but his right arm seemed to crack against the steps.

"Damn it!" he shouted. I wasn't sure where the microphone was, but I'd no doubt that everyone could hear him. He managed to push himself up with his left arm until he knelt on the stage.

"Are you okay, Kenneth?" Mayor Dermot approached him while still on the platform.

"I'm fine," Tarzal said, more softly but somehow the microphone, wherever it was, picked up his voice. "I will be, at least—when I find the imbecile who dared to spill milk where I was likely to fall in it."

EIGHT

"DOES THAT MEAN YOU'LL have seven days' bad luck?" I could see the horror on the mayor's face.

Obviously he, at least, was superstitious. Was Tarzal superstitious enough to buy into that kind of curse even though it was a lot more lenient than the seven *years'* bad luck for breaking a mirror?

If Tarzal was rattled, he didn't admit it in front of this crowd. "Not I," he said calmly. He'd pulled himself back to a standing position on the stage and was so tall that the top of his head reached the same altitude as that of Mayor Dermot, who still stood on the platform. "Whoever tried to curse me that way—well, I hereby state that, like I suggested before, I, the expert on superstitions, now turn that around so that whoever did it will be the one who experiences bad luck."

I heard a lot of muttering in the audience, then someone—a man I hadn't noticed previously—stood and said, "Can you do that? I've never heard of anyone turning a superstition already in play on someone else, either good luck or bad."

"This show is over," Tarzal said, without responding directly. "Remember, this is Destiny. My town. My superstitions. Things happen as I say. Now, everyone leave."

I noticed that Preston had come onto the stage, at its edge. As Tarzal began to limp off, Preston hurried toward him, arms out as if ready to steady his partner. I couldn't hear what Tarzal said since he didn't project or speak into the microphone, but Preston backed off.

Did anyone believe Tarzal—that he knew so much about superstitions, that he was so much in charge of them, that he could change existing scenarios, turn them against others?

Surely no one who was a true believer would buy into that. And the rest of us agnostics—well, I didn't accept what he'd said, either.

I saw a woman at the side of the stage taking pictures with a tablet computer. She also typed something onto it, then made notes onto a real notebook, like a media person. I saw them often in L.A., but here? I guess they could be anywhere.

Tarzal didn't seem to notice. He edged past his partner, who just stood watching him. He made his way backstage, then, as the audience continued to file out of the auditorium, he appeared again on the same level as those in the front row.

The front row. I thought I'd seen Martha there, in a wheelchair. Was Tarzal, or someone else, going to help her?

I had to check on her.

It wasn't easy making my way to the front through the crowded aisle beside me. The rows of red plush seats were emptying fast as the chattering, determined audience headed for the side doors. I succeeded, though, and when I saw Martha just sitting there, pale but with an irritated expression on her face as most people hurried by her, I was glad I'd fought the hordes.

By then, Tarzal stood near the base of the stage, waving a cell phone in one hand as he talked to Preston, the mayor, and others, and was among those ignoring Martha.

"Rory!" she exclaimed, standing up. "I'm so glad to see you. I made a lot of noise to get released from the hospital late this afternoon and was able to convince one of the nurses to push me over here in this nasty contraption a while ago." She waved one of her yellow sweater-covered arms toward the wheelchair. "I told her I'd call my nephew to push me home if I didn't see someone else who'd do it. I'd figured Tarzal or Preston would, but they're both preoccupied." She nodded toward them.

Everyone else had left the area where I now stood looking down at Martha. Despite her slight pallor, she appeared a lot better than when I'd visited her at the hospital.

I'd also told her when we'd spoken that afternoon, after my call to Bev, that I could stay in Destiny for a while. She was aware that, at least for now, I would manage the Lucky Dog Boutique for her.

She must have left the hospital a short while after we'd spoken, but she had sounded iffy to me about when she would be able to return to her home upstairs from the shop, let alone start running the place again.

"I'll be glad to push you back to your place," I told her now, and she looked relieved and sat back down again.

As I moved toward the back of her chair, I saw Police Chief Justin Halbertson arrive with some uniformed cops. They entered through one of the doors from which much of the audience had exited.

He stopped beside Martha's chair, and I saw surprise on his face as he looked from one of us to the other. "What are you two doing here?"

"I could ask you the same thing," I said. "I'm a visitor and was told it would be good luck for me to see the Destiny Welcome show as soon as possible."

I was becoming familiar with his expression: a half smile, his dark, arched eyebrows raised over his blue eyes in a way that all but shouted skepticism. "And you believed in this potential good luck?"

"Doesn't matter. It was definitely a night of bad luck for one of the speakers, Kenneth Tarzal. He slipped coming down from the platform on the stage. Said some milk was spilled there."

"Yes, he called the station and asked for an investigator to come and check whether the situation was intentional."

"And that's why you're here."

He nodded. "My guys will look at the evidence, take pictures, bring in any milk containers they see, and check for fingerprints to try to figure out how the liquid got there."

I couldn't help my amused smile. "So that's what the police department of a specialty town like Destiny does? Investigate the origin of spilled milk?"

He gave a short laugh. "Yes, that kind of thing has real meaning around here. I'd better go observe what my guys are doing. Will you be in town much longer?"

"She's decided to manage the Lucky Dog for me till I'm better," Martha inserted.

"That's excellent news." Justin did, in fact, look happy about it. His apparent pleasure made me feel all the better. And I felt sure Martha could have called on him to get her home if I hadn't been there and willing to help her. "Then I'll be seeing you around."

"That'll be nice," I said. "Now, Martha, let's go back to your place."

On our walk back to the Lucky Dog Boutique, I asked Martha more about the Destiny Welcome show. "Do other townsfolk sometimes participate?"

We strolled leisurely along the still crowded sidewalk, beneath the streetlamps in the shapes of old Gold Rush lanterns. Some restaurants and bars were open, but the stores we passed were all closed.

Rather, I strolled, pushing Martha in her wheelchair. I couldn't worry about the wheels touching the cracks in the sidewalk but I managed to avoid walking on them, just in case.

"Sure." She proceeded to fill me in on which town council members spoke, sometimes instead of the mayor. Shop owners and tour company managers sometimes got up on stage, too, to welcome visitors—and encourage them to frequent their businesses.

"Have you ever done it?" I asked.

"A few times, especially when there are a lot of folks in town with their pets."

I had to ask. "And Tarzal. I assume, considering his notoriety with respect to superstitions, that he's pretty much always one of the main speakers?"

"Oh, yes, but he's been less welcome lately. He used to talk more about how real superstitions were. Lately, he's been giving the kind of talk he did tonight more often. Like, his research has shown him that superstitions are wonderful things, but believing in them may be … let's say, foolish. Everyone in town has been chewing him out about it, and he apparently promises each time that he'll go back to his original kind of talk, but he obviously doesn't always do that."

Interesting, I thought.

I also wondered if he genuinely believed that, thanks to slipping in milk, he would now experience more bad luck.

I didn't wish that on him, of course, but I'd have to pop over to his store soon and ask if there'd been any consequences. Or anything in his life that, if he were superstitious, he would consider to be bad luck.

I did wonder, though, about how the milk had been spilled. Whoever had done it must have entered the stage area behind the curtain before the show began. But how had they known where to put it? And when had they had the chance to do it without being seen? Maybe it had been an accident. Or not.

And Tarzal wasn't the only possible target of the milk, was he? Anyone present at the theater that night could have gone that direction and spilled it. The fact that some people in town didn't like some of his current presentations probably had nothing to do with what had happened.

Unless...

"When the show is given that way, is Tarzal the only one who goes up onto the platform on the stage?"

"Pretty much," Martha said. "Most people just stand at the front with the microphone and interact more with the audience. He seems to want to get away from them a bit and pace up on the platform."

So maybe he had in fact been the milk's intended target.

And the possible impending bad luck it brought?

Well, we'd just have to see.

We soon reached the sidewalk nearest the Lucky Dog Boutique as well as the Broken Mirror Bookstore, which was also closed. I'd seen no indication that either Tarzal or Preston lived there, though there were a couple of floors above the store.

Martha directed me to the rear of the Lucky Dog and used a key to open the back door. The place was becoming more familiar to me, but I was glad to be entering the storeroom with a healthier Martha rather than worrying about finding her here again, ill.

She directed me to push her wheelchair among the stacks of items stored there until we reached a door along the wall near the one that separated this room from the rest of the store. She used a different key to unlock it, then kicked the footrests on the wheelchair out of her way and stood on the floor.

"Be careful," I told her.

"Of course. And I will need your help to get upstairs."

She flicked on a light, and I saw the stairway that must lead up to her apartment. It was narrow, but wide enough for me to stay at her side while she proceeded slowly upward, holding onto the handrail while I kept an arm around her to help keep her steady and moving.

She did really well on the stairs, and it didn't take us long to reach the next floor. She flicked on more lights and I was delighted to see how cute her apartment was, with well-maintained living room furnishings that must have come from the time even before Martha was a child, ornate, plushy antique chairs and a sofa, as well as wooden end tables and a coffee table—and a modern, though not huge, TV.

Fortunately, her small bedroom was on that floor. She offered me a drink of water from her kitchen, which I declined, as we passed it on the way down the hall. She took a bottle of water for herself from the fridge, though, and carried it with her. She needed even less help here than on the stairs. Then, though she didn't seem pleased about it, she allowed me to help her maneuver her slight, aged body out of her clothes and into a robe.

"I'll be just fine now." She showed me that her bathroom was right next door. "The nurses gave me a sponge bath at the hospital so I won't have to shower, at least not till tomorrow." She was leaning against the wall, but stood up straighter. "I want to thank you, Rory. For everything. For staying here to help with the store as well as for helping me get home and upstairs tonight."

"You'll be all right here?" I asked. "I'll come in early to help you with breakfast. And I assume you'll just stay upstairs here until you're all better, right?"

"I've got some help coming tomorrow that the hospital scheduled for me. They'll check on me, bring me food if I need it, that kind of thing." She didn't sound thrilled, but what she said made me feel a lot better.

"I'm glad," I said. "And while I'm around, you can call on me, too, to help out if you need it."

"Like I said, I want to thank you." She moved a bit and gave me a brief hug. "Now go on back to your B&B. I know you've got a wonderful little lucky dog there waiting for you. Goodnight, Rory. I'll see you tomorrow."

I hesitated only a minute. "You have your phone with you?"

"Yes," she said. "And its charger. I'll be able to call for help if I need it—which I won't. But thanks again, for worrying about me this time."

I laughed.

And then I left.

———

Martha was right. Pluckie was waiting up for me to return to the Rainbow B&B. So was Serina. She was in a room just off the lobby, in the other direction from the dining area, watching TV while sitting on the sofa. I gathered that Pluckie had been on it with her, too.

When I used my key to enter the lobby from the outside, I noticed right away that the lights were still on there and in the room next door. I popped my head in and saw Pluckie pulling at her leash.

I was glad she was restrained like that, much better for keeping her safe as well as away from annoying anyone coming in late with her effusive greeting.

"Hi," Serina said, standing up. At this hour, she wasn't in her usual Gold Rush-era outfit, but instead wore modern two-piece pajamas in a print with horseshoes on it. Her light brown hair was loose now about her shoulders. "How did you enjoy the Destiny Welcome?"

"Well, I'm not sure the show was a harbinger of good luck." I told her about the incident with Tarzal and the milk. "But I did find it interesting—and definitely welcoming to outsiders." I also mentioned walking Martha and her wheelchair home. "Now, come on, Pluckie. Let's go for our last walk of the night. Thanks for watching her for me, Serina. Was she a good girl?"

"The best."

Once again let free, my little black and white dog leaped up on me, showering me with affection that I knelt to return. Then I grabbed her leash and we went outside for her last short walk of the night.

Soon, we were back in our bedroom, and I got ready for bed. My PJs were frilly and blue and somewhat ordinary. Maybe I'd get some with good luck symbols before I left Destiny.

I gave my longish blond hair a final brushing for the night, and then I lay down, too tired even to read myself to sleep. I turned out the lights, feeling Pluckie jump into bed beside me.

I'd fallen asleep. I was fairly sure of it.

But Pluckie began moving in the bed and woke me. "Go back to sleep, girl," I said without checking the clock for the time.

I closed my eyes again—and then I heard it, what must have awakened my sweet pup.

Somewhere in Destiny, a dog howled loudly into the night.

Pluckie barked this time, and I shushed her—even as I heard the howl again.

Was that an omen of some kind? An occurrence that would say something to the superstitious people around here?

I'd have to check it out in the morning.

———

I didn't have to check it out, at least not look it up. Others at the B&B talked about it over breakfast.

A howling dog was an omen of death, to those who believed.

I'd wait and see if anyone in town was reported dead today. I hated even the notion of that.

It reminded me too much of my Warren and his walking under that damned ladder. Not that I'd heard any howling dogs then.

For now, I ate my eggs and muffin, drank my coffee, and prepared to head to the Lucky Dog Boutique with Pluckie, who'd already been outside and eaten. I wanted to arrive at the store before it opened.

Only Pluckie didn't let me get there. Not right away.

We walked to Destiny Boulevard with no incident.

As we passed the Broken Mirror Bookstore, or at least I tried to, Pluckie pulled on her leash. Hard. She wanted to go into that store.

Having had her also insist on my going into the back room of the Lucky Dog and showing there was good reason for that—an ill Martha—I obviously had to obey her.

Or at least try. It was too early for the bookstore to open. Maybe I could peek into the windows.

But I first tried the front door. Oddly, it was unlocked.

And as I opened it, Pluckie went inside and sat down. She was the one to give a small howl this time. She sounded scared.

The store wasn't quite dark, since some illumination came in through the windows, but no lights were on inside.

I felt icy fingers of fear tiptoeing up my back. What superstition did that evoke? I had no idea.

But Pluckie began inching forward on her leash, toward the side of the store where the windowed office enclosure was located. And as I looked inside, I gasped.

There was just enough light in there for me to see someone lying on the floor.

Not Martha, of course. A man. A tall man, it appeared. He faced away so I couldn't see, but I thought it could be Tarzal.

"Tarzal?" I called out as I entered. "Are you okay?"

I smelled something then—curdled milk, and worse. I saw some on the floor near Tarzal's face. I also saw shards of glass around the floor near him. Broken mirrors? The pieces reflected what was near them.

Not only that, but as I drew closer I saw that a large piece of glass protruded from Tarzal's chest. Blood oozed from it.

"Oh, no," I cried. "No."

I bent and put my fingers on his neck, holding my breath, hoping I'd at least feel a pulse the way I had with Martha.

85

I didn't.

I pushed a little harder, and his head moved—but not because he'd moved it.

His eyes were open. Sightless.

And I knew that Kenneth Tarzal was dead.

NINE

Trying not to hyperventilate, I called 911—for the second time since I'd arrived in Destiny. Had the last time been only two days ago?

I made myself look away, toward filled bookshelves instead of Tarzal. I needed to be able to talk, not gag. Or cry.

I was standing now, and I'd grabbed Pluckie, picked her up so she couldn't get near the man who lay on the floor. She'd tried, though. Maybe that awful odor had enticed her. But fortunately, she hadn't stepped in the blood. A good thing. No bloody pawprints for the police to look into.

And no need for me to clean those paws.

And why was I worrying about that now? Was I in shock?

I was glad when my phone call was answered. Did I speak to the same dispatcher? She certainly sounded the same, at least at first. This time I didn't make her guess the location. I knew that the Broken Mirror Bookstore was on the 1300 block of Destiny Boulevard, like the Lucky Dog Boutique.

The address. The 1300 block. Thirteen was supposed to be bad luck. Was it?

It certainly had been since my arrival here.

"What's the nature of your emergency?" the dispatcher asked as calmly as the last time.

"It looks like a murder! Tarzal has been stabbed. There's blood. A broken mirror—a real one, not just the name of the store." I gave a gasping laugh as I said that, almost hysterically. That's what would matter in this town—the actual broken mirror.

No. I truly was becoming hysterical, and I had to calm myself.

"A real broken mirror? Oh, my!" the now-distressed voice exclaimed. "Seven years' bad luck. Whose? Can't be Tarzal's if he's already…" She stopped, maybe realizing how unprofessional she sounded. I'd have laughed even more, if I didn't feel like crying instead.

Superstition over reality… the norm around here.

The last time I'd called the emergency number I hadn't mentioned Pluckie, the lucky black and white dog, or maybe I'd have gotten the same reaction then.

"Please stay on the line, miss… What was your name?"

"Rory. I help out at the Lucky Dog Boutique next door."

"Rory. Remember to breathe, Rory."

"Thank you," I said as calmly as if she had just said she would come to the Lucky Dog to do some shopping. Good. I was getting hold of myself… maybe.

I did as she said and took a conscious deep breath, which was probably a good thing. I wasn't sure I had been breathing otherwise.

"Now, is anyone else there with you?"

"No," I said. "At least I don't think so." Was she asking whether the killer was still around? I shuddered, which made Pluckie move in my arms.

Surely my wonderful little dog would be reacting differently if any other person was present. But right now, she was licking my chin, acting as if we were the only two beings in the world. I hugged her closer.

"Good," the dispatcher said. "Okay, carefully go outside and wait there. And stay on the line with me." Silence for a few seconds and then I heard her talking to someone else, muffled. Part of sending help here, or was she letting other people know about the broken mirror?

I didn't obey her. Instead, I hung up and immediately pushed in an additional number—the one Justin had given me to stay in touch with him.

He hadn't anticipated this reason, I was sure. Neither had I. But the police chief needed to know about this. And it wouldn't hurt to tell him immediately.

It might help me, too, to get him here sooner.

"Hello?" he said right away. "Rory?" I'd called on his cell, and he must have recognized my number on caller ID. "Are you okay? I'm just getting word that you're at the Broken Mirror Bookstore—and that there's been an incident there."

"I'm fine," I assured him—and myself. Right? I *was* fine, or at least I would be, maybe once I actually did go outside. "I called 911 and I think help's on the way."

"It is—and it includes me. I'll be there as soon as I can. Just be careful." And then the connection ended.

Be careful? Well, sure.

But his words reminded me—as if I'd forgotten—that what had happened here did not appear to be an accident. Tarzal had been stabbed.

Okay, it was time. Pluckie and I were going outside where there'd be lots of other people.

I heard a siren then. Maybe more than one.

"You know what?" I said to my dog, hugging her even closer. "Things around here are going to get crazy. You don't need to be here, especially since your paws are clean. Let's go next door."

I put her down, held her leash, and led her out the front door without looking back to where Tarzal lay.

As soon as we got outside, I saw a black cat stalking at the side of the bookstore. So did Pluckie, but I got her to heel and stay quiet after the first lunge and bark.

A black cat. It hadn't crossed our path. But had it crossed Tarzal's?

I used the key I'd been given to open the Lucky Dog's door. It was only around nine A.M., though it felt like I'd been around this area for hours. I needed to leave Pluckie here. What was I going to do with her? I couldn't just shut her in the store loose. Other people would come in and she could sneak out the door. Or maybe she'd get into treats on the shelves. She had an excellent nose, especially for stuff she was interested in.

She was crate trained. Maybe this shop sold crates and I could—

But I gasped aloud as Pluckie pulled ahead on her leash. We weren't alone in the shop after all.

But it wasn't Millie or Jeri who stood there getting ready to open for the day.

It was Martha. Downstairs, when she was supposed to be recuperating up in her apartment. She was standing and holding onto the cash register's counter, dressed in a blue blouse and dog-print skirt. Her gray hair was mussy but she had apparently run a comb through it.

"What are you doing here?" my voice squeaked.

"This is my store," she responded, her words a little slurred. Was she okay? Letting go of the counter, she took a couple of steps toward me without appearing too rickety. "What's wrong, Rory?"

Should I tell her? She had to be friends with the men who owned the shop next door, and she was infirm. Maybe telling her would be harmful.

But she would hear about it soon enough anyway. It might as well be from me.

"We were on our way here—Pluckie and I—and Pluckie told me we needed to stop at the Broken Mirror," I began. "And—well, Martha, those sirens? They're because I had to call 911. I—we—Pluckie and I, we found Tarzal lying on the floor. And I think he's in worse condition than you were when we found you."

Her wizened hand went to her lipstick-reddened mouth. "Is he ... is he going to be okay?"

"I think he's dead," I said, then hurried over to grasp her in my arms so she didn't fall. But she felt fairly strong and sturdy as I held her.

"Oh, no," she wailed. "And he and I were ... well, we were talking business. That's why—never mind. I need to go see him."

"No," I said firmly. "The authorities are on the way and may need to treat next door as a crime scene." Surely she, like me, had seen enough TV to know how crime scenes were treated.

"A crime scene. Then—someone hurt him?"

"I think so, but it'll be up to the cops to figure it out." The siren was louder now, but then broke off. The EMTs and cops or whoever'd been sent must be here. "I was just bringing Pluckie over to protect her and keep her out of the way. Could you do me a favor and take care of her?" Giving Martha a mission might help to keep her stay clear for her own sake.

"Of course, dear." Her voice trembled. "But let me know what's happening. Please."

I'd stepped back and started removing the end of Pluckie's leash from my arm. "You'll be okay here? Do you want me to get you anything?"

"No, I'll be fine."

Giving her Pluckie's leash to hold, I went back into the storeroom anyway and got Martha's wheelchair from where I'd left it last night. "Here. Sit down and relax, at least."

She leveled a vaguely irritated look at me from soft hazel eyes surrounded by wrinkles of concern and age. "Relax? You think I can relax after what you've told me?"

"Sitting's better for you than standing. I didn't think you were even allowed to come downstairs yet. Didn't you say the hospital was sending some kind of home care attendants to help you today?"

"Yes, but they can help me out down here, too. I was getting claustrophobia already. This will be much better."

Maybe, I thought as I left Pluckie in her care to head back next door. But I wasn't so sure.

In fact, I was afraid that Martha's coming downstairs that way, considering what had happened to Tarzal, was a big mistake.

Did I think she could have killed him? Of course not—not even if she wasn't as frail as she obviously was.

But she clearly was able to walk on her own.

And what I thought wouldn't make a bit of difference in what the authorities thought.

———

"There you are." That was the first thing Justin said to me as I saw him outside the door to the Broken Mirror. "I was just about to call you." His severe frown marred the usual good-looking nature of his face, and I stopped immediately. Was he going to accuse me of something? "With what happened in there—well, I had some concerns about you."

Instead of getting defensive, I felt a trickle of warmth begin inching its way within my body. He'd been worried about me —and not about what he thought I'd done.

That was sweet, especially coming from the local police chief, whose force was starting to investigate what looked like a murder.

"Thanks," I said as offhandedly as I could. "I admit to having a bad case of nerves right now."

"Not surprising. We'll need you to describe everything that happened from the time you got up this morning till now—and focusing on finding the body."

The body. That was who and what Tarzal was now, at least to the cops.

Maybe that was how they managed to deal with seeing death often.

How many of the deaths that occurred here in Destiny were murders? Coming from Southern California as I did, killings weren't as rare as they should be. But here?

I didn't ask. Not now.

"Okay," I said, though I swallowed hard at the thought of reliving every moment of today.

"I'll get one of the investigation team members over here. I'll stay with you, if you'd like."

"Oh, yes, I'd like that." I felt a bit relieved. Not that Justin could protect me from my emotions, but maybe I could control them a little better if I tried to act like a normal human being to impress him.

As long as I stayed in Destiny, it wouldn't hurt to have the chief of police as a friend.

"So let's—" Justin began, but he stopped. I looked in the direction he did toward the crowd of people amassing in front of the store.

Pushing through them was Preston.

As well dressed as I had seen him before, he maneuvered his way through the noisy onlookers—were there any members of the media present yet?—and joined Justin and me near the door.

"What's going on here?" he demanded. "Where's Tarzal? Did he do something to bring in a crowd—schedule an unplanned book-signing, or ..." His voice dropped off as he looked from Justin's face to mine and back again. "What happened?" he croaked.

"I'm sorry to tell you, Preston, that it appears that Tarzal has passed away," Justin said. Nice way of putting it. But then Justin added, "It was an apparent homicide. Possibly a murder."

My turn to look from one face to the other. I gathered that Justin, in his cop role, also watched Preston's reaction, to see if he did something that made it obvious that he was the murderer.

But as I looked at Preston, I saw his face go as white as his hair. He reached out but there was nothing to grab onto to steady himself. I didn't know the guy well, but I felt sorry for him. I took his arm and felt him put a lot of weight that way. Could I continue to support him?

Fortunately, Justin took his other arm. "Come on," he said. "Let's go inside."

I wondered, with all the blood on the floor where Tarzal lay, if that was a good idea, but Justin was in charge.

He maneuvered both of us through the door but then kept us moving around the perimeter of the displays and tall bookshelves to the door to the rear storeroom.

That was where we wound up.

I found it interesting that Preston moved away quickly, approaching a carton on some shelves against the wall. He brought out a copy of Tarzal's superstition book.

"I'm not sure how we should behave in the situation of a murder," he said. "I have to look that up."

He turned immediately to the end of the book and began scanning the back pages. I'd noticed the index before. It was very detailed, incorporating all the subjects of superstitions that Tarzal had written about.

But then he looked up directly at Justin. "I have to know. How did he … how was he killed?"

"It appears that he was stabbed with a sharp piece of glass. From a broken mirror. But that's not certain yet, so please don't pass it along."

"A broken mirror," Preston repeated. "In the Broken Mirror Bookstore. How appropriate." He paused, and I noticed that there were tears in his eyes. He must have been close to his partner. And maybe what had happened wouldn't completely sink in until he'd done his superstitious research and thought about reality. "And of all murder weapons, that could be the best, at least under these circumstances."

"What do you mean?" I had to ask.

He turned his gaze on me. "Assuming that the killer, and not Tarzal, broke it, then that person will be doomed to seven years of bad luck. Unless he—or she—grabbed one of the five-dollar bills along the wall and made a sign of a cross." He looked from Justin to me and back again, but he couldn't find an answer to that on either of our faces—but I now knew what those framed bills were there for. Preston shook his head. "Their bad luck, if it happens, won't bring Tarzal back, but at least it would give me a tiny bit of solace."

"Oh. Right," I said. Maybe that meant the killer would be identified immediately.

Or maybe Tarzal had been the one to spill the latest batch of milk and break the mirror without grabbing the five-dollar bills. He'd certainly suffered some pretty bad luck.

He was dead.

"Here," Preston said after opening the book and turning the pages until he reached the one he apparently sought. "Superstitions about murder. First of all, seeing one, or finding a body, or passing a murder victim, is bad luck."

"So we all are subject to bad luck?" I tried not to scoff. That superstition was too obvious. How could finding a murder victim be good luck?

Besides, although I'd discovered Tarzal, everyone here—except maybe Preston—had seen his body, most likely passed it. Did that mean bad luck would follow every one of us?

And surely, if there were any validity to that one, there'd be a whole lot of anecdotes out there about cops and crime scene investigators and coroners and everyone else who dealt with murder victims staggering around forevermore with horrible luck once they'd worked their first case.

"Yes," Preston said. "Also, the blood shouldn't be removed, and the body will bleed again in the presence of the murderer. Oh, and Chief?" He looked straight into the face of Justin, who stood beside me, his expression a lot more neutral than mine.

"What?" Justin said. He was standing near a tall stack of crates, his arms crossed.

I remained near him, my hands clenched at my sides. I was still trying to keep control of my thoughts, my emotions. Did I really need to hear these superstitions about dead people?

How might they have applied to Warren?

At least he hadn't been murdered.

"If there's going to be an autopsy," Preston continued, still looking at Justin, "be sure to tell whoever does it that the image of the murderer will remain on a victim's eyeballs forever."

"I'll mention that," Justin said dryly.

If that one superstition was true, and those who did autopsies knew how to access those eyeball images, solving murders would be a lot faster and more predictable than it seemed to be now. But maybe the right scientific techniques hadn't yet been established. Or they were kept secret by those who'd figured them out.

And all those superstitions about blood. They clearly couldn't be true.

Now, thinking again about—what else?—superstitions, I recalled that Tarzal had attempted to turn the superstition about spilled milk on whoever had left the bottle there for him to run into. That was a major blow, in my mind, against the validity of superstitions. Or maybe it was a sign they were real ... sometimes.

Tarzal, despite trying to change it, had been the one who had experienced bad luck.

And if I remembered my view of his dead body correctly, there was more spilled milk on the floor near him—in addition to the blood that wasn't supposed to be cleared ... Right.

"You know," Justin said, "since this is Destiny, all of us in the police department have been made aware of a lot of superstitions. Not that we'd tell the tourists, but not every one of us really buys into all of those ideas. And just in case they're real, one rule of the department is that we each need to wear an amulet to ward off the bad luck and bring us some good luck instead." He reached into the front of the blue uniform shirt he wore and pulled out a chain. At its end was a small bronze charm in the shape of an acorn. "It's a real acorn," Justin said. "Dipped in something—bronze, maybe, or a representation of it. Acorns are supposed to bring good luck, deter old age, increase lifespan, all sorts of things. I chose this one. Others wear rabbits' feet, wishbones, horseshoes, whatever."

I looked into his eyes. He appeared amused. I still doubted that he believed in superstitions, but he did believe in his adopted town of Destiny. That, most likely, was why he and his fellow cops wore good-luck symbols more than because they believed ... but they probably figured it wouldn't hurt.

"Hey, I like that," I said, not sure whether I did or not. "I think that, while I'm staying in Destiny, it wouldn't hurt for me to get some kind of good luck amulet. One related to black dogs would probably be best."

"I'll bet Martha—you—sell some. Ask the part-timers who help out. They'll know."

I recalled the charms and things locked into the case near the cash register. Customers were told they would foster good luck. I'd have to ask if that was supposed to be true.

"Chief? Is it okay for me to interview Ms. Chasen now?" A young woman in a black suit had just come through the door from the shop. She had a dark complexion and was around my height of five-six but appeared a little heavier. Or maybe some of that was from cop gear. Despite the suit, I noticed a utility belt around her waist.

Chief Justin didn't wear one despite being dressed partly in uniform, with his blue shirt and dark slacks. But presumably he could grab one if he needed it—or rely on his underling cops to do any dirty deeds requiring guns, like protection or catching crooks that were required.

"Rory, this is Alice Numa," Justin said. "She's one of the detectives investigating Tarzal's murder, and she wants to talk to you about what you saw."

TEN

I WASN'T SURPRISED. IN fact, Justin had indicated I'd need to be interviewed. And I realized that what little I knew probably had to be analyzed along with evidence and other witnesses' descriptions of when they had last seen and talked with Tarzal.

Preston, at least, could talk about when he'd been with Tarzal after last night's performance. And maybe others who'd attended could add to the description of what had become Tarzal's last day.

But the idea of my rehashing this so far short yet significant day, moment by moment, wasn't exactly at the top of my preferred to-do list.

My wishes didn't matter, though. The Destiny PD needed to solve a murder. I'd been the first person to stumble onto the victim—fortunately not literally.

And I'd never have done that at all if it hadn't been for Pluckie.

"This storeroom is as good as anyplace else around here to talk," Justin told Alice. "It's relatively quiet, although we'll need to keep people out while we conduct interviews. We won't touch anything so our folks can also check it for any evidence later. Preston, I think we'll talk to Rory first, although you're on our list, too."

"I doubt I know anything helpful," he said with a frown on his aging face. "But of course I'll talk to you later. My poor Tarzal." He closed his eyes for a moment, then opened them again. "I don't know what I'm going to do around here without him. But I'll do all I can to help you find his killer. For now, in case you need these …" He walked around some nearby shelves. I heard something grate on the concrete floor, and when he reappeared he was carrying three collapsed metal chairs.

"Thanks." Justin took them from him. "Please stay nearby—although we'd like you to remain outside the store while it's investigated as a crime scene."

"Oh. Yes. Well, I … I think I'll go and get a cup of coffee and bring it back. Is that all right?"

"Yes, but be sure to give your phone number to Alice, here, before you go so we'll be able to get in touch with you."

He provided a number, unsurprisingly with an 805 area code which covered a lot of territory in this part of California, and then walked slowly out the back door of the storeroom, his shoulders slumped.

Justin set up the chairs in a corner. On one side were stacks of boxes labeled with book titles—mostly Tarzal's. On the other side were metal shelves with books stacked directly on them.

Surrounded by two cops as I was, I felt hemmed in. I inhaled the dusty storeroom aroma. It reminded me a bit of the Lucky Dog's back room, but Martha definitely kept it cleaner and free of dust, unlike this place.

"All right, Ms. Chasen," Alice said. "You need to know that our conversation will be recorded. I'd like for you first to give your full name, then to tell us where you were before you came here and describe why you came in. Please just start talking, and if necessary we'll interrupt you with questions. Do you understand what I just described?"

Obviously all that was for the recorder—and to show that I was giving up any rights to object to both talking and having it saved for posterity.

That was okay. I, in fact, wanted to do my part to figure out what had happened to Tarzal.

And surely I wasn't under suspicion—was I?

I looked at Justin when I said, "My full name is Aurora Belinda Chasen, but you both can just call me Rory." I didn't mention that my initials were "ABC" because my parents had a sense of humor and always claimed they wanted me to learn the alphabet early. "And—well, before I start, I know enough from TV and all that you haven't given me my Miranda rights. I'm assuming that's because I'm not a suspect—right?"

Justin's grin was so cute that it almost alarmed me. Was I being set up? But what he said put me more at ease. "Oh, you can be certain, Rory, that if you say anything suspicious that could change. But no, at least for now, you're not under suspicion of anything other than being an important witness. Now, please go ahead."

I described hearing a dog howl last night. That was relevant here. This was Destiny.

They'd probably heard it, too.

Then I told about waking up at the Rainbow B&B, throwing on clothes to take Pluckie outside—and yes, I described each of her eliminations with too much detail. They wanted information, and I'd give it to them.

I told them about returning to my room, feeding Pluckie, and then going downstairs to eat my own B&B breakfast. Justin already knew that I'd committed to stay in town to help Martha so it was no surprise to him that I then headed, with Pluckie, to the Lucky Dog Boutique.

"You say you had your dog with you?" Alice asked.

"That's right. She's the one, in fact, who yanked me on her leash toward this bookstore when I tried to pass. She senses when things aren't right."

I looked at Justin, and he informed his detective that Pluckie had alerted me of Martha Jallopia's distress a couple of days ago in the back room of the pet boutique.

"You and your dog seem to be finding a lot of trouble around here," Alice remarked. Her dark hair was clipped at the nape of her neck, and her face, though attractive, seemed to have even sharper features than if she'd had bangs adorning it. Her stern expression made me uneasy.

Was I going to be a suspect after all?

"Unfortunately," I said, "that seems to be the case."

"Where is Pluckie now?" Justin asked.

"Next door. I walked her over there after calling 911 and you. I didn't want her either to be in the way here or to get tromped on during the investigation."

"At the pet store?"

"That's right."

Alice looked at Justin. "Shouldn't we have one of our crime scene team take a look at her, in case she got some blood on her or is somehow able to provide other evidence?"

Justin nodded. "We can go see her when we're done here."

I didn't object but let them know I'd kept her away from Tarzal and his blood, as well as the broken mirror and spilled milk.

Next I gave them a moment-by-moment description of finding Tarzal, seeing the blood and milk and glass shards, including the one protruding from his chest. I described my horror, my calls for help, then walking Pluckie next door. "I'd planned to secure her in a crate till I got back there, but instead I left her in Martha's care."

"Martha? Did you take your dog upstairs?" I couldn't quite read Justin's expression. Did he think I decided to bother an infirm woman by insisting that she take care of my pet?

"No," I said. "I'd helped her upstairs last night and assumed she would stay there. She told me she had day care workers coming in to help her today. But when Pluckie and I got there this morning, she'd managed to make her way downstairs. She insisted on taking care of Pluckie for me. And by now, Millie's probably there to help out, so it should be okay."

"Okay? I'm not so sure … Tell you what," Justin said. "Finish your description now, then we'll go with you to check on Pluckie."

And Martha too, I was sure.

I wished I knew what Justin was thinking—since he didn't look at all happy.

———

I didn't have much more to say about my own saga after that. In maybe five minutes, I'd finished.

"Let's check on whether Preston's back," Justin told Alice. "We'll talk with him as soon as we return from the pet store."

She nodded and preceded us outside. Sure enough, Preston had returned, standing just off his property toward the front of the bookstore. With him was the mayor, and they were engaged in conversation with a man I didn't recognize. But like the woman I'd seen at the Destiny Welcome, he seemed to be taking pictures and making notes. Another possible media person? Alice went over to them and returned a minute later.

"Preston said fine," she told us. "He's not going anywhere."

All three of us walked next door. The boutique was open, and we went inside. Millie was the first to greet us. "Oh, Rory, Martha told me that you were the one who found poor Tarzal. How awful!"

I nodded. "Yes, it was." I didn't need to give her any further description.

When I looked around at the displays of superstition-related pet paraphernalia, I had a different sense than when I'd been here before. I felt as if I needed a new boost of good luck and might even receive it here.

Especially— "Where is Pluckie?" I asked Millie. "And Martha."

"Here we are." Martha was sitting in her wheelchair toward at side of the store, and Pluckie sat on her lap. Around them were the displays of dog leashes and collars decorated with superstition symbols.

"I didn't know you were mobile enough to get downstairs by yourself, Martha," Justin said, rushing over to her. "I'm glad you made it okay."

"Me, too," she said.

I joined them and lifted Pluckie from Martha's lap. I wasn't exactly buying into superstitions, of course, but I wanted whatever good luck my mostly black dog could impart to me right now. I'd become aware that some superstitions involving black dogs suggested bad luck, but they had nothing to do with Pluckie. I hugged her close, feeling her warmth and the fuzziness of her coat against me, and she licked my nose.

I smiled, feeling at least a little better.

I realized then that Alice had started to ask Martha some questions.

Yes, of course she knew Tarzal. She'd heard from me what had happened to him.

"Did you ever wind up having that meeting you'd been planning the day you got sick?" That was Justin's question.

"Tarzal and Preston came to visit me in the hospital, so, yes. Sort of."

Justin nodded. "And how did that meeting go, Martha?" His voice was soft, his expression somehow pained-looking.

What was going on?

"Not well. I put them off, of course. But Tarzal's attitude—well, just because I'm getting older and had a physical problem, he thought that would be enough to convince me to sell out to them right there. And of course I wouldn't do that."

"So you argued." Justin sounded sad.

"How did you know that?"

"Never mind that," he said. "Martha, I have to ask you, because if I don't someone else will. You were able to get downstairs by yourself. I'm not sure how mobile you really are. But—Martha, did you go next door this morning when you saw Tarzal arrive and argue with him again?"

"Justin Halbertson!" Martha was obviously so agitated that she didn't know what she was doing. But she rose from her wheelchair with no hesitation. Which made me cringe for her, knowing what was going on. "Are you accusing me of murdering Kenneth Tarzal?" she stormed, taking a step toward him.

She must have realized then what she was doing. She quickly moved back enough to sink again into the chair, but the damage was done.

Did she have enough energy and strength to go next door, as Justin had asked?

If she were wise, she would demonstrate her infirmity now to its fullest extent, but that might be too late. She may have blown that alibi by her anger.

"For all our sakes, I'm going to give you your Miranda rights now before asking you if you did kill Tarzal," Justin said gently, and proceeded to tell Martha she had the right to remain silent and to have an attorney present. "We're not going to arrest you, at least not now, but we would like to talk to you a little more," he finished.

"Darn it!" Martha exclaimed, tears pouring down her dry, withered cheeks. "I knew I was going to have bad luck today. I tripped going down the stairs. I caught myself, fortunately, but tripping on the way down is a bad omen." She shook her head slowly, sadly. "As soon as I heard about what happened to Tarzal, I knew I'd be blamed."

ELEVEN

I WANTED TO HUG Martha. To comfort her. But I probably could do neither just then, at least not well.

I did the next closest thing, though. I carefully put Pluckie back down in her lap on her wheelchair. Martha was the one to do the hugging then. Pluckie, licking the tears off Martha's face, was the one to handle the comforting.

I also wanted to shake Justin. How could he possibly think that poor Martha, whom he claimed to care for a lot, could be a murderer? Even if she'd wanted to kill Tarzal—and why would she?—she surely couldn't have gotten next door to do it, then broken a mirror and stabbed him.

For one thing, she was too superstitious to break a mirror for any reason. Wasn't she? Although she'd undoubtedly have known that other part—that touching a five-dollar bill and making the sign of a cross counters the curse of a broken mirror.

Even so, Tarzal had been bigger than her and could have defended himself. Unless, of course, she'd been so angry with him that adrenaline had given her extra strength.

Was I talking myself into the possibility? Of course not. No way could I visualize this poor, frail woman striding into the bookstore to do the foul deed. Or maneuvering her wheelchair there. If she had done the latter, at least, wouldn't someone have seen her?

Yet she had managed to get downstairs by herself. And I'd seen her standing and moving. Was some of her infirmity an act?

Enough. It wasn't up to me to either convict or defend Martha. But if I'd had to, my choice would have been the latter.

After she'd been read her Miranda rights, Martha appeared to play games a bit. Justin and Alice both asked her questions, mostly about how she felt but also about the last time she'd seen Tarzal.

I assumed the answer was last night, at the Destiny Welcome, but she didn't mention that.

In fact, she kept manipulating around Pluckie to put her hand to her mouth, then pretending, as kids do, to zip it shut. Was that a superstition? It hardly mattered.

She clearly was exercising her right to remain silent.

Plus, her eyes seemed to be dulling, her few words slurred a bit. Was whatever had made her ill affecting her again? Or was this an act on her part to make the cops leave her alone?

I wasn't sure, but I definitely didn't want her to undergo another attack of illness now—or, for that matter, ever.

I had no control over her future. But I could help her at this moment. "I think that's enough," I said to Justin and Alice, my hands on my hips and my expression as belligerent as I could make it. "At least for now," I added when both of them aimed frosty glares at me.

Heck, I didn't care what they thought of me. My first impressions of Justin had been favorable, but he'd been eroding them by his latest pushiness.

"All right," Justin finally said. "We'll wait before asking you anything else, Martha. But we will be questioning you further."

"Fine. Then I'll lawyer up." She looked toward me. "That's what they say on those crime-related TV shows, right?"

I smiled at her. "I've heard it there, too."

"Meantime," Alice said to her, "please don't leave town or do anything else that would make it difficult for us to reach you."

"Like have another physical problem?" I grumbled.

"Yes, that could make it hard on us," Justin said with a wry smile. "It would make it even harder on you, Martha." His voice was softer now. "So, for both our sakes, please stay well." To my surprise—or maybe not—he approached her, bent down, and kissed her cheek.

Which gave Pluckie the opportunity to jump up a little in Martha's lap and try to give Justin a kiss, too, I supposed. "Down, Pluckie," I told her.

My dog sent me a sad look. Justin's look didn't appear much happier. "We'll be in touch," he said. "Bye for now."

I wondered whether, next time I saw or heard from him, if it would be in relation to Tarzal's murder. Why else? Because he had been a friend of Martha's but now wanted to arrest her? Maybe, since he'd twisted my arm a bit before, he would want to do some more of it to make sure I stayed around to manage her store for her.

What, for the next twenty years to life?

———

A little while after the police contingent had left, some customers walked into the Lucky Dog—several sets, more than just Millie could handle.

After I asked Martha if she was okay enough for me to leave her alone near the cash register, she shooed me toward the visitors. "Sell them lots, dear."

I hoped that by saying that she wasn't jinxing me into selling nothing. But she knew jinxes better than I did.

And believed in them, unlike me ... usually.

In fact, this time, she apparently sent me over there with luck instead—good luck. The two couples, all friends who had traveled to Destiny together, were both breeders of purebred dogs. One of the couples' female dogs had had a litter of Scottish terriers a few weeks ago, and the other couple had Boston terriers.

Each couple had grown children at home taking care of their babies—both puppies and some grandkids as well. They wanted to bring home items to sell with their pups when they were old enough to find new homes, things that would ensure their luck and longevity. Oh, and yes, for the grandkids, too, but they'd look for those kinds of things somewhere other than the Lucky Dog Boutique.

Both couples spent so much money that I wondered whether their puppy sales would cover the costs. On the other hand, they could probably sell the decorated collars and leashes, the specialized plush dog toys in the shapes of lucky items like rabbits' feet and shamrocks, and everything else to the people who'd feel lucky anyway getting to bring their new family members home with them.

Millie's customers finished shopping first, so when my group finally left with the arms of all four of them hung with plastic bags with Lucky Dog logos on them that were filled with lots of fun, lucky stuff for puppies, I stepped over to Martha. "How'd I do?" I asked her.

"Very well," she said, "as I knew you would."

Millie joined us, too. "Hey, good job," she said to me. She still looked quite young to me, but I'd been impressed, too, with how well she did around here, helping customers and selling them stuff that they must feel obliged to buy if they wanted their pets to remain lucky. And filling me in on shop procedures.

"Thanks," I said. "Back atcha."

She smiled, lighting up her smooth, pretty face. In fact, all three of us were smiling at one another.

But one of those smiles looked a lot more tired than the others.

"Martha," I said, "how about if I help you upstairs for a rest? Then I'll go out for a short while and bring back lunch for all of us. Okay?"

"Okay," she said with a nod.

I put Pluckie back down on the floor. "I'm going to attach the end of her leash to those hooks on the counter again," I told Millie. I didn't want my dog running up and down the stairs around Martha and me—and perhaps tripping the older woman when what she needed was stability.

"Sounds good," Millie said. "Is it okay if I give her a treat or two?"

Pluckie knew that word. Her long black ears perked up. "I don't dare say no now," I said with a laugh. "But please don't overdo it."

I hooked her leash up to the counter near the cash register, then returned to where Martha remained in the wheelchair. "Are you ready?" I asked.

"As ready as I'm going to get." Her visit down here, plus her earlier confrontation with Justin and Alice, had apparently tired her a lot. I helped her out of the chair and over to the door that hid the stairway. We started walking slowly up the steps, with Martha again holding the handrail as I helped to support her. She was warm and bony and seemed utterly fragile. I had no idea how she'd made it downstairs on her own before.

And attack Tarzal? No way.

Unless she was just acting now…

"We've got to be careful," she said.

"I'm sure you don't want to trip again going up the stairs," I responded. I wondered if she was still concerned about whether her earlier misstep had brought her bad luck.

"It's better to trip going upstairs," she contradicted. "That means there'll be a wedding in your family soon."

"Oh." I wasn't sure what else to say. That certainly was different from the other superstition.

As we continued our slow progress, Martha added, "Also, ignore it if Millie or Pluckie seem to want you to go back downstairs before we reach the top. It's bad luck to turn around on a stairway."

"Interesting," I said. "Are there any other superstitions about stairs?"

"Probably, but I only know a few." Martha stopped walking, apparently to catch her breath, and I waited with her. "Here's another one. It's bad luck to meet someone else on stairs, but of course that can happen anytime. The best way to ward off the bad luck then is to cross your fingers."

"I see. I'll have to remember that."

"Ah, but will you pay attention to it? I still have the impression, Rory, that you don't really believe in superstitions, even though you've seen quite a few come true in the short time you've been in Destiny."

"I'm still learning," I said noncommittally as she started to move again.

"Mmm-hmmm, I know you are."

I thought about what she'd said, though. I had seen superstitions in action since arriving in this town, but had any really come true?

Martha herself had gotten lucky, perhaps, thanks to Pluckie. Kenneth Tarzal had gotten unlucky, but someone had killed him and perhaps had planned to make it appear that some evil omens had come to pass.

I'd heard that dog howl the night Tarzal died, but that could have been planned by the murderer, too—a recording, perhaps.

Too many maybes. And I wasn't yet convinced.

But neither was I convinced it was all a sham. And I still wanted to know for sure if the damn ladder walk had in fact somehow affected my beloved Warren.

Not that it would make a difference in my life either way. As I kept telling myself, I just needed closure.

We finally reached the top of the stairs, and I helped Martha walk the short distance into her charming, antique-filled living room. She sank immediately down onto her plush sofa and closed her eyes, taking a deep breath.

"Are you all right?" I asked her again.

"I'm fine. And thanks for helping me up here."

"Should I call the hospital to see if they're sending you a helper today like they promised?"

"They are," she said. "I phoned them before to ask them to wait till afternoon."

Interesting. When and why had she done that? Not that it mattered.

"Then I'll head back downstairs," I said, "and go get us some lunch. How about a sandwich or a salad?"

"Fine. Whatever's easiest for you to grab." She opened her mouth again, apparently deciding whether to say something or not.

"Is there something else?" I asked.

"Well... yes. I'm not going to tell Justin, even though I know he's had my best interests at heart, at least before. Right now, I can't trust him. He may not want to arrest me, but he's thinking about it. And I probably shouldn't tell you, but..."

Was she going to admit to killing Tarzal? Couldn't be. That was crazy.

"It's up to you, but you can be sure I won't reveal anything you tell me." I hoped—unless the silence got me into trouble.

"I know, dear. You've been nothing but good luck to me, you and Pluckie. I know that won't change. The thing is... well, I didn't kill Tarzal, but I had even more of a motive than Justin or Alice know."

I sank down on the other end of the sofa. "What's that?" I asked hesitantly.

Surely a better motive hadn't led to her actually doing anything, had it? She'd said not, but...

"Well, when Tarzal and Preston came to see me in the hospital, they said the visit was instead of the business meeting they had intended to hold with me before I got sick. They want to buy my shop, you know. I don't want to sell, and they knew that, too. Tarzal... well, he asked to speak to me alone, so Preston left for awhile. You know how Tarzal was so revered as the expert on superstitions. He said then that he'd make me sell."

"By some kind of superstition?" I asked. Sounded odd—but this was Destiny.

"Yes. By his book and the publicity he got. He was always writing magazine articles and blogs and stuff. And he said that, if I decided not to sell right away, he'd start talking up some really bad superstitions about dogs and buying things for them and whatever else his research had unearthed. That way, no one would come into the Lucky Dog Boutique because it would be bad luck, and when business got bad I'd have to sell out anyway."

"That's awful," I said.

"It gets worse," Martha said, tears appearing in her tired hazel eyes. "I didn't physically kill him, you understand, but I did curse him loudly. Yelling at him. Invoking every bad luck superstition that I could think of. So even though I wasn't his murderer, I did cause Tarzal's death."

TWELVE

I HUGGED MARTHA YET again, tried to reassure her that she shouldn't blame herself. Wishing bad luck on someone was not the same thing as murdering them.

Except, perhaps, in Destiny—if one happened to be a believer.

Like Martha.

I realized I couldn't convince her. Maybe if we knew who'd really committed the miserable act of stabbing Tarzal to death Martha would feel at least a little better.

Or maybe not.

I determined, as I walked down the stairs a short while later, to at least keep my ears open. If I heard anything that could lead to solving Tarzal's murder, I'd have to talk to Justin again. That wouldn't necessarily be a totally bad thing, even though I was mad at him and despised his attitude toward Martha.

Martha. Going down the stairs.

Just in case, I held onto the railing to ensure I wouldn't trip. No need to tempt fate, even if I didn't believe in it...

When I reached the bottom of the stairway and walked into the store, I saw that Jeri had arrived.

I realized that, as temporary manager, I'd better get a better knowledge of the staff's schedule. That would help me figure out mine as well.

"Hi," I said to both Jeri and Millie. "I'm heading out to buy lunch, which I'll bring in." Would they tell me that today was another day they'd go out for lattes? But Jeri's arrival had been later than the morning they had gone off together. "What would you both like? Oh, and any suggestions where I should go?"

"Wishbones-to-Go," both said nearly simultaneously.

"I don't think I've seen that place," I said hesitantly. "Is it good?"

"Perfect for lunches," Jeri said. She was wearing another Lucky Dog Boutique T-shirt today, a bright green one. Her shoulder-length black hair was pushed back from her face by matching green hair clips. "You can eat in, but like the name says they also make meals to go. Great meals, in fact." Millie added, "And you do get—"

Again both of them said together, "Wishbones to Go!"

"It's down the street and around the block," Jeri said, pointing toward the door, then crooking her index finger toward the right. "On Fate Street."

"Not as many tourists go there as locals," Millie said. "But it's always pretty crowded at lunchtime anyway." Her grin was huge, lighting up her smooth face beneath the straight bangs of her dark brown hair that otherwise hung straight, brushing her cheeks.

"I'll give it a try," I said, then asked them each what they wanted. I grabbed a pad of paper from a shelf beneath the cash register counter and made notes. Jeri wanted what might be the place's specialty, a turkey sandwich, on wheat with cheese and lettuce and ranch dressing. Millie wanted roast beef. Since I hadn't known where I was going, I didn't know what Martha might prefer, but both her helpers said she'd love chicken on cheese bread with everything on it, from lettuce to olives to pickles and more. "Great," I said. "I'll be back as soon as I can."

I had to wait at the door for some customers to enter, and I greeted the family of four plus a Great Dane with a hearty welcome. "One of those nice ladies will help you," I told them, sweeping my hand toward where Jeri and Millie stood.

"Thanks," said the mom.

I hurried out onto the sidewalk which was, as apparently usual for midday, quite crowded. I turned toward the right, as Jeri had pointed, and started down the block toward Fate Street. I knew which one it was since my B&B was on it, too, but in the opposite direction.

As I passed the Broken Mirror Bookstore, I eavesdropped on a couple of conversations in which people talked about whether it was unlucky to be on this street at all, since there'd apparently been a murder on it last night. They'd heard about it, and seen it mentioned in national news and on the Internet. Apparently the superstition-related murder in Destiny had gone viral.

I thought about what I could say to reassure the tourists but I was the wrong person to say anything. I was far from an expert on superstitions. I certainly didn't think it was bad luck to be here. Those of us walking beneath the warm sun over Destiny were still alive, and presumably most of us were healthy.

And then it dawned on me. I could say something.

I turned to the trio of senior ladies who walked just behind me discussing the murder. "You know," I said, "I think it's always good luck to cross your fingers. It wouldn't hurt, considering what's said to have happened on this street." I lifted my right hand from where it had hung near the large purse I carried with its strap over my shoulder and made an obvious point of crossing my middle finger over my index finger.

"Oh. Of course," said the white-haired lady farthest from me, and she did the same thing, followed by her comrades. "Good idea," she told me.

I smiled, turned back the way I'd been heading, and continued on.

Too bad none of them had dogs along or I'd have told them all about the good luck of visiting the Lucky Dog Boutique.

Maneuvering through the crowd, I reached Fate Street, turned right, and immediately saw the Wishbones-to-Go restaurant. That was where I headed.

As my helpers had warned, the place was busy. There weren't a huge number of tables, but all were filled with people whose loud chatter sounded happy. Or maybe that was just wishful thinking on my part, since I needed some cheering up.

The tables were decorated with number holders to show servers which order to take to each table. The metal stands weren't ordinary, though. The frame at the top of each was shaped like—what else?—an unbroken wish bone.

I didn't try to figure out how to get a table, though. Instead, I headed for the line that led to a counter where take-out orders were being filled.

That was the best place for me to be, as it turned out—and not only so I could get the food I'd bring back to the pet boutique for Martha and the staff.

It was an even better place to eavesdrop on conversations about Tarzal's murder than the street had been. Especially since I got the sense that a lot of these people knew each other, as Jeri and Millie had suggested. They seemed to be townsfolk who'd also known Tarzal. A few, though not many, looked familiar.

When I first got into the line, it stretched nearly out the door. Immediately in front of me were two people who appeared utterly businesslike. The woman wore a silky-looking, peach-colored dress, and the man wore a shirt and tie and dressy slacks, although no suit jacket. They kept their voices low, but I could still hear them.

"I hate to say it, but I really think we should find a way to capitalize on his death," the man said.

"Good idea," the woman replied, her tone enthusiastic. "It shouldn't be too hard. The media are publicizing not only the murder, but that he was stabbed with a broken mirror. A broken mirror," she said in emphasis. "Our tours already drive past the Broken Mirror Bookstore, and it's a landmark. Now we need to make sure our guides add to their talks about how even the town's expert on superstitions couldn't stop one from coming true and killing him, that kind of thing."

"I know," the man said. "I'd suggest that we script it, though, so it comes out right."

Interesting. So these two must own, or run, one of the town's tour companies.

We'd moved forward a few steps by then. Neither of them would know me. It wouldn't hurt for me to ask questions as if I was a tourist—someone who might take one of their tours.

That wasn't beyond the realm of possibility anyway. If I was going to stay in Destiny for a while—and it appeared that I would—I should learn everything about it that I could.

You never knew when that kind of knowledge could help sell superstition-related pet paraphernalia.

"Excuse me," I said. "I couldn't help overhearing what you were talking about. I also heard what happened to that poor man who was apparently stabbed last night. Are there any superstitions that might identify who the killer was?"

"I'm not aware of any," said man stiffly, as if he resented my daring to join in their conversation.

"Me, neither." The woman sounded a lot friendlier. "But I'd really like to find some. We could use them . . . or at least hint about them."

"On your tours?" I asked. "I gathered from what you were saying that you give tours of Destiny."

"That's right," the woman said. "I'm Evonne Albing, owner of the best tour company in town—which just happens to be Destiny's Luckiest Tours."

Interesting. As I recalled, that was the name of the tour company on the shirt Martha's nephew Arlen had worn.

"We'd better get our guides and others who know superstitions to look into which might apply to Tarzal's murder," she continued, looking at the man again.

"I was trying to figure that out, too," said a female voice from behind me. A woman had gotten in line and edged up to hear what we were talking about, too. She appeared to be in her thirties, and she had on a T-shirt that was all black and had the golden outline of a black cat peering from it with eyes made out of shiny buttons. "But ... well, I don't know if it's true, but I heard that Martha Jallopia wasn't as ill as rumor had it."

Should I say anything? Not now. It would be better if I knew what those rumors said if I had any intention of helping Martha.

"I heard she was still in the hospital," Evonne said.

"No," the man said. "Arlen told me before he went out on today's first bus tour that his aunt was home now."

Ah. That confirmed what I'd thought: that Arlen worked for their tour company.

"Does anyone know where Arlen was last night?" the other woman asked. "Maybe he decided to help his aunt. Or himself. I hate to gossip but I heard that Martha and Tarzal weren't on the best of terms."

"If you hate to gossip," the man said, "then why do it?"

"Like everyone else in this town, I want to know what happened," she retorted. "Especially since Tarzal really represented this town to the rest of the world. All of our businesses could suffer now that he's gone."

"Unless we're able to use it, like I said." By now, Evonne sounded a bit callous.

"Well, I just want to know the truth," the other woman said. "And whatever it is, it's not likely to help me sell superstition-related clothing accessories. And, yes, I know that's insensitive under the circumstances and I'm sorry." She motioned toward her own shirt. "I'd rather that you just add my Buttons of Fortune shop to your Destiny's Luckiest Tours retail destinations."

"Is there a standard itinerary for your tours?" I asked Evonne, not sure whether interrupting right now was a good idea, but I, too, was suddenly curious about Arlen's whereabouts last night.

Had he been in his aunt's neighborhood? Did he have any motive to kill Tarzal except to try to help his aunt preserve her store? I wondered if the police would be able to tell the approximate time Tarzal had been stabbed. At night, when the dog had howled? It was unlikely Arlen had been giving a tour so late that it would rule him out as a suspect.

Did the coroner find an image of Arlen—or someone else—in Tarzal's eyes?

"Yes, each of our tours has a specific itinerary and theme," the woman said. "And we have a good selection."

"Great," I said. "I haven't taken any tours at all yet but someone recommended your company, with a guy named Arlen as the best tour guide."

I really had no idea if Arlen was particularly special, but saying so might earn me some more information.

"Really? That's good. And yes," said the man. "Like I said, our tour company is the best in town." He grinned. "How long are you here for? We could set you up with one of the tours Arlen guides within the next day or so, I'm sure. Right, Evonne?" He looked sideways toward the woman who was apparently his boss.

"I'm sure we can, Mike." Evonne looked at me. "Just give us your name and how to get in touch with you, and we'll make sure you get the tour you want."

"Thanks," I said. "If you could just give me your tour company's information, I'll call in and work out a time. I'm not sure what my schedule is right now." That should be vague enough without my having to explain who I was—and that I had any knowledge of the murder or anyone who might have been involved with it.

"Hey," said the other woman. "I saw you at the Destiny Welcome last night, didn't I?" Unfortunately, she was talking to me—and it became even more unfortunate when she said, "You went over to help Martha afterward, didn't you?"

I sighed internally as I managed a slight smile. "That's right."

"You know her?"

"Not well," I said—and was happy to see that the man and woman from the tour company had finally reached the front of the line. "I've never been here before," I told the lady from the button shop. "What would you recommend?"

She made some suggestions, including one kind of sandwich I knew I was already going to order for Jeri.

And then, finally, it was my turn and the tour company folks were gone—without, fortunately, hearing any followup on whether I knew Martha.

I decided to try the turkey sandwich, too. When my order was filled and I was ready to go—and was the pleased recipient of four wishbones to take along—the button-shop woman stopped me before stepping to the front of the line. "You're the woman with the lucky black and white dog who saved Martha, aren't you?"

I wanted to deny it, or at least ignore her. But if I was going to help Martha, I needed to meet more people and get their respective takes on who might have been angry enough to kill Tarzal.

If nothing else, I didn't want to antagonize anyone who might have a pet and frequent the Lucky Dog Boutique.

"That's right," I said with a weak smile.

"I'm Carolyn Innes, owner of Buttons of Fortune. I sell all kinds of buttons, including special ones that can bring luck to people. I heard you're going to be running the Lucky Dog for a while for Martha. I'll pop in there soon. We'll talk."

THIRTEEN

THE LARGE WHITE PLASTIC bag that I carried had a logo on it—a wishbone, of course. As I walked back to the Lucky Dog with that bag full of sandwiches and, yes, wishbones, I wondered what Carolyn Innes and I would have to talk about.

Did she know something that would help me to boost the boutique's business or save Martha? Or would she only push buttons—hers or mine?

I'd probably encourage the conversation, though. She'd seemed pleasant enough. It wouldn't hurt to have another acquaintance and potential friend here in Destiny. In fact, the more people I got to know here, the better, for Martha's sake and my own.

I didn't know how long I'd be staying, and a diversity of friends and conversations might ultimately help me find the answers I'd come here seeking.

Or not. The longer I remained here, the more I was questioning whether answers existed.

More to the point, though, it was good for me to become acquainted with as many people as possible who knew Martha and Tarzal. Maybe something I heard would help me to learn the truth about his death. And preferably, that would be something that I could pass along to Justin so he could arrest someone other than the sweet senior lady who'd already gone through so much... so I could plan when to leave here.

It turned out Martha was going through even more that day. When I reached the store, Millie, who'd been waiting on some customers, quickly excused herself. Her expression told me it wasn't starvation that made her approach me so quickly.

"What's wrong?" I asked while heading to the counter to soothe Pluckie, who was pulling on her leash.

"Chief Halbertson is upstairs in Martha's apartment," Millie said, the frantic expression on her youthful face aging it quickly. "I told him when he came in that she wasn't feeling well, but he called her and I guess she said it was okay for him to come upstairs."

"Drat." I looked at the bag in my hands, then opened it. Fortunately, the girl who'd waited on me at Wishbones-to-Go had wrapped the sandwiches well and labeled each one. I was easily able to remove Millie's and Jeri's, along with some packages of dried apple chips. I hadn't brought drinks since we kept water bottles here. I handed the sandwiches and chip bags to Millie. "Here. I'll take Martha's up to her and do a bit of eavesdropping—or interrupting—whatever seems most appropriate."

Her smile eased some of the concern on her face, allowing it to look once more as if she was barely out of her teens. "Great. Thanks, Rory. Everything at the shop is fine now, by the way."

I looked toward Jeri, who was leading a couple of guys with their arms full of dog toys toward the cash register. "Looks that way," I said. "Good job." Then I hurried to the stairs with a newly released Pluckie following.

I heard voices before I was near the door to Martha's apartment. Neither sounded raised nor particularly upset, although the female one was considerably softer than the male. As soon as I reached the door, I knocked on it. "Lunch is served," I called, thinking Justin might let me in more easily that way than if he thought I was only coming to protect Martha and give him a hard time.

The door opened immediately. Justin stood in front of me though, so I couldn't easily slip into the apartment.

A wave of something pleasant surged through me as I saw him. A bad sign. Yes, I knew I'd felt an unwelcome bit of attraction to him, but that could only lead to further complications in many respects.

I didn't want it, and it certainly couldn't help Martha.

I reminded myself once again why I was in Destiny, and Warren's face in my mind turned my mood sad and my smile chilly.

"Well, hi." I tried to put surprise in my tone, as if I hadn't expected to see him. "I just picked up some food. Would you care to join us for lunch?" My sandwich was large enough that I could share it, and I suspected that Martha wouldn't want her entire sandwich, either.

It wouldn't hurt to act friendly toward Justin, to throw him off guard a bit if nothing else.

"Come in," he said, not responding to the invitation.

"Thanks." I might as well act polite, no matter how I felt.

Martha was in her living room, seated at the end of her fluffy yellow sofa. I hurried toward her, and so did my dog. Pluckie immediately rubbed against her, asking for a pat which she gave.

Was Justin giving Martha a hard time? Wearing her down so she'd confess to something she hadn't—probably—done?

The expression on her pale, lined face as she looked up toward me appeared more determined than defeated. That surprised me.

"Here's your sandwich." I pulled the larger wrapped package with all the works on it out of the bag and held it out toward her.

"Thanks, dear," she said without reaching for it. "Why don't you go into the kitchen and get us all some plates? I heard you tell Justin he could join us for lunch, and I'm willing to share mine."

"Me, too," I said.

"Oh, and get us some bottles of water while you're at it."

I placed her sandwich and the bag on top of the long low coffee table in front of her.

Without looking at Justin, I edged past him and did as Martha asked. Opening the doors into several ornate wooden cabinets along the wall above the kitchen counter, I'd no trouble finding her lovely plates that looked almost antique with their floral decorations, yet appeared to be not china but modern and dishwasher safe. I also withdrew three bottles from the refrigerator and headed back to the living room.

"Here we are," I said.

For the next few minutes, we separated already halved sandwiches and apple chips onto the three plates, giving Justin portions of both of our meals. I also saved Pluckie a few bites of turkey.

Justin sat down on one of the chairs matching the sofa at the far end of the coffee table. I took a seat beside Martha and set the wishbones aside on the table. Fortunately, Pluckie ignored them. They must have been washed clean.

Then the three of us began to eat. Pluckie just lay down on the floor beside me.

"You know, Rory dear," Martha said, "Justin came here today to tell me that he already knew Tarzal and I were arguing and that the man had threatened me."

He did? How?

More important for the moment— "Martha, I don't think you ought to talk about that," I said, my voice shrill and my eyes huge and cautioning as I looked over at her.

"Well, it's true. He knows. So I gather that he thinks even more that I'm the person who killed that nasty man. But Tarzal and I were friends of sorts as well as business associates. Yes, he threatened to make up or emphasize superstitions against dogs and my shop so Lucky Dog would fail anyway if I didn't sell him the property. And no, even though I was mad at him I didn't—"

"Martha, stop!" I turned to look at Justin, who had put his plate on his lap and was calmly eating. "Did you threaten to arrest Martha? I know you read her her Miranda rights, but I thought—"

"Yes, he did," Martha said, now from behind me. "Read me my rights, I mean. He hasn't arrested me yet—at least I don't think so."

"Then don't talk around him," I said, again facing Martha. "Not without a lawyer present. Don't you know that it's bad luck to keep talking without a lawyer when you've been read your Miranda rights?" Okay, I was making that up. But around here, I figured a lot of people made up superstitions.

And Martha, being as superstitious as she was, might even buy into this one.

"I didn't know that," she said softly.

I didn't want to see Justin's expression. Would it be angry? Possibly, but if so that was too bad.

"Do you have a lawyer?" I pressed.

"Yes, of course. I've had a will done and all that kind of thing since, as much as I hate to admit it, I am getting a bit older. I was afraid it would bring me bad luck to do something like that, but Emily assured me it was good luck to be prepared for something that would only happen far in the future."

I assumed that Emily was the lawyer, and I liked her already. "Good," I said. "Then why don't you do as Justin suggested and not say anything else until you've talked with Emily?" I didn't know if Emily was the kind of lawyer who only dealt with estate planning but she could at least suggest someone with criminal law experience to Martha if she didn't handle it.

"That's actually a good idea," Justin said from behind me. "No, I haven't arrested you yet, Martha. And I hope I don't have to. But you know I'm not just a cop. As chief of police, I have to keep the rights and interests of the people of Destiny at the forefront of everything I do. I hope you really didn't kill Tarzal, but we're still collecting evidence and I have to tell you …" He paused. I had already turned back to him yet again, trying to read his blank yet official looking expression.

"Tell me what?" Martha urged.

"That at least for now, you seem to have the most to gain from Tarzal's death. The best motive. And possibly opportunity, since you weren't stuck here upstairs."

I sometimes watched cop shows on TV. What Justin hadn't mentioned yet was means, so I did. "Do you really think she had the means to kill him? I mean, I know that anyone theoretically could have broken into the Broken Mirror Bookstore last night or this morning with Tarzal there and actually smashed that mirror that had only been symbolically decorated to look broken before. That part includes Martha. But she's ... er, senior." I suspected she didn't like to be reminded of that. "More important, she's been ill. Plus, she's a lot smaller than Tarzal was. Do you really think she could have stabbed him?"

"If she took him unawares." He put his plate back onto the coffee table and stood. I moved it onto one of the end tables since it still had a sandwich on it and Pluckie eyed it with interest.

"I don't suppose the autopsy indicated any image of who killed him in Tarzal's eyes," I had to add. Maybe things like that actually did occur in Destiny.

Justin aimed a wry grin at me. "What do you think?" The question was clearly rhetorical since he continued, looking toward Martha, "Is it okay if I go into your bedroom? I'd like to make sure there's no bloody clothing there."

"What! Is this an official investigation?" I was utterly indignant now. "You need a warrant, don't you? Or—"

"That depends," he said. "And ... well, okay. My informality could work against both of us." He moved around to look down at her. "For now, just tell me you're not hiding any evidence in your closet or bathroom or any other place up here."

"Remember what I said about it being bad luck to talk without—"

"You do realize," Martha interrupted me in a prim voice, facing Justin, "that, yes, I was found downstairs after poor Tarzal died, but I'd have had one heck of a time taking bloody clothing or whatever up here, then getting back to the store again to wait for people to come in."

"I've thought of that," Justin admitted. "And I've already had guys checking the outside garbage bins and all. That's part of the reason I haven't arrested you. The other, even more important reason, is that I don't want to because I care about you, Martha. A lot. Even if you had a good motive I'd rather look for other possible suspects, but I have to do my job and report to city officials and even the media. So I can't lay off you completely or tell my detectives or officers to do so, at least not yet." He walked over to Martha, bent down and kissed her cheek. "I'd better go. But it'd be a good thing for you to listen to those Miranda rights and what Rory had to say. Get a lawyer on board ... just in case. That's bound to be good luck."

He started to leave, then bent to pick up the remainder of his half of my sandwich. He'd already eaten his portion of Martha's and most of this one, too. "Thanks for lunch." He took a couple of final bites.

"You're welcome," I lied. As he walked out the door, I said to Martha, "I'll be right back," then followed him.

———

Justin knew that Pluckie and I were behind him on the stairs. As soon as I started down behind him, he turned around but said nothing, just continued going down.

I wondered whether he'd have bad luck if he tripped on the steps because I pushed him.

No, I wasn't as angry with him now as I was at first. He was performing a balancing act of sorts.

He obviously cared about Martha. I'd learned that before, when he'd tried so hard to get me to stay here and help to run her shop until she got better.

But he was also a peace officer faced with helping to solve the most heinous of crimes: murder of one of the citizens of the town he served.

Never mind that the town was an especially unique—and strange —one.

Maybe its theme of superstitions would even stand in Justin's way somehow.

Or help him.

Help him ... I could do that, sort of. If I helped to figure out what had really happened in order to help Martha, then that would be to Justin's benefit, too.

But I wouldn't tell him what I had in mind. Weren't the cops on TV and in mystery novels all bent out of shape when amateurs butted in to try to figure things out?

He stepped into the shop but didn't hurry to the door. Instead, he seemed to wait for me.

"Come outside with me for a minute, will you?" he asked.

Although both Millie and Jeri appeared to be waiting on customers, I saw their eyes fasten on Justin and me, at least for a moment.

I didn't know what he had in mind, but maybe having the potential of being overheard wasn't a good idea. "Okay," I said, then hurried to the counter to grab Pluckie's leash and fastened it onto her collar.

We were soon on the crowded sidewalk in front of the Lucky Dog's multi-paned display window. We could be overheard, too, but people here wouldn't know us.

But then Justin led Pluckie and me around the corner, to the sparse and empty area between the stores. I gathered that this narrow space was not kept up either by the store owners or the city since the paving was full of cracks I tried to avoid.

"Please do give Emily Rasmuten a call," he said, and here, where we were sort of alone, I could hear him despite the nearby din. "That's her full name, and she's with Destiny's largest and most prestigious law firm, Eldred and Rasmuten. Not that there are a lot of firms here, and 'large' means more than a couple of attorneys, unlike in L.A. where you're from. Just tell her what's been going on. She'll have heard part of it anyway. Let her know that you've been talking to Martha and that Martha's ready to hire a lawyer regarding the death of Tarzal. That'll mean Emily's firm won't take on any other clients who might be suspects, for one thing. For another, Emily's a nice person as well as a good lawyer. She'll know how to approach Martha in a way that will encourage Martha to retain her despite her insistence on her own innocence."

"She is innocent," I retorted, then let my frown soften in the face of Justin's sad smile. "You know that, but I realize you have to do your job."

"I have to follow up regarding all potential suspects," he said. He seemed to be examining the pavement beneath us, or maybe watching Pluckie, and his lips were pursed as if he was upset. But then he looked up again. "I shouldn't mention it to you, but it'll probably be in the news anyway. People heard Martha yelling at Tarzal when he visited her in the hospital. It was so loud that a nurse who's related to one of our patrol officers even called him to tell him about it. But apparently Preston went back into the room, they quieted down after that, and none of my officers were sent to look into the matter. Even so, that adds to the things that look bad for Martha."

"Oh," I said, choosing not to mention that Martha had told me about that—and that she had cursed Tarzal. "Okay, I'll call Emily."

"Thanks." He looked up then—right into my face. He still appeared solemn. "I also heard … You're here in Destiny, aren't you, Rory, because someone you cared about walked under a ladder and subsequently died?"

Shock sent a lightning bolt through me. "How did you hear that?" But I realized immediately what must have happened. Since I'd arrived here, the only people I'd mentioned it to were Tarzal and Preston. Tarzal most likely hadn't said anything about it to Justin before he died, but the police chief might have questioned Preston about Tarzal's death—and Preston might have brought it up then, although I'd no idea why.

I hadn't told the two men to keep it quiet. And even if I had, they might have talked about it anyway. It was, after all, superstition related.

How did I feel about Justin knowing about it? I wasn't sure. After my initial shocked reaction, I now felt numbness creeping over me.

Justin was still looking at me, his expression sympathetic.

Trying to appear casual, I forced my tone to lightness. "Did Preston mention that?"

Justin didn't acknowledge it verbally. Maybe he couldn't, if he learned it in an interrogation. But he didn't deny it, either.

So I assumed it was true. "That's actually correct. It made me curious, so I came here to figure out how superstitions work—if they do.

I mentioned it to Tarzal and Preston just in case they had the answer. They didn't."

"What's your conclusion, then?" Justin asked softly.

"I don't have one yet. Still looking. If you've got any answers for me, I'll be glad to hear them."

"I think you know that, as important as superstitions are around here, I'm still a bit of an agnostic. But if there's anything I can do to help—"

"Nope," I cut in. "But thanks. I think I'd better get back to the shop now."

"Sure," he said, aiming another sympathetic glance my way that almost made me cry.

Instead, I shrugged. "See you around, Justin."

"Right."

I had a sudden urge to grab his arm as he turned to leave the small walkway we occupied, but I wasn't sure what to say to him. Assure him, wrongly, that I was fine?

There was one thing I could ask. "I'd appreciate it if you'd keep what you heard to yourself," I said. But that probably didn't matter, if Preston was telling the world—or at least the world of Destiny.

Justin faced me again. "Of course. And I won't let anyone jump to conclusions about Martha, either. You can be sure of that. We need more evidence than we've found to arrest anyone."

"Thanks," I said.

This time, Pluckie and I were the ones to start walking away. As we did so, I realized that, even in the face of a really difficult situation, Chief Justin Halbertson seemed like a decent guy.

I just hoped I had the same impression of him later, as I figured out a way to dig further into the murder to find out who really did it and ensure that Martha was cleared.

And then … would I go home?

No. I meant, then I *would* go home. Whether or not I felt convinced that the ladder superstition had anything to do with Warren's death.

But even as I thought that, I realized that Destiny was digging into my psyche like a leech. Or maybe starting to hug me close, like a snuggly new fleece jacket.

Were there superstitions that involved leeches or fleece jackets?

Gritting my teeth as I grinned at that thought, I turned the corner, reentered the Lucky Dog and patted my own lucky dog on her head.

The sooner I found a good way to get all the answers I needed for Martha and myself and leave here, the better.

FOURTEEN

Inside the Lucky Dog, I realized nearly immediately that I'd left the four intact wishbones upstairs on Martha's table. Would that constitute good luck or bad? Most likely, forgetting wishbones had no consequences. Breaking them supposedly did.

I'd use them as an excuse to go back upstairs to talk to Martha in a little while. For now, I had a phone call to make.

I left the helpers in the store assisting customers while I picked up Martha's laptop from the drawer under the counter and went back into the storeroom, with Pluckie close at my heels. I could have asked Millie or Jeri for the information I needed, but I didn't want them to know that I was seeking it.

I needed attorney Emily Rasmuten's phone number.

Doing an online search, I had no trouble finding the website for the local law firm Eldred and Rasmuten. But when I called on my cell, I was told that Ms. Rasmuten was in a meeting and would have to call me back.

She of course would have no idea who I was, so I explained that I was helping her client Martha Jallopia at her pet boutique and was calling on Martha's behalf. I hoped that would be enough to get her attention.

When Pluckie and I returned to the main part of the store, Jeri approached me. Several people were wandering around looking at things, but none seemed particularly ready to buy. Millie was with one couple by the area with cat toys representing superstitions.

"We both managed to eat our sandwiches," she told me. "Just let us know how much we owe you."

"For today, it's on me. Not that I'll feed you lunch every day I'm around, but since I'm temporarily in charge I want to show how much I appreciate your help." I grinned, and she smiled back.

But her expression looked a bit worried. "The thing is," she said, "we suggested Wishbones partly for their food and partly—"

"—for their wishbones. Sorry. I left them upstairs with Martha. I'll get them from her in a little while."

"Oh, that's okay." Jeri looked relieved. Had she thought I'd left the restaurant without them? "I'll go get them. I can give her a run-down on how sales have been since she went upstairs before. Even when she's around and running the store, she always likes us to report. Often."

"Fair enough," I said. "She seemed tired, though, so you may want to call first."

"Okay."

Before she could make the call more people walked in. I immediately headed in their direction, as did Jeri.

Back in L.A. at the large chain store I ran, I seldom was needed to be one-on-one with our customers. Since I'd started out as a sales associate on the floor I knew what to do, but I was a bit rusty now.

I was also enjoying it.

But when the pair of young couples I was helping asked me the meaning of some of the superstitions represented by the stuffed animals and other dog toys, I was a bit stumped. "They all represent good luck, of course," I said, glancing down at my own lucky black and white pup. Otherwise Martha wouldn't be selling them. But what aspects of good luck were indicated by a dolphin, a wolf toy, a toy that was a wolf's tooth, a football, and a doggy necklace with stuffed beads?

I traded places with Millie, who was talking to her customers about the brands of cat food we carried. Pluckie joined me, her nose in the air as she scented some of that food. I wished I could hear what Millie said to the people I'd just left.

I also realized I had a lot to learn about superstitions if I was going to stay in Destiny for any length of time—including deciding which amulet that we sold made the most sense for me to buy and wear—the luckiest.

I decided to dash next door the next moment I had here without customers. I'd read through Tarzal's book quickly before coming here after taking it out of the library, thanks to the suggestion of my friend Gemma. But now I needed my own copy.

And maybe I should hurry up and take that tour I'd discussed in line at Wishbones-to-Go earlier. Especially if I could schedule it with Martha's nephew ... and find an opportunity to talk to him about other things, too. Like his aunt. And his opinion of Tarzal's trying to twist Martha's arm to sell this place.

He'd indicated when I first met him that he was prepared to start running the Lucky Dog if Martha needed him. He had even attempted to help customers. Was he prepared to do something intense to keep the store in the family?

If he'd killed Tarzal, that was a good reason for him to stay away from here ... for now. But not forever.

The people I was now with, a mother with two little girls, seemed pleased to buy a couple of different kinds of canned cat food that had four-leaf clovers on the label.

Cat food. The black cat outside. Was it feral, or did it belong to someone? And did it really portend—or cause—bad luck?

When I had finished ringing up my customers' purchases—and sneaking Pluckie a small part of a treat—I also helped take the money of the people I'd started waiting on before. They'd chosen to buy a stuffed football and a dolphin.

Jeri then went to help Millie with her customers. Otherwise, the store was fairly empty—unusual, but a good, if hopefully temporary, opportunity.

I went over to Jeri and whispered in her ear that I had to run a brief errand. I asked her to keep an eye on Pluckie, now leashed to the counter, which she agreed to do. And then I left.

I didn't go far, just headed to the bookstore next door. It was filled with customers, too—not cops. Apparently its investigation as a crime scene had been completed.

This shop was crowded, too, and noisy. Since this was Destiny and the shop was all about Tarzal's book on superstitions, I'd seen it busy before. But it appeared even more nuts today.

Because people wanted to visit a murder scene? Speculate on why the world's possibly foremost specialist on superstitions could have somehow triggered such a run of bad luck that it resulted in his killing?

I gathered that the only salespeople there had been Preston and, formerly, Tarzal. I saw Preston talking with people at the far counter beyond the book displays. He looked pale and stressed.

Of course he would. His partner was gone.

Could he have had something to do with that? But why would he?

To help Martha, I could speculate about Preston's motive to kill Tarzal. He'd have had the opportunity and the means. He was probably strong enough to stab another man in the heart with a broken piece of glass, especially if the act wasn't expected.

But why? I assumed the business partners were also friends despite sometimes bickering. Even so, I'd imagine Preston was on Justin's list of suspects but the cops didn't appear to be zeroing in on him. The evidence must not point to him—at least not the way it pointed, circumstantially or otherwise, toward Martha.

I didn't know if Tarzal had any relatives nearby. Maybe Preston had been the person closest to him.

I couldn't help thinking about my own loss. Again. And I tried to ignore the fact that Justin had some awareness of it.

My Warren's parents, brother, and sister survived him. They all lived in Boston. In L.A., I'd been his closest survivor, and it had hurt. Still did, even though we weren't related. We'd been engaged but hadn't set a wedding date.

I didn't know how long Tarzal and Preston had been business partners. Time didn't matter. Closeness did.

I made my way through the crowd to the large table that held Tarzal's superstition books. Not many were left.

I supposed that the publicity surrounding his murder might bring people in to buy his book as a collector's item, if nothing else.

I kept my ears open, in case someone said something that could lead to a new suspect or clue, but the snatches of conversation I heard mostly centered around trying to figure out exactly where the evil deed had occurred.

Sighing, I again maneuvered among the closely packed people and approached Preston at the cash register.

I'd only met him a few days ago. Then, he had appeared like a suave, though aging, man. Now he looked more aging than anything else. He still wore a nice suit but it seemed to hang on him as if he had already lost weight. His face was drawn, and the wrinkles I'd seen there before seemed to have given birth to a whole new litter of additional ones.

Preston finished taking money from the guy ahead of me, who picked up his plastic bag with a book or two in it, stuffed his receipt into it, and headed into the crowd. Preston then looked blearily toward me.

"Oh, hello, Rory. How are you?"

"Okay," I said. "But more important, how are you?"

His thin lips moved slightly toward his right side in a half smile. "I've been better."

"I figured." I handed the copy of *The Destiny of Superstitions* that I'd been carrying toward him. "I need this."

His eyes narrowed as if in confusion. "You need it?"

"I'm staying in Destiny a while longer and, though I read it before I got here, I can't remember all the superstitions in it. To survive here I'll need a reference book."

Bad choice of words I realized immediately: survive. I wasn't concerned about ending up like Tarzal—though without knowing who'd killed him and why, maybe that was naive. But Preston didn't react to it.

"Okay." He reached for the book and the credit card I held out, scanned the book's barcode and my card, then put them on the counter as the receipt printed for me to sign. "Here," he said, handing everything to me.

He was acting like a robot, doing all the right things but with no reaction, no emotion.

I didn't know him, not well, but I really felt bad for him. The guy was clearly grieving.

"Thanks," I said as we finished the transaction. I put my credit card away, then tucked the receipt into the book without asking for a bag. Not yet moving away so he could deal with the next customer, I said, "By the way, did you tell anyone about what I told Tarzal and you—I mean, why I came to Destiny? The ladder superstition?"

"Well, yes," he said. "Was it a secret? I didn't tell too many people, but…"

But more than just Justin, I gathered. "It's okay. But, Preston, as I said, I'll be in town a while longer helping out at the Lucky Dog next door. If you need anything, even just to talk, just let me know."

His eyes widened in surprise, as if I'd tried to seduce him. His smile this time lifted both edges of his mouth, although not much more than before. "Thank you, Rory. I appreciate that." He didn't say whether he might take me up on it, though. Instead, he held his hand out around my side, reaching for the next person's purchase.

I was through here … for now.

Or so I thought. As I reached the door, a man took a sideways step to block me. "Rory?"

I blinked, trying to place him. I thought I'd seen him before but wasn't sure.

And then, as I glanced down at his hands at his sides, I realized why he looked familiar. He was carrying a tablet computer.

He was one of the two people I'd seen and, because of their photo and note-taking, thought might be media folks.

"That's me," I said. "Excuse me." I tried to maneuver around him, but he didn't budge.

"My name is Derek Vardox. My family owns the local weekly newspaper, *The Destiny Star*. It's mostly a fun rag where we talk about our townsfolk and superstitions, but we do include real news if it affects Destiny." He paused, looking down at me with curious brown eyes. "You found Kenneth Tarzal's body, didn't you?"

"That's right. I've had to talk to the police about it, but I don't have to talk to you." I'm not usually that impolite—but I'm also not usually confronted by the media. I didn't want my picture or quotes to appear in this man's publication or anywhere else.

"That's true," he said. "But I want as much information as possible to make sure we get everything right. And since I've heard that the authorities seem to be zeroing in on poor Martha Jallopia as their main suspect … well, I like Martha. I go to her shop often since I have a couple of Labs at home, and I just don't see her killing anyone."

I inhaled deeply. Did he know I was running the Lucky Dog for her now? Probably, if he knew my name and that I'd found Tarzal. The information was out there if he asked questions, which, as a reporter, he undoubtedly did.

I stared at him, trying to convey no emotion at all in my expression. He had a full head of sandy-colored hair and a fairly nice-looking face with a longish nose and high cheekbones. He wore a gray knit shirt over dark trousers. His interested expression didn't quit as he cocked his head and continued to regard me intensely.

"Look," I said. "I don't want any more publicity over this. If you promise to refer to me only as an unnamed source or whatever, I'll give you the short version of what I know."

"Fair enough." He smiled expectantly and raising his tablet. "Let me record this for accuracy only. I won't use your likeness or voice. Okay?"

"All right." I paused. "I don't want you to use my dog's name or refer to the fact that I'm trying to help Martha at her shop or anything else. But for your information only as you do your research, yes, thanks to the keen nose of my dog Pluckie, who seemed insistent about going into the bookstore as I tried to pass by, I found poor Mr. Tarzal. I called 911. You've probably learned from the police that he was stabbed by a shard from a broken mirror. It was...sad. Horrible." I looked at him. "That's all for now, but I'm glad you want to help Martha. I don't think she's done anything wrong. And if you keep your promise not to name me, I'd talk to you again. But right now I have to leave." Mostly because I'd had enough, and people inside the shop were staring at us.

"Fine," he said. "I know where to find you."

———

I'd only taken a few hurried steps onto the still-crowded sidewalk outside, trying to escape Derek Vardox and my thoughts, when my cell phone rang. I pulled it from my jeans pocket.

It was the same number I'd called a little while ago—the lawyer. Or at least her office.

"Hello?" I said.

"Hello, Rory? This is attorney Emily Rasmuten. You called me before about Martha Jallopia."

I moved from the sidewalk and into the area between the two stores where I'd last spoken with Justin. It was late enough in the afternoon that there were more shadows than light here. "Thanks for returning my call." I started to tell her the dilemma of Martha being considered a suspect in Tarzal's murder.

"Yes, I've heard about it. So has everyone in town and probably beyond here, too."

Partly thanks to the *Destiny Star*, I figured, although I was aware that the murder had also appeared in some broadcast media and online and there'd been some speculation as to who'd done it.

"I gather she's been read her Miranda rights," I said, "even though she's not under arrest … yet." I didn't want to give any details of my conversations with Martha or Justin. "She told me that you represent her on some other matters. Do you handle criminal cases, too?"

"Yes," she said. "Destiny's a small enough town that the few attorneys here don't specialize too much." She paused. "Did Martha say she wants to hire me to represent her on this matter, too?"

"We've talked about it," I said. "She's not been well and is pretty much confined to her home above the Lucky Dog Boutique, although she has come downstairs a bit." I didn't want to get into the fact that she happened to have gotten downstairs at a particularly bad time. "I told her I'd call you for her. She's got access to her phone, so it would be great if you'd call her back."

"Yes, she and I would need to talk for her to retain me. And I won't want it to appear that I'm soliciting her business."

"Well, she said she wanted to talk to you, so it shouldn't hurt for you to call her."

"Right. I will. Thank you, Rory. You sound like a good friend."

"I hope to be. I don't know her well."

"But—well, rumors do flow through this town like any superstition," she said. "I heard that you and your dog saved her life before, and you may be helping to save it again."

She couldn't see my brief shrug. "I liked Martha from the moment I met her. I don't think she could have hurt Tarzal."

"But she has a motive."

That wasn't a question. And I wasn't about to respond anyway.

"I will get in touch with Martha. Thanks for calling, Rory."

I pushed the button to hang up. And then I realized there was someone else I wanted to talk to, the sooner the better. I'd stuck a business card into my pocket when I'd gotten it at the Wishbones-to-Go, and called Destiny's Luckiest Tours. This time, I left a message for Arlen Jallopia to call me. He was apparently out giving a tour just then. He might be working late tonight, or not. I hoped to talk to him as soon as possible.

While I was on the phone, I reserved a spot on one of the tours Arlen was scheduled for the next day. One way or another, I'd at least get to see him. To talk to him alone? That remained to be seen.

———

I got the call back from Arlen a short while after I'd dug back into helping customers at the Lucky Dog. Fortunately, the people I'd been with were still making up their minds about some decorative collars and leashes they were trying on their cocker spaniel—a dog Pluckie seemed to like a lot. In any event, I was able to walk away to the side of the store to answer my phone, still keeping an eye on them to make sure Pluckie wasn't bothering them.

"Hi, Rory? This is Arlen Jallopia. I got your message. Is everything okay with Martha?"

"Mostly," I said. "But I'd like to talk to you about her. Are you available to join me for dinner?"

"Sure," he said. "I'd like to talk to you, too."

FIFTEEN

ARLEN HAD TOLD ME his last tour that day ended at six thirty. We decided to meet at the Shamrock Steakhouse at six forty-five.

Millie was leaving the Lucky Dog around six o'clock, but Jeri said she would be there to wait on any late-day customers and close up.

I really liked the young ladies Martha had chosen to be her assistants. They were teaching me a lot as well as making sure that the Lucky Dog remained lucky with its touristy patrons. I'd gathered that the store remained profitable and that Martha could afford to pay me a salary, as promised. I nevertheless pondered some ideas to make it bring in even more money.

Pluckie and I soon reached the Shamrock Steakhouse and saved a table outside on the patio. The air was cool, but not cold. Another pleasant evening here in the area just south of the mountains in the Los Padres National Forest.

But it was nearly seven fifteen. Arlen was late.

I wondered if this was an aberration or his norm. Would he have retained his job as a tour guide if he was habitually late? Unlikely.

Maybe he had underestimated the time it would take him to get here from wherever the tours met. Or maybe his being late now was some kind of message to me. Assuming I could figure it out. Of course a lot of people didn't think twice about running half an hour or more late. I considered calling him, though, to make sure there hadn't been some kind of misunderstanding.

"Can I get you something besides water while you're waiting?" My server this evening was different from the one who'd taken care of Justin and me a couple of nights ago. He wore the same kind of tall green hat as well as a vest and other clothing with shamrock decorations. Four leaf clovers. Symbols of good luck.

What the heck? It was late enough in a day that had had some pretty rough moments. Hard to believe it had just been this morning when Pluckie and I had found Tarzal... "Yes, please," I said, and ordered an Irish ale on tap, as well as more water in a dog bowl for Pluckie.

She wasn't the only dog on the patio this night, either. There was a German shepherd under a table in the next row, and two small white terriers a few rows over. None seemed particularly interested in my pup or each other, a good thing in an environment like this.

I studied the menu. I intended to eat here this night whether or not Arlen showed up.

Was there any kind of superstition about being stood up for a meal?

"Hi, Rory," said a voice from behind me. "Sorry I'm late." Arlen squeezed around the nearby occupied tables toward the seat across from me. He bent to pat Pluckie on the head. "My last group of

153

tourists was gung-ho on getting a whole bunch of pictures at our last stop, so we were behind schedule. I didn't think I'd be this late, though, or I'd have called you."

At least he was apologetic and polite. And I was probably overreacting because of the emotional and difficult day I'd had, my concern over Martha—and having been the only person on this patio who didn't have another diner with her before Arlen arrived.

"That's okay," I said and realized I meant it. Most of my angst before had been unnecessary, and now I could relax.

Arlen's appearance still reminded me a bit of a TV actor—maybe not one, but a conglomeration: young and pert and trying a bit too hard to look cute and sexy.

He asked our server for a beer, too. "Did you order your dinner yet?" he asked.

"No."

"I can recommend the sirloin tips pretty highly. The T-bone, too. Although if you prefer something lighter, their steak sandwiches are great."

"I had a sirloin the other night," I told him. "I liked it a lot, so I may just stay with the tried and true."

"Oh, you've been here before?"

"I ate here on my first night in town." I didn't explain that I'd been with the chief of police, who, at the time, had been wining and dining me partly to convince me to help out Arlen's aunt while she recuperated.

When our beers arrived along with some delicious Irish soda bread, Pluckie sat up and sniffed the air. I gave her a tiny taste of bread and she settled back down with what appeared to be a contented sigh.

I looked at Arlen. I hadn't exactly thought this through. I didn't want to ask him if he happened to have killed Tarzal because the man wasn't getting along with his Aunt Martha, or maybe for some other reason. But I could at least sound him out to learn if he knew about their argument.

"I thought we should talk," I said, "because I'm concerned about your aunt. She seems to be healing, although it's only been a couple of days. I'm concerned that she's not taking the best care of herself."

"You mean because she's walking up and down the steps at her place when she's not supposed to?"

Had one of the store staff told him that? Or had Martha herself? Turned out to be the latter.

"That and other things," I said. "How'd you know that she'd been negotiating the steps?"

"I talked to her before," he said. "When I heard that Kenneth Tarzal had been murdered. She was upset because apparently the fact she'd been able to get downstairs on her own despite just being released from the hospital made her a suspect."

"That's my understanding, too," I said. "But I don't really understand what they think her motive could be." That wasn't true, of course, but I wanted to see if Arlen knew.

He did. His expression grew solemn. "I think it's pretty insubstantial, but Aunt Martha did tell me she'd had some business meetings planned with the men next door. She was doubtful they'd go well because she thought Tarzal and his partner Preston were going to twist her arm to give up the Lucky Dog Boutique. She intended to resist all temptation and was hoping to convince them instead to go after the property on the other side of their shop, around the corner."

"I suppose she may have been hoping for that result when she first saw Pluckie and said my little black and white dog was a good omen for a business meeting."

"Right. But she refuses to acknowledge that, whatever the guys at the bookstore were hoping to build on the property there, they wanted it all to face onto Destiny Boulevard, not around the corner."

I hesitated. "You know that... well, I understand that Tarzal threatened her with making sure to publicize bad luck superstitions about dogs and the Lucky Dog Boutique so it would close anyway if she didn't cooperate."

"She told me."

Our meals came then. Arlen, too, had ordered steak—a T-bone. That had been the most expensive meal on the menu.

And I suspected it would be on my nickel. We hadn't discussed who'd be paying. Since meeting here had been my invitation, he might be expecting that I'd treat.

I just hoped I'd get something useful out of him.

"This is great," I said a few minutes later after my first bite of meat. "How's yours?"

His smile told me it was good even before his words did. "Delicious. Anyway, Rory, I guess you may be wondering what I thought of Martha's arguing with Tarzal and Preston. I was all for it, since I doubted they'd pay her what her property is worth. She bought it years ago when she moved to Destiny and opened the store. Things have only gotten better in town, so I'm sure she'd make a hefty profit on it—but the Lucky Dog's really profitable, too. Yes, she could move it, but it's a great location."

"Then you supported her position." And didn't like Tarzal's? Better yet, didn't like Tarzal?

Could Arlen have been the killer to protect both his aunt and her property?

"Yes, I did. I really like Destiny. I moved here after visiting Aunt Martha when I graduated from college three years ago. I wanted to get even closer to her, you know? She doesn't have kids, and the poor lady is growing older. I wanted to help her."

Or inherit from her? He didn't say that, but I read beneath the lines.

He sighed, then drank some more beer, his eyes on me. "I know you're doing a good job helping her with the store, Rory. You've got a perfect background for it. But I wanted her to hire me at least part time so I could learn the business better."

And maybe step in to run it now that his aunt was ill, even before the possibility of inheriting it? Or maybe he'd thought—hoped?—that time was fast approaching.

What a cynic I was. But it was interesting that Martha hadn't taken her nephew under her wing after he'd moved to Destiny. Maybe she didn't trust him—at least not to run her beloved boutique as it should be managed—even though, the first time I'd seen him, he had tried to be helpful.

But not even a part-time job when the guy was obviously interested? Why? And he'd said he would come visit her once she was home, but if he had I wasn't aware of it.

I'd have to approach the question of Arlen carefully, but I would ask Martha one of these days.

"Then you didn't think she should even have listened to Tarzal and Preston's latest offer?" I asked.

"Listen to it? Yes. I doubt it would have made sense, but if it did I'd have helped Martha find another location for the store and move into it. But I'd have done a better job at it if I knew more about the business first."

He actually made some sense. And at this moment, I didn't really think that Arlen had killed Tarzal to help his aunt or himself—even if he hoped to run, and possibly inherit, the pet boutique.

I blinked and grabbed my own beer glass as I decided what to say next. I decided not to issue an invitation for a part-time job without discussing it with Martha, but I didn't intend to stay forever and she would ultimately need help, maybe someone who could take charge.

Yet if she'd already considered Arlen, then rejected the idea, I needed to know why—and honor it if it made sense.

At the moment, I couldn't think of what else to say on this subject. So, instead, I said, "You know what? I've reserved a spot on one of the tours you're giving tomorrow. Why don't you tell me a little bit about what I'll see?"

———

By the time we finished eating, I was even more eager to take the tour of Destiny. I gathered that no matter what else Arlen was, he was a smooth, comedic, and fun tour guide.

Plus, Destiny, with all its superstitions, was one really fascinating town.

I'd been right about Arlen's expectations of being treated to dinner. But that was okay. I still needed more information from and about him. Right now, though, I couldn't throw him in front of Justin as the best murder suspect in town.

That meant I had to keep looking. And asking questions. And learning more about this town's good and bad luck symbols and who believed. And who didn't.

The server brought our check. I looked at it and paid with a credit card.

"Thanks, Rory," Arlen said. His smile was all movie-star smooth, and I felt like he might have been trying to flirt with me. Or at least manipulate me.

"You're welcome," I said, then quickly stood. Pluckie rose, too, and looked at me, wagging her tail. "You're right," I said to her. "We'll go back to our B&B and I'll get you your dinner." She wasn't starving, though. I'd given her small bites of my steak.

"Where are you staying?" Arlen asked.

"The Rainbow Bed and Breakfast."

"Good choice." We'd made our way to the gate of the patio and he opened it, letting Pluckie and me go through first. "Anyway, thanks again and I'll see you tomorrow." He walked away.

Pluckie apparently thought it was a fun time to jog along the street, since she ran ahead of me. Fortunately, at this hour and location, there weren't as many people on the sidewalks as I was used to seeing.

We made a couple of stops for Pluckie to do her usual sniffing and piddling but soon reached the Rainbow B&B. At last. I hadn't been here all day. It felt like this morning, when Pluckie and I had found Tarzal, had occurred ages ago.

We walked under the horseshoe and into the lobby, only to find a small crowd of people there surrounding the owner, Serina. Among them was Carolyn Innes of the button shop whom I'd met at Wish-bones-to-Go—which reminded me I'd better ask tomorrow if Jeri had retrieved any wishbones from Martha.

Carolyn was near the back of the group. After picking Pluckie up I edged toward her. "Hi," I said. But noticing that all eyes were on Serina behind the check-in desk, I looked there, too.

In her usual Gold Rush–era frilly outfit, Serina held on as if about to fall over. Her brown eyes were reddened, and her smooth cheeks appeared damp, as if she'd been crying.

"What's wrong with Serina?" I asked Carolyn.

"We're all here to support her," Carolyn said. "It's so awful for her." Her eyes were teary, too. She still had on the black cat and buttons T-shirt I'd seen her in earlier that day.

"What is?"

"Kenneth Tarzal."

"She knew him?" Not surprising in this relatively small town.

"Shhh," Carolyn whispered. "Yes. They were engaged a while ago."

"Oh. But they aren't—weren't—now?"

Carolyn aimed her chilly blue-eyed gaze at me. "No, but they were starting to date again to see if they could resurrect what they had. And now poor Serina will never know."

"What a shame," I said, even as I wondered whether Serina did in fact know—and may have had a motive to kill her ex-fiancé.

SIXTEEN

Pluckie and I soon headed upstairs to our room, but I could hear the crowd below for a long time.

I didn't sleep well that night, and it wasn't only because of Serina's noisy supporters trying to help her grieve into the wee hours. Even when those hours were no longer so wee, I lay with my eyes open in the dark, for a while at least.

When the sun shone through the window, though, I found myself waking up, so I must eventually have fallen asleep.

Heck, considering how my mind roiled, why had I slept at all? With the help of my lucky dog Pluckie I'd discovered a dead body— had it really been only yesterday? So much had happened since then.

I'd spoken with a number of people, any one of whom could have been guilty of Tarzal's murder. Others who'd been mentioned could be, too. I'd been questioned myself by the cops.

And I'd unofficially taken on the job of trying to clear the one person I just couldn't make myself believe had been the killer—even if Martha had one of the most credible motives.

And not to mention diving further into my current actual job of managing the Lucky Dog Boutique, even as I continued attempting to learn more about superstitions, whether or not I ultimately believed in them. Sure, people wanted to control their worlds. Their luck. But could they? For now, at least, I remained a skeptic.

Tarzal's murder had nothing to do with the broken mirror in the Broken Mirror Bookstore, except as a convenient weapon for his killer … right?

Or would the killer now suffer bad luck, assuming he or she hadn't followed the ritual of the five-dollar bill to counter what could happen after breaking a mirror?

Heck, were there any superstitions about being unable to sleep after learning of a murder? I grabbed the book written by the murder victim and looked in the index.

My movement stirred Pluckie, who'd been sleeping at the foot of my bed. I didn't think she'd lost any rest last night.

But she wasn't worried about all that had gone on yesterday, and maybe she knew she passed along good luck to those crazy humans around her.

I sat on the edge of the bed looking up the pages containing sleep superstitions. But none seemed to apply. They mostly seemed to be about the direction in which a bed faces—and I had no idea of the direction of the one I'd been sleeping in. Or whether moonlight beamed directly on a sleeper's face, which causes nightmares. Or if a mirror reflects on you while you're in bed, your soul will be stolen.

Balderdash!

I didn't try to read the supposed origins of those superstitions but slammed the book closed, which disturbed Pluckie yet again. This time, she jumped off the bed and stood on the floor looking at me expectantly, tail wagging slowly. She knew I was awake—and that meant it was time to take her outside for a walk.

I dressed quickly, figuring I'd shower later, after she was comfortable. For now, we went downstairs.

I heard nothing in the room where food had previously been served at this hour. Apparently, after the horrible night Serina had had, this day the inn was for bed only, and not breakfast.

Pluckie soon finished with her morning necessities. We went upstairs so I could feed her, then get ready to leave. I hurried so we could get to the Lucky Dog long before it was supposed to open. I intended to take a tour of Destiny that day. But before I left, I wanted to make sure all was going well at the shop I now managed.

———

"This is sweet of you, Rory," Martha said a while later as she bit into a biscuit filled with egg, cheese, and bacon.

I'd called to see if she wanted me to pick up anything for her breakfast. There was a 7-Eleven convenience store sort of on my way—the only chain store I'd seen so far in Destiny, but I could understand why an operation with that kind of name would be welcomed here. I'd stopped on my walk to the Lucky Dog with Pluckie and picked up coffee and breakfast sandwiches to go.

"No problem." Sitting at Martha's small kitchen table, I reached down to give Pluckie a little taste of muffin, then looked back at my human table companion. "How are you feeling today?"

Martha didn't look as well as yesterday. I had a feeling that I wasn't the only one who hadn't gotten much sleep.

"Just fine," she said though, smiling so brightly that the lines on her face turned into tighter pleats. "You're here awfully early. What do you plan to do before the shop opens?"

"I'll just check the inventory on the computer to see if we need to order anything."

"I'm impressed." Martha raised eyebrows darker than her gray hair. "You know how to run our system already?"

"In the rare times when customers aren't around, Jeri and Millie have shown me what they know." Jeri had been the most helpful. Not only was she the older of the two assistants but she'd also gotten a degree in business administration. Plus, she'd worked at the Lucky Dog for a couple of years and had helped at her family's retail shop since she was a kid.

I wondered why Martha hadn't chosen her to run the place in her absence. Jeri seemed a much better bet than Arlen, who admitted to knowing nothing about the store, and at least somewhat better than Millie.

Why me, instead?

But Jeri only worked at the Lucky Dog part time. I'd gathered from what she'd said that her relatives swallowed up a lot of her time in helping out at the Heads-Up Penny Gift Shop.

Martha confirmed it. "She's a good girl. I'd have asked her to help out more while I was healing if I thought she could, but I've asked that even before and she's said no. Her family really needs her some of the time at their shop, too."

That answered my question about Jeri ... but not about Arlen.

"I also wanted to get everything I could done early, before Millie or Jeri gets here. Guess what I'm doing today." I grinned at her.

She looked puzzled. "I haven't a clue. Tell me."

"Well, it looks like I'll be in Destiny for a while, and the more I know about the town and its superstitions the better, so I'm taking a tour. Now, guess who my guide will be."

Her eyes opened wide but I couldn't interpret her expression. "Arlen?"

"That's right. I've heard really good things about him as a tour guide."

I hoped that opened the door enough for her to jump through and tell me what she thought of her nephew—and why she hadn't taken him on to train as a part-time employee.

"I've heard that, too, dear. I've never taken his tour, so you'll have to tell me all about it."

"I will," I promised. "He seems like a nice enough guy, and I gather he cares a lot about his aunt." I waited, but Martha didn't comment.

Taking a last bite of my sandwich while saving a bite more of the biscuit for Pluckie, I stood, grabbed my coffee, and said, "I'd better get downstairs."

"Okay, but first—just so you know, Millie came up here and got the three other wishbones from yesterday, but I want to break the fourth one with you to see which of us will have good luck today."

"Oh." Not a good idea. I certainly didn't want the larger part to be mine since Martha believed in such things. On the other hand— did I want to tempt fate?

She reached into the pocket of her jeans and pulled out a substantial-sized wishbone. "Okay, make a wish." She closed her eyes, and when she opened them she held out the wishbone.

Had I made a wish? Well, yes, in a way. I wished that we would both have good luck today and forever, no matter what the results of this little activity.

Just in case, I tried to manipulate the wishbone as we both pulled on it to ensure that Martha got the big end.

She didn't.

That upset me a bit, though not much. She was the one who believed. But she would also be sitting upstairs here today, unlikely to get into more trouble … I hoped.

And me? Well, I didn't intend to get into any difficult situations, either. And since my wish should theoretically benefit both of us, I should feel fine about this.

I almost convinced myself.

Standing, I looked at Martha. "I can't tell you my wish since that might cause problems, but you have no need to worry. Just in case, though, call if you need anything." I didn't make it a question.

"But you won't be here." Her wan smile said that was supposed to be a joke.

"No, but if you call the store's number, you'll get one of your assistants, and everyone's ready to help you. You know that."

"Yes," she said, her smile real this time. "I know that." But then her expression morphed to sorrow. "Everyone but the police."

That made me want to contact Justin and relay Martha's state of mind to him. Surely he couldn't really consider her guilty. Especially since he'd seemed to care for her so much. But I realized he had a job to do, procedures to follow, no matter what his emotions might have told him.

With Pluckie at my side, I went back down the stairs to the store—careful not to trip. Not that I believed in the bad luck superstition Martha thought had jinxed her enough to make her a murder suspect. But I could really hurt myself, and maybe Pluckie, too, if I happened to fall down those steps.

It was just a little past nine o'clock, so I was a bit surprised to see Jeri inside the store. "Good morning," I said as Pluckie dashed over to greet her, tail wagging.

"Hi. I can't stay long right now, but Millie will be here soon. I'll return late this afternoon to help out, though. I hope that's okay."

I considered pressing her a bit for what her family's ongoing expectations were in her other part-time job but didn't think this was the best time. Instead, I motioned for her to join me at the computer after pulling it out from its locked home beneath the counter, and we went over my latest inventory questions. I was delighted that she had a lot of the answers, and we ordered some more pet foods and decorative collars and leashes since we were starting to run short.

I was also glad when Millie came in a short while later. I'd still be around for about an hour, but I wanted overlap in who was there. When I told her about my upcoming tour, she laughed and clapped her hands. "You'll love it. And guess who'll be the next expert on superstitions around here."

"Not I," I said, but was glad that she clearly had no qualms about being left alone today to mind the store.

She also promised to take good care of Pluckie, since I didn't think it would be appropriate to take her on the tour.

When I was ready to leave, I let Millie know. Then I fitted the loop of Pluckie's leash around the hook near the back counter once more, just so I'd feel more at ease that she wouldn't follow anyone out the door. Like me.

I was somewhat surprised as I strode back to the front of the store to see Millie moving some of our products for sale around. "Just want to call people's attention to them some more," she said.

But wouldn't most patrons think it bad luck to have a clowder—yes, that's the name for a group of felines—of stuffed black cat toys in their paths as they entered the store?

I didn't say anything, though. That would at least get our customers' attention—and I hoped it would be in a good, superstitious way.

———

The offices of Destiny's Best Tours were on the other side of town, but I walked there anyway. I might have been able to arrange to be picked up nearer the Lucky Dog, but it was a nice morning, and I also wanted to get another personal view of the town before I heard about it from Arlen's perspective.

As always, the sidewalks were crowded. One of these days I'd have to stop in City Hall and see if there was any printed literature or website that kept track of numbers of people who came here. Maybe even that guy Derek's weekly paper, the *Star*, collected statistics. I'd need to check.

I enjoyed my walk—although I was more in a hurry than most of the pedestrians so I had to squeeze around them, even as I tried to avoid stepping on cracks as I noticed others did, too.

Why were so many people interested in finding out about superstitions? Was it only curiosity about this little town that made tourists flock here?

How many others came as I did, hoping for answers in situations where it looked as if some superstition came true?

Maybe I'd learn that on my tour.

I walked until I reached Luck Street. I used a crosswalk to get to the opposite side of Destiny Boulevard. Did people ever cross their fingers for luck when they got into crosswalks?

I smiled at my own silliness as I proceeded up Luck Street to a building with a large parking lot where several tour vans were parked, all labeled, "Destiny's Luckiest Tours."

I glanced at my watch. My tour wouldn't leave until ten, and I still had about twenty minutes. I decided to wait in the building.

As I pulled open the glass door at the front of the smooth concrete building, I saw Evonne Albing, the owner of the tour company whom I'd met at Wishbones-to-Go, behind the front counter. A lot of people were in line, presumably signing up for tours or checking in like me.

Evonne, in another smooth and attractive business dress, seemed somehow to sense my presence. Ignoring the people in front of her she stood, smiled, and called out, "Hi, Rory. Welcome. Are you ready to experience some of Destiny's greatest luck? Get ready for your tour!"

SEVENTEEN

"Thanks, Evonne." I hurried to the front of the line and shook the hand she held out. She grasped mine warmly for an extra second before letting go.

I smiled at her, all the while wondering how she knew who I was. Sure, she'd recognized me, but how did she know my name?

When I'd met Evonne in the Wishbones-to-Go line, she'd introduced herself, but when she told me to give her my name and a time I wanted to take a tour, I'd demurred. She'd left before Carolyn Innes from the button shop indicated she recognized me for assisting Martha after the Destiny Welcome show.

Well, this was a small town, and I was now more than a tourist. Besides, Arlen knew who I was. But even if he'd described me to Evonne, that didn't mean she would recognize me.

Heck, why did I care? This was Destiny, home of superstitions. Maybe there was more woo-woo stuff here, too—like inherent psychic abilities.

I considered asking her how she knew my name, but Arlen stepped through one of the doors behind the long counter. "Hi, Rory," he called, then joined Evonne.

She was looking at a computer screen in front of her. I noticed that Arlen had an earbud in. I couldn't tell whether Evonne did, too, but they both had similar electronic gizmos clipped to their shirts that could be microphones.

Was there a camera here somewhere? Probably. This could have been as simple as his seeing me on a screen in a back room and telling Evonne, via the electronics, who I was.

Impressive to superstitious tourists, maybe, if they pulled the same act on them. I wasn't impressed.

"Hi, Arlen," I finally responded. "I was just over at your aunt's—upstairs. We had breakfast together." I considered telling him about the wishbone but decided against it. He was supposed to be the expert on superstitions around here, not me.

Besides, depending on what happened today on our tour, if neither Martha nor I had any particular good luck, that might prove to me that superstitions had no merit.

"How is she?" he asked. His red shirt with the Destiny's Luckiest Tours logo on the pocket hugged surprisingly buff arm muscles.

"Improving, I think."

"Great," he said. "Now excuse me while I gather our tour group together."

Arlen meandered around the crowd for a little while. I saw a display of tour brochures and others for Destiny shops, plus a stack of *Destiny Star* newspapers.

I picked up a paper as well as information on some of the shops and restaurants that I recognized, noticing that the Broken Mirror

Bookstore was represented here, but the Lucky Dog Boutique was not. I'd already started considering ways to increase the shop's business. If such a thing didn't exist, I'd have to do something about it.

Arlen made an announcement requesting that everyone on the ten o'clock Meet Our Destiny tour get together outside at the van in the parking lot nearest the door. "I'm your guide," he told us. "Follow me."

The van seated a dozen passengers. Arlen directed me to the driver's side, right behind him. "You should be able to see fine from there as we drive, and you can get in and out quickly at our stops. Oh, and feel free to ask me any questions. I might even have answers."

The other seats filled quickly. Considering the number of kids and couples and the Destiny totebags carried in, I figured that everyone else was a tourist.

Arlen ran through a list of people who'd reserved seats. Then he further introduced himself. "Hi, everyone. Welcome. I'm Arlen Jallopia, and for the next couple of hours I'm going to give you Destiny's Luckiest Tour."

He quickly explained that he had roots here thanks to a family member who'd moved to town years ago—Martha, I was sure, but he didn't identify her. He'd only been here a comparatively short while but had been enthralled by Destiny's origin and history and all the superstitions personified by stores and people's beliefs.

"We'll mostly drive past points of interest, although we'll get out and look around at a few sites. Feel free to ask questions anytime … although if the place and timing could bring any of us bad luck, I reserve the right to let you know that and refuse to answer."

He gave a big wink and a wave, then said, "Everyone have your seat belts on? Good. It's bad luck around here not to wear one while riding in a car or driving. So … let's go!"

He got behind the steering wheel, put on his own seat belts, and started the engine.

As he drove out of the parking lot, he tested his elongated van's public address system. Everyone could hear him.

Sitting beside me was a guy who appeared to be in his twenties, with longish blond hair and a short beard. "Is this your first time in Destiny?" he asked, his smile wide.

"Yes," I said. "Yours?"

He nodded. "I've wanted to come here ever since I was a kid and first learned to cross my fingers for luck. I'm here with some other guys majoring in sociology at Cal State Fremont. We're all doing papers on offbeat things people believe, and coming here is part of our research. My name is Barry."

He held out his hand expectantly, and I shook it. "I'm Rory."

Our van was about to turn onto Destiny Boulevard in the area of town I assumed was its civic center. I'd been there at the nearby Break-a-Leg Theater for the Destiny Welcome, and next door was City Hall. Beyond that was a matching, though smaller, building I assumed was the police station. A bunch of official-looking cars were parked in front of it.

That must be where Chief Justin Halbertson hung out when he wasn't harassing old ladies or chatting with—or interrogating—younger ones.

Okay, maybe that wasn't fair. He was just doing his job. And I had an urge to talk to him and ask how their investigation into Tarzal's death was progressing.

Instead of turning toward town, Arlen turned right. "We'll come back this way," he said into his microphone. "But first thing I want to show you is Destiny's most hysterical—er, historical—area."

I knew Arlen was supposed to keep his tour light and even act as a comedian, so maybe there actually would be hysterical humor in what he first showed us.

For now, he started telling the story I'd heard previously about the origin of Destiny: Its founding by two California Gold Rush Forty-Niners who'd found gold after dashing to the end of a rainbow and had fallen in love with superstitions.

"Now, you may have heard that story before, including that where those panners found gold wasn't around here. But did you know that they chose the location for Destiny after chasing the end of another rainbow?"

That part I hadn't heard, and I gathered that most, if not all, others on the tour weren't aware of it, either.

"Where I'm taking you now," Arlen said, "was where they ended up—way up in the surrounding mountains. Settling there and planning a town would have been difficult, if not impossible, so they looked around and found a much more suitable locale, which is where Destiny is now. But I'm going to show you a place beloved by those of us who are true superstition freaks, where Destiny could have been located."

I assumed the miners hadn't suffered bad luck by choosing a slightly different location or Arlen would have mentioned it. We went up winding roads that sometimes made me hold my breath in fear that we would tip over and roll down some pretty steep mountains even with guard rails at the edges. But eventually we reached a

174

flat and paved area that was also surrounded by cliffs. A few other tour vans were parked there, too.

"Let's all get out and breathe deeply," Arlen said. "And close our eyes and think of how superstitions can come true."

We exited the van, and, along with a crunch of the tourists here from our group and others, I looked at a large sign posted at the end of the parking lot, near a path up the side of a mountain. It described the Forty-Niners, their luck in finding gold thanks to rainbow number one and their decision to found Destiny near the end of rainbow number two—which they happened to claim was right here.

Interesting. I closed my eyes, breathed in the light, fresh mountain air, and tried to open myself to the possibility that superstitions really were real.

But when I opened them again, I still—unsurprisingly—had my doubts.

Arlen came over to me. "What do you think, new resident of Destiny? Are you convinced?"

"Convinced enough to tell customers at the Lucky Dog Boutique how lucky they'll be if they buy stuff for their pets there."

He laughed. "Fair enough. And now I can tell why Aunt Martha picked you to manage the place. I guess." His smiled appeared to turn momentarily bitter but he looked away quickly. "Okay, my gang," he called out. "Let's get back into the van and continue our tour."

The rest of the tour was pretty much what I expected. On the way back to town, Arlen spouted tales of other superstitions that had supposedly come true for residents over the years, indicating that carrying a rabbit's foot, or wearing the traditional something old, something new, something borrowed and something blue at a wedding brought good luck. Black cats crossing the paths of some people had supposedly caused things to go terribly wrong in their lives—and the worst wrong of all was that several people had had to move away from Destiny thanks to the evil caused by nasty, road-crossing black cats.

Including the one I'd seen?

All very interesting, and I could understand why people who believed in superstitions could assume that their good or bad luck resulted from some occurrence they'd been warned about.

But I still didn't hear anything that made me certain at last that Warren's ladder incident had definitely led to his death. Or that it hadn't.

If he'd believed in that superstition, then maybe so—since he'd be expecting something to go wrong. But that would also mean he'd have been more careful and would not have walked under that ladder in the first place.

I sighed as I often did while thinking about my loss. My confusion. My Warren.

At least this time I didn't cry.

Before heading into the heart of town, Arlen drove by some landmarks in the civic center that I hadn't seen before, including the local library. I promised myself to tell my friend Gemma about it. Better yet, I'd visit it first.

There were also schools near there, from elementary through middle school and high school.

"Do the schools here teach superstitions?" asked my seatmate. I imagined that would be important to his research for his sociology paper.

Arlen responded that each grade level did, in fact, teach something about superstitions appropriate to the age of the children. "I have to admit," he said, "that from what I've heard the students are told that even though Destiny is built around superstitions, they may not be real, so the kids are advised to think for themselves."

"I'll bet they believe in superstitions anyway," called a female voice from behind us.

"I'll bet they do, too," Arlen said with a laugh.

Soon, Arlen reached the beginning of Destiny Boulevard again. Once more, everyone got out. This time, we received a brief tour of the Break-a-Leg Theater where the Destiny Welcome had been. Arlen recounted tales of performers over the city's history who had or hadn't given the standard exhortation set forth in the theater's name to one another. Some shows had done well—but the actors or musicians in others had met mysterious fates that the locals of the time had chalked up to someone instead wishing them good luck and thereby bringing on just the opposite to those in that highly superstitious profession.

Back in the van, Arlen drove slowly down the street, pointing out various stores that I had already noticed or visited, describing their wares, their owners, the superstitions behind their names—and encouraging the tourists to visit them and spend money. All good for the town's economy, I was certain.

We reached the area where the Lucky Dog Boutique was, followed by the Broken Mirror Bookstore. Arlen immediately launched into a description in a deep, mournful tone about the town's foremost superstition expert Kenneth Tarzal, who'd written the most famous book ever on superstitions. And how, somewhere in the middle of the night only a short while ago, he had gone into his store and actually broken a mirror.

And how a shard from that mirror had given him the bad luck he then expected—when someone used it to kill him.

There were gasps and nods and murmurs from the time Arlen began his sad, if exaggerated and partially made-up, spiel. Of course everyone there must have heard the story. But what I heard in this group of strangers wasn't going to help me figure out the truth behind Tarzal's murder ... was it?

I listened as people speculated. Asked questions, like who had the most to gain by using that piece of mirror to kill Tarzal. Was he married? No. Did he have a girlfriend? Not then. How about his business partner? Yes, he had one but the town's speculation was that the man had had more to gain by keeping his superstition-expert partner alive. Were there other people who'd fought with him? Well ... that was still being investigated.

I was glad that Arlen didn't get into that any further. Maybe that was because one of the primary people who'd quarreled with Tarzal was, of course, Arlen's aunt.

Then ... how about someone no one would suspect, someone who had been harmed by a superstition that, if he'd known about it, or hadn't known about it, could have protected himself? Someone who might blame the world's superstition expert and decide to avenge him or herself on the book's author.

Now, that was an interesting angle that I hadn't previously thought about. But if it was the actual situation, how would I ever learn who had that kind of grudge and acted on it?

Still … well, it was a different approach. It gave me a reason to go, after this tour, to the police station we had passed a second time a while ago and check in with Justin, mostly to say hi.

But also to throw this additional idea into the mix of suspect-seeking.

EIGHTEEN

THE TOUR WAS OVER. Arlen parked in the lot beside the Destiny's Luckiest Tours offices, then stood, thanked everyone for coming, and wished them all the best of luck during their stay in Destiny and forever after.

He climbed out of the van and helped people down the steps—accepting tips from some of them.

I didn't give him one. After all, I was becoming a friend—sort of. Besides, I'd treated him to dinner.

In the parking lot, I said goodbye to my seatmate, Barry—and invited him and his fellow students to the Lucky Dog Boutique after telling him that I was its manager. He admitted to having a dog at home. "Who knows?" I said into his grinning face. "You might find some of the superstitions about pets represented in our goods interesting enough to include in your class projects."

I didn't mention its proximity to the Broken Mirror Bookstore, but Barry's friends who were hanging out with us kept checking a tour brochure of Destiny's Luckiest Tours, including a map depicting the town's layout. If they hadn't noticed before, they'd now see how close the two shops were.

Maybe curiosity about the murder would bring them in, even if shopping for doggy gifts didn't.

As that conversation ended and people drifted out of the parking lot, I stepped up to Arlen to say goodbye. "This was a really great tour," I said to him. "And do come by the Lucky Dog anytime to visit." Maybe I'd find a way to get his aunt to agree to let me hire him part-time to see how he worked out—the better for giving me more flexibility to go home sooner if all went well. If nothing else, seeing him around there would give me a better way of eliminating him— or not—as a murder suspect.

I started walking back toward the edge of town—to the home of the Destiny Police Department.

As I walked, I pondered what to say to Justin, assuming the police chief happened to be at the station. How should I approach the subject of whether he'd finally wised up and realized for certain that Martha was innocent, and figured out who'd really killed Tarzal?

And if he hadn't any definite answers yet, what was he doing to investigate people besides Martha?

As always, the sidewalks were crowded, and I overheard snippets of conversations—many about superstitions, none about the murder.

Should I give Justin a rundown of my own thought processes, the people I'd met or thought about as perhaps not getting along great with the murder victim—like his former fiancée Serina?

I didn't want the killer to be her, either, of course. I liked the owner of the Rainbow B&B.

And I didn't want it to be Arlen, or Preston, or anyone else I'd met here so far. Therefore, the idea of it being some unknown subject who'd had a grudge thanks to a superstition gone wrong really appealed to me.

The police station appeared to be a mini-version of the lovely, antique-looking City Hall next door, all marble-looking exterior with archways and domes.

I walked up the steps and into the lobby, which was busy but less crowded than the sidewalks. Most people hovering nearby appeared upset, shaking their heads or talking on their phones in angry tones. Had they suffered bad luck in Destiny, in the form of some kind of theft?

I imagined that kind of criminal behavior was especially frowned on in this town where tourists ruled.

A few uniformed cops stood behind a long desk partly behind glass off to the right, probably the station's greeters. Presumably those in the lobby had already checked in and were waiting to be called to speak to an appropriate officer.

I started walking toward that desk, preparing to ask if the chief might have a few minutes to talk to me, but soon stopped.

Was I starting to believe in superstitions or bad karma? I was wondering if I should have crossed my fingers before coming inside here. Or used my wishbone wish for something more productive than general luck—like, ensuring that I didn't see Detective Alice Numa here, or at least not before I'd spoken with Justin.

Unfortunately, despite my wish, my luck wasn't particularly good that day, at least not in that respect. I didn't even have time to turn and dash out.

Detective Numa looked toward me, and our eyes met. Even as I aimed a polite smile at her, I sighed internally.

She'd been talking to one of the people behind the greeting desk before she'd turned. As before, she wore a professional-looking suit and a chilly frown. Her hair was still pulled severely back from her face which might have been attractive had she allowed herself real smiles now and then.

She made a final comment to the person she'd been speaking with and started walking in my direction.

Damn. Well, all she'd done before was to interview me in Justin's presence about how Pluckie and I had found Tarzal's body, and ask what else I knew concerning his death, which was nothing. And to question me about Martha and, presumably, question Martha about me when she had interviewed her, too, as a potential witness … or killer.

Despite whatever emotions were at play in the minds of the people in the waiting area, they all seemed to know better than to stand in Alice's way. The sea appeared to part as she walked toward me.

I stood my ground—even as my mind churned about what reason to give for my being here.

Heck. I could be honest. I was here to see her boss. She didn't have to know what I wanted to talk to him about, though she probably could guess.

"Hi, Detective," I said as she finally got close enough to confront me. "Looks busy around here today."

"As it is everyday. This situation isn't our norm, though. Most of the people here were on a tour bus that came in from out of town, and someone apparently slipped into it and stole things while this group was at lunch. Outside of Destiny, I might add." Her smile looked complacent, as if she knew for a fact that bad things like that didn't occur in her town.

Murders, however, did. I didn't remind her of that.

"Anyway, I assume you're here to discuss something about the Tarzal homicide," she continued.

Yes, but I didn't want to explain to her that I had more questions and wanted to run them by the chief. "Actually, I just took a tour of Destiny and was walking back to the Lucky Dog. I started to pass by near here and thought I'd stop in. Is Chief Halbertson available?" If she thought this was a social call and I merely wanted to flirt with Justin, that was fine.

She frowned. "Yes, but I'm sure he's busy."

"I'm not surprised, but I'd still like to see if he could say hi. I'll just go check in at the desk."

"Don't bother. He's—" She stopped talking, and her frown became one deep scowl that pinched her eyes and mouth even more. She was looking over my shoulder, so I turned, fairly certain of what—or who—I'd see.

Sure enough, Justin had just entered the room. He stood at the doorway that appeared to lead into the bowels of the station. "Hey, everyone," he shouted, loud enough to get the attention of the people in the area. "Please make sure that the officers over there—" he pointed toward the desk, "—have your contact information, a description of what you lost, and how long you'll be in Destiny."

Lost? They'd been ripped off, but I supposed that was police-speak, a euphemism for what the jerk stole from you. Or maybe it was phrased that way because they'd have even worse luck recovering their stuff if the theft was described as what it was in this town of superstitions.

"We're in close touch with the Ojai police, who actually have jurisdiction over this incident," Justin continued. "We'll be working with them both to apprehend the suspects and to recover your property. Meantime, thanks for your information and your patience."

I doubted that any of those grumbling people was patient, but I did appreciate Justin's good, potentially calming attitude.

Some people started to swarm him, but a few uniformed officers and people in suits came over, apparently to help ease the pressure off him.

As he moved away from one couple, he spotted me. I smiled and nodded, and he started walking toward me.

"Looks like he's at least going to say hi," I murmured to Alice.

"Guess so. And I've got to go talk to some of these folks." Her tone sounded more resigned. "I assume you don't have any more information on the Tarzal homicide, do you?" Her tone was still soft, as if she wanted to convince me to tell her, if I had any, before passing it along to her boss.

I figured I'd be nice. I'd also tell the truth—sort of. "Sorry, no. If I did, I'd let you or Chief Halbertson know right away."

"Okay." She walked away with a nod toward her boss as he reached me.

"Hello, Rory." The expression on his handsome face was slightly contorted, too—not in the irritation I saw on Alice's face, but with more of a question. "What brings you here? I assume you weren't on the tour bus with these folks?"

"I did take a tour," I said, "with Arlen Jallopia and Destiny's Luckiest Tours. I felt pretty lucky afterward so I figured I'd stop in here and see if you were around. My luck held out, since here you are."

I was laying it on pretty thick but this was, after all, Destiny, where luck was everything.

"Well, welcome. I don't have a lot of time right now, unfortunately." As he continued to look down at me, he began to smile. "How about joining me for dinner again? You can tell me what you like and don't like about Destiny now that you've learned more about us."

The idea had crossed my mind, too. It would probably be better to interrogate him gently in a social situation than here. "Sounds great."

We made arrangements for him to stop by for me at the Lucky Dog at around closing time, seven tonight.

———

We were busy that afternoon, but not overwhelmed. Jeri wasn't around, but I let Millie wait on most of the customers, although I stepped in frequently when it appeared she needed help.

Millie assured me she had retrieved the wishbones from Martha's while Jeri was there, and they had used them appropriately. She didn't tell me what her wish had been, what size of the bones she'd wound up with, nor whether her wish had come true.

Of course Pluckie stayed at my side. And when I had a few minutes, I sat down behind the rear counter with Tarzal's superstition book.

I hoped to find a clue in it about whom he might have irritated, but that of course wasn't the tome's purpose.

Even more, I sought superstitions that we could incorporate into more products at the Lucky Dog Boutique.

There certainly were a lot of superstitions about dogs. Maybe I could figure out a way to have a black-and-white dog figure resembling Pluckie made into a business card holder, to ensure that the person using it would have upcoming luck in meetings with whoever picked up one of his or her cards from it. Of course that might not work, since the superstition was that it was best to have a black and white dog cross your path on your way to a business meeting.

Or I could add plush toys resembling Dalmatians, since they were thought to be lucky.

Hey, I realized. I was really getting into this. Into the Lucky Dog Boutique, at least. Not necessarily into the underlying superstitions.

I went upstairs to check on Martha, too. She seemed a bit restless, which I took as a good sign of her healing. Also, an aide sent by the hospital had visited her for about an hour.

Eventually, store hours came to a close. As we got ready to lock the doors, Justin showed up.

"See you tomorrow," I told Millie as she went one direction and Justin, Pluckie, and I went the other.

It turned out that the Black Cat Inn wasn't only a hotel. It also had a restaurant. That was where Justin suggested we go for dinner. I was glad, since I might as well sample food from as many places as possible while I was still in Destiny. Justin said it had an area where dogs were welcome, so it sounded great.

"But why call it the Black Cat?" I asked him as we walked there. "Isn't that bad luck?"

"Not unless one crosses your path. I think." He looked down at me and shrugged. Obviously, despite being a Destiny resident, he didn't profess to know all its superstitions.

Or believe in them.

I saw no black cat on the way. On our arrival, I noticed that the inn itself took up most of the property, but there was a small building of matching dark stone off to the side—the restaurant, I gathered, since there was a fence around it and lights that indicated that part was an outdoor seating area.

We headed there and were shown immediately to a table in a corner of the outside patio. This place seemed a little less crowded than the rest of the town's eating facilities, or maybe this was just a slow night. There weren't any other dogs present besides Pluckie, who lay down on the pavement with a sigh.

After consulting me, Justin ordered a carafe of red wine. I noticed that he still wore his nice-looking white shirt and dark trousers, but no tie or jacket, and his sleeves were rolled up. He looked good.

For someone else, I reminded myself. I was not in the market for another man, and even if I was someday, it wouldn't be someone in a location where I intended to stay only temporarily.

We both ordered pasta dishes, mine mushroom ravioli and his spaghetti carbonara. I figured that any treats I could give Pluckie would have to consist of small pieces of the Italian bread served while we waited.

I started the conversation I'd hoped to have with Justin, about the investigation into Tarzal's death.

"It's progressing all right," he said.

"Do you have suspects other than Martha?"

"I really can't talk too much about an ongoing situation," he said.

"Maybe not," I responded, "but I can. Look, I've been thinking about this. A lot. I realize it's your business and not so much mine, but I do have an interest in it. So ... here are some people I've been looking into."

Before I started listing Arlen and Serina and anyone else, Justin reached across the table and grabbed my arm, startling me.

"Bad idea, Rory," he said. "Keep out of this. I know your intentions are good, but don't you know it's considered bad luck to poke around in something that's not your concern?"

"It is my concern," I contradicted, "since I care about Martha, and you apparently do, too, even though you still consider her a major suspect. And you know what? I don't really believe in superstitions like that."

But he did know about the superstition I'd come to this town to question...

I didn't bring that up, but I did mention my thoughts earlier, thanks to my eavesdropping, about the killer being a stranger who'd read Tarzal's book and had the superstition he—or she—had focused on go wrong. "That may be why you haven't gotten enough evidence against anyone," I said, "especially if whoever it was looked like a tourist and has already left town."

"Interesting idea," Justin said, not sounding particularly interested at all. Then, after taking a long sip of wine, he leaned toward me. "You know full well that I'm a superstition agnostic, too, Rory. But you've got to understand that, if you get in the way of our investigation, you will have bad luck. Ongoing. Because I'll have to be involved in making certain that you back off. And I can be the source of all kinds of bad luck if you cross me."

"Well, hell." I glared at him. "You know, I've been doing a lot of research into superstitions since I arrived here. And whether or not you believe in them either, I think I can be the source of your bad luck in this situation, Justin, if you try to scare me off from helping Martha. Getting her well and back at the store is the only way I can be sure I'll be able to leave here comfortably. If you want to get rid of me, let me do what I need to. I'll stay out of your way … but until and unless I know you've got things wrapped up, and in a way that clears Martha, I'm going to continue to be the black cat crossing your path."

NINETEEN

SURPRISINGLY AFTER OUR SORT-OF confrontation, the rest of our dinner conversation was fairly congenial. We talked more about Destiny and superstitions and some rather humorous kinds of crimes Justin and his police force had had to investigate.

For example, some believers would steal nearly anything made of wood so they'd have something to knock on for good luck, and often assumed that the good luck would include absolving them of theft charges.

Also, most of the stores that carried tokens of superstition had stopped carrying agate, since it was reputed to cause invisibility and was therefore a prime target of theft—although the cops were nearly always able to find the culprits.

In turn, I regaled him with a couple of my favorite MegaPets scams. No superstitions involved there, but I'd met a number of customers who thought they could get away with anything—such as computer whizzes who manufactured manufacturers' coupons for free dog food or other products and expected us to honor them.

Sure, they looked legitimate, but all staff was under orders to check out any kind of coupon they hadn't run into before. Genuine ones were nearly always used by a lot of different people and many appeared in our own store ads. It was the one-time wonders that were suspicious.

The food at the Black Cat Inn's restaurant was great. The company was even better, once we got off the topic of murder. Pluckie seemed to enjoy it, too, since she got an occasional treat from me.

But as we finished—and, yes, this time he allowed me to grab the check, but not without a slight dispute about it first—I had to go back to our earlier topic of conversation since we hadn't resolved anything.

I took my final sip of wine first and looked him straight in the eye. "I really don't want to step on anyone's toes, Justin—especially not yours or any other cops, particularly since I don't know what superstitions there may be about that—"

"But you're going to stick your very pretty nose into official business as often as you want to," he finished for me. "And, no, I'm not sure if there are superstitions that involve noses, either."

"Sounds as if I'd better check on superstitions involving body parts," I said as I picked my credit card and receipt out of the tray the server had brought back after I'd paid.

"While you're figuring out how to do my job as an amateur." He didn't phrase that as a question.

"I'm an excellent pet store manager," I said. "I've no intention of becoming a cop, amateur or otherwise. But if things occur to me that might help Martha—and therefore let me feel more comfortable about choosing when I leave here—then I'll have to look into them."

"You could just tell me about them. Assuming there's some sense to them." Those blue eyes of his bored into me as if he was attempting to figure out my thought processes.

"That's the big 'if' about the whole thing," I countered. "You undoubtedly look at the murder and potential suspects and everything involved by using officially approved reasoning and protocol. Maybe it won't be so bad for someone like me to look at things from a less official angle." I paused. "And if that helps to clear Martha, how bad could it be?"

His rueful smile called more attention to his dark five-o'clock shadow. No, actually, his eight-o'clock shadow. "I'd like her to be cleared as much as anyone, Rory. You know that. Maybe more than anyone else. But it can only be done by our finding an even more compelling suspect, and so far—"

"So far, you've got a lot of suspects," I inserted. "Maybe a whole town full. And beyond." I stood, and so did Pluckie, who rubbed my right leg with her sweet little body. "We'll go back to the B&B and get you your real dinner now, sweetheart," I told her.

"The scope isn't quite that wide," Justin told me as I started skirting around other diners and walking out of the patio area.

"Maybe you should let the scope widen in your mind," I said, turning my head back toward him. "Anyone who was in this town that night could be a suspect."

"You?" He smiled, which softened the suggestion a bit.

"Maybe," I said, which resulted in that grin melting. "If I happened to have had motive, means, and opportunity. Aren't they what you look for?"

"You and everyone else had the means," he reminded me unnecessarily.

We were on the sidewalk now. It was less crowded than before, but people nevertheless still filled it. Pluckie pulled toward the side of the nearest building and squatted.

"Anyway," I told Justin, "I didn't do it, but you get my drift. And it's not really my intent to do your job. But if—"

"If you find a way to clear Martha and get out of town, you'll do it. I get that."

"Good." I wanted to ask when I'd see him again if I didn't call with an idea about a new suspect. I liked the guy and our repartee. Plus, it was important to me to be kept informed—to the extent I could extract stuff from him—about how the investigation was going. But I figured I could always call him and make up an idea to get him to scoff at it and maybe counter with something real. "Anyway, see you around. Oh, and one of these days I really want to meet Killer."

"I'm walking Pluckie and you back to your B&B," he told me in a tone that didn't easily allow for denial. "And I agree. Sometime soon, when I'm off duty, I'll bring him into the Lucky Dog and all four of us can go for a walk."

———

Justin walked us up to the door and I hurried to use my key to open it. This had felt the most like a date between us than any other get-together we'd had so far, and I didn't want to get into the awkward position of having to duck away from a goodnight kiss.

But Justin didn't even get close as I pushed open the door. Instead, he just said goodnight and left. Which made me feel unhappy and even a little ashamed. We were more than acquaintances by now. Friends. Platonic friends, which was how it should be.

Even so, my feelings were hurt. I might not want anything more, but I wanted Justin to want more. Maybe.

I realized I was confused about my reasons for staying in Destiny and helping Martha. But I was even more confused, at least tonight, about what I wanted from Justin.

A relationship? No. Too soon.

But if I believed he was genuinely attracted to me, that might help me continue my life without Warren—*might* being the key word.

"Hi," said a voice as Pluckie and I walked through the lobby toward the stairway. A female voice. Serina's.

"Hi," I said in return, my voice soft and sympathetic. "How are you?"

Did I really think she'd tell me? When I'd lost the man I loved, I'd thrust away most of the advice I got to talk about it and kept my thoughts pretty much to myself, except sometimes—such as with my dear and kind friend Gemma.

But that was me.

"I'm doing okay." But Serina's tone belied her words. She came around the welcome desk toward me. She wasn't in one of her standard Destiny Gold Rush outfits, nor was she in pajamas. Tonight she wore a long-sleeved but short blue dress in a print with the lucky number seven in various sizes and colors on it.

Impulsively, I drew closer to her, with Pluckie, still on her leash, following me. I gave Serina a hug. "I know how hard it is to lose someone close," I said. I regretted it at once since I didn't want to explain whom I'd lost, but fortunately she didn't ask.

"Yes," she said softly. "And the thing is, I feel even worse that we'd been arguing before. We wasted time that we could have spent together."

She seemed so mournful that I couldn't really consider her a suspect in Tarzal's murder … could I?

They had been arguing, after all, even if they were attempting to reconcile.

But that left open the question … "What were you arguing about, if you don't mind my asking?"

I figured she'd mind a lot, but instead of jumping on that she walked toward the small room just off the lobby and sank onto its sofa. I followed and joined her on the couch, and Pluckie, good dog that she is, lay down by my feet on the ornate area rug on the hardwood floor.

Serina looked toward me, her light brown eyes red from crying. That area of her face was swollen, too, which erased her wrinkles but nevertheless made her appear older. "What else, around here? We argued about superstitions."

I shouldn't have felt surprised, but I did. "What about them?" I urged, though I was fully prepared for her to tell me to mind my own business.

But she apparently needed to talk. "He'd lived in Destiny for about ten years. He'd researched some of his book on superstitions before moving here and apparently it taught him that this was the place to be if he wanted to specialize in the field. I've lived here most of my life, so I met him as soon as he arrived. The way I grew up and learned to deal with the town's main focus was that I could believe whatever I wanted, but I had to portray total belief and adoration of superstitions to the world—and that portrayal, if nothing else, helped me actually to believe."

She looked at me as if wanting approbation for her belief. I nodded out of encouragement for her to keep talking, not necessarily because I bought into what she said.

"That was Tarzal's manner, too, at first," she continued. "But recently, he began doubting. The rationale he told me was that yes, he'd been lucky, but his luck had resulted from his own intelligence and diligence. It had nothing to do with crossing his fingers or anything else he wrote about. He was considering moving away again and revealing all—even though there really was nothing to reveal. People either believed or they didn't—their choice. And that choice didn't really control their lives or luck, but just how they interpreted what happened to them. The more they believed, the more foolish they were." She sighed. "He really hurt me by his attitude, not only about superstitions, but that he could leave this town—and me—to make his point."

"I see," I said. "I'm sure the whole thing really was hurtful."

She nodded. "Especially to someone whose destiny revolves around Destiny, like me." She gave a small smile.

That gave her a motive to kill him. But it wasn't proof.

I couldn't help asking, "Do you have any idea who'd wanted to hurt him? I mean, I guess anyone in town who also loves or makes a living from superstitions could be on that list, but who do you really suspect?"

She hesitated. "Martha, maybe, since they were in some negotiations to buy her property. And if they'd been successful ... well, Tarzal was finally leaning toward staying after all. That was why we were attempting to reconcile."

I wondered what had changed his mind, especially considering how he'd disrespected superstitions and the town at the welcome meeting.

"The police are apparently looking closely at Martha," I said tactfully. "But if it wasn't her, who else do you suspect?"

"Have you met Martha's nephew Arlen?"

I nodded.

"He's another possibility, since I have the impression he'd like to take over the Lucky Dog someday."

Nothing new there. But I just tilted my head a little to encourage her to continue. "Anyone else?"

"As you said, it could be nearly anyone. I've even considered our police chief. I know you've met Justin Halbertson. What do you think of him as a possible killer?"

I knew my eyes widened. "He's one of those who's looking closely at Martha. Why do you suspect him?"

"Oh, Tarzal and he were always bickering about Justin's going after tourists who committed minor crimes in the name of testing superstitions and their luck. Tarzal said that they should be left alone —and in fact their petty crimes should be publicized outside of town to encourage even more people to come and visit since even petty crooks would have good luck here and wouldn't be prosecuted."

Interesting to hear, especially after my earlier dinner discussion with Justin.

"That's quite a motive," I said. "I'll have to ponder it. I have to admit that I'm trying to help Martha clear herself, even though Chief Halbertson wants me to keep my nose out of it." My pretty nose, was what he'd said. Which was sweet. Sort of. And I probably shouldn't have admitted as much as I had to Serina, whom I now considered to be a suspect, though not the most likely.

I wasn't considering Justin to be a suspect, though. Not for such a dumb reason.

Or maybe I just wanted him to not be guilty even more than I believed in Martha's innocence.

"I figured you were, since you're helping to manage Martha's store now. I assume you still don't have an idea how long you'll be in town."

"Martha seems a little better," I said, "but if she's arrested for murder she'll need help longer. And that's one of the reasons—besides just liking the nice lady—that I'd love to help figure out who really killed Tarzal."

I realized that, if Serina was guilty, I'd just given her a reason to attack me, too. But I already knew I had to be careful in my quest for the killer. Even someone I didn't suspect could come after me if whoever it was thought I might stumble onto something that would reveal them as the murderer.

"I'd love to help," Serina said quietly. "Maybe knowing who it is would help me reach some kind of closure about losing him."

I knew just how she felt, of course. My search for closure was different from hers but just as necessary.

"If you think of anything helpful, let me know. Although if you learn of something that could be actual evidence, you should contact the police."

"Chief Halbertson?" she asked wryly.

"Well, if you really consider him a suspect, you might instead contact Detective Alice Numa. She's the one who questioned me after I found poor Tarzal."

"That's right." Her voice was even softer now, a husky whisper. "You found him. You and your adorable dog." She moved a bit so she could pet Pluckie on the head, causing a massive tail wag. "I won't ask you how it was. I've heard plenty about it. But ... you poor thing. I know there was blood."

Time to change the subject.

"Well, it's been a long day," I said, standing. Of course Pluckie did, too. "I need to get as good a night's sleep as possible. Guess I'll see you at breakfast?"

"Yes," Serina said. "That's a given on all days of the week —except when I was awake with so many people around trying to help me the other night." She paused. "And if I happen to dream of any possible suspects, I'll definitely let you know."

TWENTY

Pluckie was entitled to one more walk before we went to bed. She told me so by pulling toward the door.

By the time we returned to the B&B, the lobby was empty. We didn't need to say goodnight to Serina again.

But just thinking about her and her recent loss poked my psyche about my own loss.

Oh, Warren, I thought as Pluckie and I walked upstairs and into the empty hallway. *What would you think of my pilgrimage to Destiny to try to learn the truth about what really happened to you?*

He'd have been so sweet about it even as he recognized how nuts I was. He'd have attempted to distract me—maybe by a trip somewhere else.

Or finally planning our wedding.

I quickly unlocked our door and Pluckie and I walked inside. I closed it again and leaned my head against it with my moistening eyes closed. Why was I torturing myself tonight? Thinking like that would never help me move forward.

Learning more about Destiny and its superstitions? And how, perhaps, the ladder superstition had—or had not—affected what had happened to Warren?

Hey, that was my goal. And I'd always been goal directed.

Holding my emotions at bay, I went to bed that night determined to—of all things—sleep.

And as I dropped off surprisingly fast, my last thought was that at least I'd already looked up the superstitions about sleeping.

———

I grabbed a quick breakfast at the B&B the next morning, mostly because I wanted to see Serina again before I left for the day.

She was there, reigning in her small but crowded dining room as if nothing was on her mind except making sure her guests got all they wanted to eat—and enjoyed it. As I dished some orange and grapefruit slices onto my plate, she said, "Good morning, Rory. I hope you slept well."

"I did, thank you," I replied, finding it interesting that Serina seemed the perfect hostess, not acting at all as if she remembered our somewhat emotional discussion last night.

Or maybe she was even better than I was at compartmentalizing her brain and thrusting emotional thoughts aside at times when they'd be particularly awkward.

I glanced down toward where Pluckie pushed against my leg as if to remind me that her own breakfast, though it might have been good, was only dog food—even if it was an excellent and healthy brand—and she deserved more. "I've got a biscuit here," I told her. "I'm willing to share some of it." Which I did.

We soon headed out toward the Lucky Dog. As always when we reached Destiny Boulevard, the street was already busy.

Always? I had to think for a few seconds to confirm it, but Pluckie and I had been in Destiny only a matter of days. Less than a week.

It seemed like forever. So much had happened since our arrival, not the least of which was finding Martha ill.

And finding Tarzal dead.

"Good morning," said a female voice as Pluckie and I waited to cross the street outside the Wish-on-a-Star Children's Shop. I turned and recognized the speaker: one of the women who'd been at Serina's support party. She was sweeping the sidewalk in front of the shop and greeting people—possibly its owner or one of its sales staff.

"Good morning," I said. "Is this your shop?" I didn't mention that I'd wished upon the fake falling star in its window a few days ago. Too hokey.

But my wish had come true. I'd wanted some sign about whether to stay in Destiny any longer and help Martha run her shop as she healed.

I'd gotten all kinds of advice from people about remaining.

And I'd felt I had no choice after Tarzal died and Martha's ability to get back to running her store turned even more tenuous when she became a suspect in the killing.

I hated to think of the murder as a sign, but—

"Yes, this is my place." The woman fortunately interrupted the odd direction my thoughts were taking. "I'm Lorraine Noreida, and my husband Brad and I own Wish-on-a-Star. You're Martha's friend who's helping out at the Lucky Dog, aren't you?"

"That's right." I stepped toward her and offered my hand, maybe not the best idea since she had to shift the broom and a dustpan from her right hand into her left. "I'm Rory Chasen."

Lorraine looked like hardly more than a child herself, slim and model-pretty, with high cheekbones, a smooth complexion, and golden hair that was a short but unruly cap around her face. She wore—what else?—a pink T-shirt with a shooting star on it and the words "Wishes on stars come true."

"I know. I saw you at the Rainbow B&B the other night and you were pointed out to me. Your little dog there was good luck in saving Martha, right?"

Word did travel broadly around here, at least about things relating to superstitions. But I knew that already.

I nodded, but she might not have seen it since she had bent to give Pluckie a pat. "That's right," I said.

She stood up, shifted the things in her arms again, and shoved her right hand into the pocket of her beige slacks. She pulled something out and handed it to me. A penny.

"I found this penny heads up on the sidewalk this morning. I'd like you to give it to Martha."

"Of course," I said. It seemed so typically Destiny.

But it was even more than I originally thought. Lorraine continued, "In case you're wondering, all of us Destiny residents go around seeding the area, so to speak, now and then. We want tourists to find lucky coins so their luck will be increased, and so will their love of this place. We want them to have fun here—and keep coming back. Not surprisingly, the owners of the Heads-Up Penny gift shop started it some time ago."

That was Jeri's family's shop.

Lorraine paused to look at my hand, where I still held the penny in my open palm. "Maybe," she continued, "since you're running the Lucky Dog for now, you'll want to do that, too, one of these days."

"Sounds like a good idea," I said noncommittally, although my mind suddenly started racing about other kinds of good-luck stuff I could make sure tourists found around the shop I now managed.

"The thing is," Lorraine continued, leaning forward on her broom, "I haven't put any coins out in a couple of days and this is the only one I've seen. I'm not sure where it came from or who put it in front of my store." She straightened. "Doesn't matter. It's still good luck. Even more good luck since it appeared out of nowhere. Anyway, I need to get back inside before we open, but I'm sure I'll be seeing you around."

At a children's shop? Well, I might need to go make another wish, and before I did I'd stop inside to say hi. And make sure no one was watching my lunacy.

But it was certainly no greater lunacy than believing a heads-up penny brought good luck, was it?

"Hope so," I said. "I don't have any kids to buy things for, though." I'd hoped to someday with Warren.

"I'll introduce you to ours one of these days. Twin boys, in preschool, thank heavens. It was hard before when they were babies and we usually had them at the shop with us. See you soon, Rory."

"Bye." I gave Pluckie a slight tug on her leash and we maneuvered around visitors to reach the curb and soon crossed the street.

Another shop owner. Another resident of Destiny.

Another believer in superstitions.

Believer or not, I was beginning to feel like a real resident myself. Was that a good thing?

Were there any superstitions about settling into a new town?

I laughed at myself as I unlocked the door and Pluckie and I entered the Lucky Dog.

I inhaled the faint scent of catnip as I always did in the shop and continued to smile.

———

I called Martha right away, then Pluckie and I went up to say good morning and hand over her lucky penny. Could my wish for both Martha and me on the large half of the wishbone yesterday have resulted in her having the penny handed over to her today?

Gee, with a thought like that, who knew how soon it might be before I actually started thinking like a real Destiny citizen?

Martha was delighted with the penny and said she'd call Lorraine a little later. She was looking good and said she felt well, too—and didn't really need the aide who would be coming later today to check on her and help her bathe. She'd already had cereal for breakfast, plus instant coffee. I told her I'd get her some of the real thing if I had time to go out and buy any later.

Then Pluckie and I returned downstairs and I logged onto the computer to check inventory and wait for our ten o'clock opening time. Millie had let me know she wouldn't be there until around eleven that morning. That meant that Martha—and I—would have to wait a while before that coffee break.

As it turned out, I actually didn't get to leave until a late lunchtime. When I called Martha, she sounded delighted when I offered to bring her a sandwich from Wishbones-to-Go as well as coffee. I also told Millie, who'd arrived right on time, that I'd get lunch for her as well.

I left Pluckie with Millie, since the Lucky Dog had only a few customers when I walked out the door and into the tourist crowd. I immediately looked down at the sidewalk, seeking cracks to avoid and heads-up pennies to pick up. Plenty of the former; none of the latter.

I supposed Wishbones-to-Go was always busy, at least around mealtime. The line was as long as last time.

I saw some familiar faces in that line, too, as I joined it, including Carolyn Innes from the button store who was just in front of me. She wore a different T-shirt than the one with black cats and buttons I'd seen her in the last time I was there. This one was luminescent green and had a white rabbit on it with button eyes and two large lucky feet still attached.

"Drat," she said, turning to face me. "I meant to stop in at the Lucky Dog before. Tell you what, Rory. I'll walk back with you after we pick up our food. I need some things for my own dog —plus, I'd like to talk to you."

"Sounds good," I said. "And will you tell me what the superstitions involving buttons are?"

"Of course. They're my favorites, but I'll bet you could guess that."

I looked beyond her. The line was moving quickly again, but there were at least half a dozen more people ahead of her. A wonderful aroma rose from behind the counter, undoubtedly one of the reasons for the place's popularity. Maybe the scent wafted outside and enticed people in like the Pied Piper's piping lured rats to follow him.

What an awful analogy, but I realized I was thinking more in analogies these days—not just superstitions.

"How's Martha?" Carolyn asked. "That's the main reason I'd like to visit the shop, especially if she's receiving visitors upstairs. She's a friend, even though we don't always see eye-to-eye about superstitions." Carolyn had leaned her slim body close to me, and the last part of what she said was a whisper. Interesting. Was she a doubter like me? And why even hint at that to a stranger?

"Martha's improving all the time. And since she is a real superstition aficionado, I gather that you're not?" I kept my voice low, too.

She laughed. "You haven't been in this town long enough to learn all about it." She spoke softly. "But there are basically two factions of shopkeepers. We all have one thing in common: we want to make money off superstitions and tourists' interest in them. But one group consists of believers. And then there are the rest of us."

Like me! Maybe I'd found a genuine ally. "I thought that might be true," I said. "Then you're one of those who doesn't believe?"

"So far I've got more hope than proof. I won't ask which side you're on—but I'll figure it out, I'm sure. I may be foolish, but I kind of broach this subject with every newcomer to town to let you know that, however you feel, you've got friends." She changed the subject then and started talking at normal volume. "So tell me about Martha."

"I saw her this morning. She was waiting for her aide of the day to come and help her out, but she'd rather be on her own."

"That's what she may be telling people, but I doubt it," Carolyn said. "If she gets help, that means she at least looks like she's still sick—and the sooner she heals altogether, the sooner she might be arrested." The volume of her voice was muted once again.

"Is that the rumor?" I asked with interest.

"I'm pretty sure it's reality. There are factions developing about that in this town, too." She grinned. "We're just like the federal government—opposing sides to everything, with our feet dug in." I smiled again. I liked this woman and her irreverent attitude. "Anyway, some locals are sure she did it and is faking her illness."

I couldn't tell from Carolyn's amused but noncommittal expression if she was one of them.

"Well, I don't think she did it," I said. "Not that I know everyone around here or who might have had it in for Tarzal, but there are so many others with potential who'd have been better able to— Well, never mind." I realized that others in the shortening line had stopped talking, and a couple were looking at us. "It's not really my business," I finished.

"Sure it is," Carolyn countered. "It's everyone's business in this town, and yours especially since you're running Martha's shop."

Fortunately, she had reached the front of the line. She ordered her lunch. And in only a few minutes, I was ready to walk back to the Lucky Dog with my own bags and coffee cups.

Carolyn was waiting outside for me. "Okay, let's go to your shop. Time to see Martha. Plus, I've got two dachshunds who're my family. I don't need anything superstition-related for them, just some good food."

"I can certainly help you with that."

"I know. I always buy their stuff from the Lucky Dog. And—well, I hope it stays open, Rory. Will you hang around indefinitely if Martha's arrested?"

I didn't want to get into that. "We'll see." I had to ask. "Did you consider Tarzal part of your faction of Destiny citizens? Expert or not, he sounded skeptical to me."

We'd reached the end of the block on Fate Street and turned onto the more crowded sidewalk of Destiny Boulevard.

Carolyn shook her head, but the slow movement looked more sympathetic than negative. "He should have kept his mouth shut. I think he'd started out as a believer—or at least he wanted it to look that way. But either his opinion or his attitude changed. And talking about it may have been what got him killed —if Martha didn't do it to protect her property."

Interesting. "I did gather that some people were concerned about what would happen to Destiny and its businesses if superstitions stopped being considered real, and Tarzal's opinion could have added to that."

"Right." Surprisingly, the word almost exploded from Carolyn. "Okay, I might not be a solid believer, but a lot of us who don't think superstitions are real still make a good living off them—so far. And Tarzal, with his notoriety, might have changed that if he hadn't shut up. Or been shut up."

Then she was glad he'd been killed?

Was this fun woman suddenly a murder suspect, too?

She must have realized from my expression or my silence what I was thinking. She laughed. "I gather from what you've said and what I've heard that you're trying to help Martha by figuring out who else could have killed Tarzal. Not me. I might not be mourning him deeply, but I didn't kill him. And I don't know who did—although there are plenty who'd do nearly anything to protect our town. You were at the latest Destiny Welcome, weren't you?"

"Yes," I said. I didn't recall seeing her there, but I hadn't met her yet then.

We had arrived at the door to the Lucky Dog. My hands were full so Carolyn reached out to open it.

"I wasn't there," she confirmed as we went inside. "But I heard not only about the milk there that Tarzal fell into and spilled and a lot of speculation about who of those present were angry enough with him to sneak in early and hide the milk that would make him trip. Martha's one of them, of course, since she was apparently wheeled there from the hospital in plenty of time."

Interesting question—one I'd also considered. But there was a curtain across the front of the stage that had been drawn back for the show. Anyone might have been able to sneak onto the platform earlier to leave the milk bottle.

"And Tarzal's reaction, trying to turn the superstition tables on the perpetrator?" Carolyn continued. "That riled a lot of people."

"Like who?" I couldn't help asking.

I realized then that there was one person who'd been there and had a very public argument with Kenneth Tarzal whom I hadn't really considered, except in passing, as a murder suspect. But he was probably the most logical one of all, especially considering all he'd said right there, in front of the world.

I thought it at about the same time as Carolyn said it. "Well, I heard that our dear leprechaun-loving Mayor Bevin Dermot wasn't happy with Tarzal that night. In my opinion, he's too obvious as a suspect. But sometimes the most obvious people are the guilty ones.

Hey, you know what? One of these days I'm going to bring you some of my goods to display here, and I'll take some of yours to my shop, if you'd like. I love black cats, although with my pups I can't own one." She'd moved through our displays and picked up a stuffed black cat toy.

My mind was still reeling, but it opened up enough to consider that she was offering an idea for increasing the business at both stores. And I was definitely interested in that, as long as I was managing the Lucky Dog.

Speaking of which, my own lucky dog, who'd been with Millie at the cash register, ran in my direction and I introduced her to Carolyn, who lavished lots of attention on little Pluckie.

Then Carolyn said, "Okay, I'll call Martha now and see if I can go up and visit her. But first, here are some button superstitions for you to cogitate over."

For the next few minutes she spouted one after another. Finding buttons was lucky, and so was receiving them as gifts—a good thing for Carolyn's business. Finding one with four holes meant you should expect good news. If you button an item of clothing wrong, you need to unbutton, take it off, and put it back on buttoned right or it's bad luck.

And more.

"Now ask me how many of them I believe in," Carolyn said as she pulled several cans of Lucky Dog Food from the shelves and shuttled them among customers to the cash register.

"How many?" I asked.

"I'll never tell." She laughed. "Okay, total these and I'll pay when I return downstairs." She hurried up to see Martha.

The store was busy, and I waited on several batches of customers. Then I totaled Carolyn's goods for her return.

And all the while, though I was too busy to focus on it, my mind kept simmering around my latest murder suspect: Destiny's mayor.

TWENTY-ONE

"I'm looking for a new leash for my dog," said a customer who had just walked into the Lucky Dog. "The superstition symbols on this one are wearing off." She pointed to the one she held, a red lead with objects stamped on it in white that were hard to recognize. They appeared to be stylized curved fists, perhaps knocking on wood, but it was difficult to tell with so little left on the woven nylon.

The short lady with curly brown hair looked familiar, but the black Labrador retriever at the end of her leash—whose head I petted as she sniffed my hip—didn't. I must have seen her on the street, at the Destiny Welcome, on my tour . . . Well, it didn't matter. She was here with her dog and wanted to buy something. That was what was important.

I glanced over at Pluckie. She'd been near the cash register where Millie was ringing up a sale of miscellaneous treats—the little beggar—but now she headed toward where I stood near the door. She obviously felt I was being disloyal. Or maybe she just wanted to meet the Lab. The two sniffed noses, both tails wagging. Good.

"We've got leashes over here," I told the lady, gesturing for her to follow me to our racks of leashes and collars. I wondered if she might be interested in some with rhinestones, or just a replacement with the decoration stamped on.

"Are you enjoying being here in Destiny?" she asked as she kept up with me.

"Absolutely." It didn't matter if that was true. I had to convey that attitude to help sell Lucky Dog products.

And, I admitted to myself, there was at least some truth to it. Destiny was growing on me—despite all the things that kept me wondering why I was still here.

"What's your dog's name?" I asked my customer. Pluckie had followed us to the leash rack.

"Charlotte," she said. "Short for Charlottetown, an actual town in—where else?—Labrador."

"Cute." I gave Charlotte another pat as Pluckie lost interest and walked away.

The lady wasn't looking at the leashes, though, but at me. "You're here helping Martha Jallopia with this store because your lucky dog saved her, right?"

"You could say that. Now, were you interested in another red leash or—"

"And you also found Kenneth Tarzal's body after he'd been stabbed with a piece of broken mirror, right?"

I didn't want to alienate a customer, but she was doing a darned good job of alienating me. "We have some attractive blue leashes, too, that would look good on Charlotte and would go with that tote

215

bag you have over your shoulder." It, too, was blue. I pulled a blue leash off the rack. It had representations of rabbits' feet on it. "This one should be pretty lucky."

"I understand that you're still trying to help Martha, and not just with this store. She's suspected of killing Tarzal and you're attempting to—"

"Who are you, and what do you really want?" I didn't quite shout. Not here, with other customers around. But I was getting quite perturbed with this lady.

Then it dawned on me where I'd seen her before. She had been taking pictures and jotting down notes at the Destiny Welcome show—after Tarzal had fallen in spilled milk.

"Everything okay here, Rory?" Millie had finished with her customers who were now leaving, and she joined me. A good thing. Maybe I'd turn this woman over to her. Was she a reporter trying to get me to talk without explaining who she was and what she wanted?

"I don't know," I said to Millie. I looked at the lady. "Is it?"

"Of course. I think I will take that one you suggested. It'll look good on Charlotte. And—well, I think you have me pegged, even though we haven't been introduced. Could we go over there for a moment?" She pointed toward the corner of the store where pet foods were shelved. At the moment, it was empty of customers.

I didn't want to, but I was curious. "It's okay," I assured Millie. "Maybe you could help those folks over there." Some customers appeared fascinated with the display of stuffed animals, particularly black cats. Millie nodded and headed in that direction, but not before aiming a quick, irritated glare at the woman beside me.

Then that woman, Charlotte, and I walked over to the more private area, with Pluckie following.

"Here's the thing," she said and began to tell me her background. Sure enough, she was a reporter, associated with the *Destiny Star*. Very associated with it. Her name was Celia Vardox, and she and her brother Derek ran it since their parents, the owners, were now part-time employees so they could travel.

"Away from the wonderful tourist town of Destiny?" I had to ask.

"Yes, aren't they odd?" Celia smiled. She appeared to be in her thirties like me, with a strong brow and wide mouth. Her brown eyes seemed to radiate friendliness and curiosity, but that could have been part of the persona she projected to get people to talk. "Now, look, Rory." She knew my name, which wasn't a surprise. "Here's one reason I'm particularly interested in you. I've been following you." Now, that was a surprise. But maybe not so much when she elaborated. "I was in line behind you at Wishbones-to-Go earlier, and I couldn't help overhearing your conversation with Carolyn Innes." She knew the button lady, too. "You were discussing Tarzal's death, and Martha, and more, once you left the shop."

Once we left it? I'd been too absorbed in talking with Carolyn, and seeing how the line progressed ahead of us, to check out people behind us waiting to be served. But Celia had followed us out—perhaps without having secured her own food? I asked.

"Well, your conversation was more interesting than a sandwich. And it didn't take me long to get through the line a second time once you'd left. Anyway—you seem to be very interested in what happened to Tarzal."

"Isn't everyone in town?" I felt my face redden—partly from embarrassment and partly from anger. My interests weren't this woman's business. And I definitely didn't want her writing about them —or anything else about me—for her paper.

"Sure, but it sounded as if you're really devoted to helping Martha. True?"

I inhaled deeply. "We've already discussed this subject a lot more than I'm comfortable with."

Her too-innocent grin looked almost evil. It was all I could do not to shudder. Or to order her to leave. But that might be bad for business, especially since even more customers had just walked in.

"Look, Rory. I'd be lying if I said that my interest isn't because I hope to do a story on this, but I'm really interested in helping Martha, too—assuming she's not guilty. Charlotte and I come in here a lot, and Martha's always so nice to us. And she carries such delightful superstition merchandise. But more than that—well, I'm curious and so's everyone else in Destiny." She leaned closer, and I resisted the urge to step back toward the well-stocked shelves of pet foods. "In fact," she continued, her voice now a whisper, "Don't tell our illustrious police chief—I know you've been in touch with Justin—"

Geez, she knew him, too. Of course. But how did she know I knew him?

She'd kept talking. "I've been taking an informal poll about who in this town is not really sorry Tarzal is dead."

I blinked. Okay, she'd done it: roused my curiosity. "And what have you found out?"

"It's about even. Lots of people seem upset because his book helped to renew interest in Destiny as a tourist destination, even if they weren't wild about his attitude lately. Others seem to think that, so what if he helped to perk up our economy for a while? He'd become dead set—so to speak—on turning it back the other way.

And, since he came up in your conversation, you may be interested in hearing the opinion of our mayor."

I wanted to throttle her for eavesdropping, even as I ached to hear her answer. "Yes," I said through gritted teeth, "I'm interested." Although, after Bevin Dermot's tirade against Tarzal at the Destiny Welcome, I had a good idea what the opinion would be.

I was right. Celia raised her head to focus her eyes on the ceiling and placed her right hand over her heart. Her left one still held Charlotte's leash. "Mayor Dermot expressed his deepest, heart-felt sorrow at the loss by this town of one of its finest citizens," she intoned solemnly. Then she looked at me. "But he did say it was too bad Tarzal hadn't simply focused on superstitions and how important they were to all of us, the way his book says, instead of starting to make fun of it all. He even suggested that could have been a reason for whoever killed him to have committed the act."

"Did he admit it was him?" I asked with a grim smile.

"Heavens, no. But—"

"But I think you ladies are butting too much into police business," said a male voice from off to my side. It emanated from somewhere beyond the nearest tall rack of shelves containing dog and cat treats.

It belonged to Justin Halbertson. I'd gotten so immersed in the conversation that I hadn't watched to see whether more customers were entering the shop.

Too bad I hadn't. The town's police chief now stood beside us while the Doberman whose leash he held traded sniffs with Charlotte and with Pluckie. I assumed that was his dog Killer, whom he'd promised to introduce me to one of these days.

Had he heard Celia's earlier reference to him, and her request that I not mention to him what she'd been about to say? I didn't ask.

But Celia glared at me as if I'd seen Justin over her shoulder and chose not to warn her.

Well, I wasn't about to defend myself. To either of them.

Instead, I maneuvered around Pluckie and Charlotte so I could reach the Doberman. "Is this Killer?" I started to stroke the dog's smooth head. He apparently liked what I did, since his long nose went up and nuzzled my hand.

"Yes. But—"

"He's beautiful." I knelt beside him. That got the other two dogs into a frenzy of attention-stealing, so, laughing, I tried to pat and hug all of them.

That fortunately changed the subject of the conversation. But Justin and Celia clearly knew each other.

"So what are you working on now, Celia?" Justin asked. "I've heard that the city is considering a major superstition-filled memorial to Tarzal. Are you going to do a story on it?"

"We always do stories on events of interest to our citizens and visitors," she said in a tone that sounded huffy. "All kinds of stories—including actual news when it occurs." She planted her hands on her hips and looked up, glaring at Justin.

"The only problem is," he said, "real newspapers aren't supposed to take sides on the issues they report on, except for opinions expressed in op-ed pieces. Not so much with the *Destiny Star.*"

"You're just embarrassed because not only did a superstition-related murder occur in our town, but you haven't figured out yet who did it. Around here, superstitions rule. You should have at least found the killer's reflection in Tarzal's eyes."

That again. The first half of what she said might be true—but not the second—despite the superstition I'd heard about it. I remained on the floor with the dogs.

"This is entirely off the record," Justin said slowly, as if speaking to a young child who might not understand what he was saying. I looked up to see that he had pasted an emotionless expression on his face. He was looking down toward the dogs and me, as if aiming his gaze at Celia would make him explode. "But here's what's going on." He blinked, then turned so he was facing Celia. "No, I'll tell you what. If you're going to put an article in your paper about the murder investigation, you can say that Destiny's police department is working on it diligently and making progress. We hope to make an arrest soon. And we're not about to go public with whether... unusual circumstances are involved in determining who the killer is."

My whole body froze. Did that mean he was about to take Martha into custody? Or was this just some garbage he was feeding to the media to take some of the pressure off?

I liked his position about the image superstition, at least. He was neither confirming nor denying it to this reporter.

"Good," said another voice, female this time, and one I recognized. Carolyn emerged from behind the shelves on the other side. "I just got back downstairs from visiting Martha. She's feeling better but we're both sure that the pressure from her being considered a suspect in the murder is slowing her recovery. Do you agree, too, Rory?"

"Most likely," I said, rising finally to my feet.

All three of us women stared at Justin.

"Then is your primary suspect someone other than Martha Jal-lopia?" Celia asked. I could sense her mind making notes on how the article she was about to write would read.

"No comment," Justin said, eliciting groans from all of us.

"Then how soon can we expect—"

"I brought Killer with me so he can help pick out which food he'd like me to buy him." Justin's gaze was now entirely on me. "Would you care to help us with that momentous decision?"

A smart and tactful way to end this conversation, I thought—even though I'd have liked to hear his answer to Celia.

"I'd be happy to." I followed him, with Killer trailing on his leash, toward the display of large kibble bags right near us.

As Justin reached the display and knelt to check out the bags, I turned toward the others and gave a one-shoulder shrug, dismissing both Celia and Carolyn.

As far as I was concerned, too, this conversation was over.

TWENTY-TWO

CAROLYN JOINED US BY the dog food display to say goodbye. "Come over and visit my Buttons of Fortune store any time," she told me. "I'll give you even more insight into the glamorous and superstitious mystique of buttons."

I laughed and said I'd be delighted—although I didn't suggest a time. I'd just have to see how things progressed at the Lucky Dog—and in my life here in Destiny.

Justin and Killer soon picked out a large bag of some of the healthiest food the Lucky Dog carried—or so I believed since I'd been addicted to researching such things as the assistant manager of my large chain pet store.

My suggestion and explanation seemed to help in Justin's decision. Especially after Killer agreed—once I gave him a small sample of the food to taste.

And since Pluckie and Killer appeared to be getting along fine, I agreed to have dinner yet again with Justin—this time with both dogs present.

By the time I was done helping Justin, Celia and Charlotte had left. Thank heavens. Just being around Celia and knowing that her mind had to be racing to figure out what she'd be writing about next made me nervous.

And I was right to be, I found out three days later when the next edition of the *Destiny Star* was published.

———

The time in between was pretty uneventful, even though it was the weekend. I seemed to be settling into an irregular routine.

Pluckie and I did have dinner with Justin and Killer that same night, a first—at least as far as having Killer along. We went again to the Shamrock Steakhouse and had an enjoyable time.

Especially because Tarzal's murder wasn't mentioned even once.

On both Saturday and Sunday, the Lucky Dog's business seemed to double, which was amazing considering how busy it had been during the week. But that was fine with me. I liked to keep busy. And I also loved seeing the success of the store I was now managing, for however long that might be.

I also got to know Millie's and Jeri's irregular schedules a little better. I nearly always had one or the other of them around to help at the Lucky Dog, and sometimes both, except when they took their outing together on one of the weekend mornings.

I saw a lot of Martha, bringing her meals upstairs now and then, getting an opportunity to speak with the aides who popped in daily, apparently whenever they felt like it. They all said she was improving, little by little. That was my opinion, too. And I helped Martha come down the stairs for short visits to the shop every day, even though I sensed that she could easily have done it on her own—as she had on the night Tarzal died.

Still, the more time I spent with the sweet senior citizen, the gladder I was that I'd taken time out of my own life to help her. She was amazingly grateful. She adored Pluckie. And her attitude toward all pets was definitely compatible with mine.

One low spot of the weekend was when her nephew Arlen popped in for a visit during one of the times Martha was reigning over the shop while sitting in her wheelchair. I got a first-hand look then at how the family love I actually saw between them was tarnished by each of them gibing at the other about what they really should be doing with their lives right now.

Plus, Arlen kept saying that, even if he couldn't help out by working here, he'd love to be able to add the Lucky Dog Boutique to his general tour itinerary but even on the specialized tours the shops that were featured always had something really exciting and unique about them.

Of course Martha's temper exploded. So did mine but I kept my tone much more civil as I pointed out to Arlen some of the superstitions about pets I'd learned about, and how they were symbolized here in items for sale such as stuffed toys, decorated collars and leashes, and all the rest. And, oh yes, people really loved their pets.

He didn't act impressed and said that it wasn't his decision anyway, but his bosses'.

Which gave me another goal to accomplish while I remained in town. I'd met at least one of those bosses. I'd find a way to go have a talk with her.

But first, I'd do something to make them take notice of the Lucky Dog.

What? Well, I pondered that for a while after Arlen left, even asked Pluckie her opinion, in between customers. And then I got it—a good idea. It would require me to leave my comfort zone, at least for a short while each week as long as I stayed in Destiny to help with the Lucky Dog.

I decided to give a small seminar one evening a week where I'd talk about pet superstitions and invite tourists and townies alike to come and discuss them.

I'd use all I could find in Tarzal's book, but there were also other resources about superstitions. I'd do as much research as I had to.

As I came up with that concept, Martha was still downstairs and acting a bit tired, so I helped her back up to her apartment. I followed her to the couch, then sat down with her.

"I have an idea to help put the Lucky Dog on Arlen's tour," I told her, hoping it wasn't premature. After all, we had no control over what Destiny's Luckiest Tour Company did or didn't feature. But I thought this could work.

"What's that?"

I described my concept. "You can come to each one, too, and talk about how Pluckie provided you with good luck when you were ill." I was really getting into this. "Maybe we can clear out an area in the storeroom and set up chairs—only a few at first. We'll have to see if this grows."

"I love it!" Martha tried to push herself up to a stand but I discouraged that. She scowled at me. "I want to give you a hug."

I helped her onto her feet and we had a short hug-fest. Pluckie joined in, standing on her hind legs and pawing at us. After helping Martha sit back down again, I knelt to hug my dog who had started all this. Kind of.

We brainstormed a little more. I decided to start this Friday, five days away from today, which was Sunday. I'd have flyers printed. I'd even buy a small ad in the next *Destiny Star*, even though it wasn't likely to appear this week.

That meant I was committing to stay here at least another couple of weeks, even if Martha's health improved enough for her to run the store—and she wasn't arrested.

But that was okay. A bit of planning ahead never hurt. It didn't commit me to be here forever.

———

So that was why the next day, on Monday, I headed for the offices of the *Destiny Star*, a few blocks to the east on Destiny Boulevard.

I brought Pluckie along. She was my good luck symbol as well as my dearest companion. She loved walks, and I think she, too, had gotten used to our having to weave in and out on the sidewalks around tourists, while avoiding stepping on cracks and looking for heads-up pennies.

I figured that, in addition to the ad I intended to buy for their website and next week's paper, Celia would be able to tell me where the nearest print shop was, where I could get flyers designed and printed. I hadn't seen one in Destiny, but even if there wasn't one here there was bound to be one in Ojai or another nearby town.

But Celia wasn't there. Derek was. I'd told him not to use my name in any articles after he'd interviewed me about finding Tarzal's body, and when I'd checked out the multiple articles about the murder in the last *Destiny Star* and its website, I'd been relieved that he had complied.

He seemed less paparazzi-like than his sister. Maybe it would be better to speak with him anyway.

I walked up to the long counter on which several stacks of the *Destiny Star* were piled. I glanced at them. The front page didn't look familiar, so I figured these were new editions.

Behind the counter were several desks where computer screens dominated everything else. The reporters and editors presumably worked here. Maybe the reporters were also the editors.

"Hi," I said. "I'm Rory Chasen. We met before. I'm helping out at the Lucky Dog Boutique."

"Of course I remember you and our discussion, too, Rory. We never used your name, if that's why you're here."

"No, it's not." I told him about my idea to do a few talks on superstitions involving pets. "I know your paper runs feature articles about various superstitions, so if you have any archived that involve animals, please let me know. I'll definitely give you credit in any talk I give that uses your information. And if you feel like it, I'd love to have you do an article on my first presentation." Then I proceeded to ask him about ads and print shops.

It all seemed to work out fine. I bought an ad for a price that wasn't outrageous. Even if I didn't get reimbursed, I could handle it, but I'd discuss that with Martha. Derek said he would design the ad for me and we discussed what it would say. I gave him my email address for him to send the proof along before I could get it printed. He also gave a couple of names of printers that weren't far away.

As we were finishing up, Celia walked in. She looked at me, then at Derek, and back again. Pluckie, who'd been lying on the floor beside me, now stood up at attention. She'd met Celia before. Why did her attitude seem so tense?

Because she sensed tension in Celia? If so, why?

"I was afraid I'd see you here," Celia finally said. "You've read what I wrote. It's good, and I didn't name names. Except for Tarzal, of course."

"What are you talking about?" I looked from Celia to Derek.

Neither met my eyes. In fact, they each glanced at a stack of the latest *Destiny Star* on the counter, then looked away again.

"Is there something in here I should read?" I reached over to pick up a paper. They were giveaways, so I just took one, then said to Derek, "I'll look forward to receiving that proof from you," and, pulling slightly on Pluckie's leash, I walked out.

I hurried back along the typically busy sidewalk toward the Lucky Dog, not wanting to be near either of them while I scanned the paper for whatever Celia had been talking about.

What had caused their odd attitudes?

Pluckie decided she needed to squat just as we got to the Baby Locks Children's Hair Salon. Nothing I needed to clean up, but I glanced at the paper while I waited for her to finish.

That was when I discovered the article.

And didn't move again until I'd read it.

———

It wasn't really an article. It was an op-ed piece on the paper's editorial page. It didn't name me or necessarily say anything that would identify me—at least not as far as tourists and other strangers were concerned.

But it did laud all of Destiny's tourists while referring more specifically to a heroic newcomer to town who'd brought her own good luck symbol—a dog—who had helped by a superstition that of course came true, to save a life. And then that newcomer remained in town and continued to try to help the person she'd saved.

Yes, the gender was specific, even if my name wasn't there.

And the article got worse. Tarzal was, in fact named—a victim of a horrible and as-yet unsolved murder with, of course, superstitious overtones. And how was that heroic newcomer involved?

Well, she'd not only tried to save that life, too—an exaggeration, since Tarzal was already dead when I found him—but when she realized that the new friend she was trying to help was a suspect, she'd started looking into who else might have done it. Now, she was doing a thorough and intensive job of it—considering friends, relatives, neighbors, officials and more.

The case was still open. No arrests yet. But the *Destiny Star* applauded that newcomer and all she was doing, and believed, as wonderful as the Destiny Police Department was, that the newcomer would be critical to solving the crime.

After all, she was good luck, wasn't she?

Plus, she was a superstition pilgrim. She had come here to Destiny to determine if a loss in her own life, when someone dear to her had walked under a ladder and died, was the result of the reality of superstitions—and everyone in town already knew the answer to that.

Well, damn, I thought. The paper may have deemed me to be good luck—to others, perhaps. But wasn't an article like this a means of clawing away any good luck I might otherwise be entitled to?

The citizens of Destiny would figure out who that applauded newcomer was.

They would even know what had brought me here—undoubtedly thanks to Preston's big mouth, despite how he and Tarzal hadn't seemed particularly interested in my revelation about why I'd come to Destiny. Maybe I should have demanded that Preston not tell anyone else when I talked to him after I knew he'd mentioned my story to Justin. But even if he'd kept quiet after that, it might already have been too late.

I didn't know who else had heard about me before this story appeared in the paper. And now everyone would know.

Even worse—well, it wasn't as if the regular media hadn't gotten wind of Tarzal's murder. I'd heard, then seen, that at first, there'd been mentions on even national TV shows, plus local Southern California ones. Daily newspapers had reported about it, too—and the situation had burgeoned on their websites and otherwise online.

It wasn't every day that a noted expert on a subject like superstition was murdered, and in a manner that supported the arcane subject he promoted.

Like the world's foremost superstition expert being stabbed by a shard of—what else?—a broken mirror.

And now, would this op-ed piece also go viral? If it did, people everywhere might attempt to figure out who "Ms. Newcomer" really was.

I never wanted any kind of publicity except for the shops that I managed.

I certainly didn't want it now.

I also wondered what Justin, who'd told me to butt out, would think now.

Not to mention the thoughts of whoever had actually killed Tarzal ...

TWENTY-THREE

I HURRIED ALONG THE half block back to the *Destiny Star* offices. In minutes, I was leaning once more against the front counter. I looked around, still holding the edge-crumpled paper in my hands.

Had both Derek and Celia assumed I'd return? Had they been watching for me from where they sat at their desks? I wasn't sure, but I thought I caught a glimpse of both heads twisting to look at whatever was so fascinating on their computer screens instead of turning to see who'd just walked into the office's front door.

I knew I must look shocked. Was I pale, or had my face gone red? I wasn't sure.

All I knew was that I was extremely upset, my breathing uneven.

I doubted there was anything I could do about what I'd read, but I could at least ask. "Interesting op-ed piece," I said to neither in particular. "Have any copies of this edition been distributed?"

"Pretty much everywhere in town." Derek looked toward me with an expression on his face that looked so innocent that I had no doubt he knew what I was feeling. "We publish our papers on Monday, so this just went out."

"We're already getting emails about it." Celia's smile was so broad that I felt certain she'd been the one to write the editorial. "All favorable. Some of them want to know who we're talking about."

"I'll bet," I said, closing my eyes. I'd no doubt that whoever didn't yet know would get the scoop from their friends who'd figure it out.

Okay, nothing I could do. The black cat was out of the bag. Or at least my smart and adorable black-and-white dog was.

I'd been handed one heck of a sour lemon. So, it was lemonade time.

Maybe I could use the notoriety—which I hoped would be short-lived—to bring in even more customers to the Lucky Dog than my anticipated pet-superstition talks would do.

And although I'd need to be careful, I wasn't necessarily in any danger from the killer ... I hoped.

"Like I told you before, please let me know if there's anything else you need for my ad," I said, forcing myself to smile. "And thanks again for the information about nearby print shops. Oh, and is it okay if I take along a few of these papers?"

I wasn't certain, but I thought I saw both Vardoxes heave sighs of relief. Had they anticipated I'd throw a hissy-fit ... or worse?

"Sure," Derek said heartily. He rose from his chair, as did Celia. "Take as many as you want."

"And if you get any further insight into who might have killed Tarzal, let us know," Celia said.

I couldn't help it. I leveled a glare at her. "I thought you media sorts figured that kind of thing out on your own. Aren't you also trying to solve the murder?" If so, maybe the killer would target them instead of me. Better yet, none of us.

For now, I didn't wait for their reactions but stalked back out of the offices.

Back on the street, I stood there for a minute or more, taking deep breaths to try to calm myself.

The piece was a done deal. All I could do now was wait and see what people's reactions were.

Were there any superstitions related to half-baked op-ed pieces that all but pointed to their subject?

What would the results be from people reading it—and recognizing who that unnamed subject was?

Endangered or not, I'd no doubt that I would find out.

―――

"Oh, good," Jeri said as I walked back into the Lucky Dog. "We've been getting phone calls and emails about some article in the *Destiny Star*. Glad you brought some copies back with you."

Good thing Pluckie was there. I hurried over to where my beloved little dog pulled on her leash attached to the counter. After placing the newspapers on that counter, I knelt and just held my girl for a long minute, glad for the distraction and her loving attention.

Jeri had already grabbed a copy of the paper and was leafing through it. "It's an editorial on the next-to-last page," I told her with a sigh.

She turned to that page, then leveled a dark-eyed glance at me. "Are you okay?"

"Read it, and you'll be able to figure that out."

I watched her face as her eyes widened, and then she frowned. Today the clips she wore to hold her long, dark hair back were copper colored, matching her Heads-up Penny Gift Shop T-shirt.

"Why didn't they just print your name in bold face and italics right in the article?" she finally burst out. "Everyone around here will know that it's about you." She looked at me. "That's not necessarily a bad thing ... is it?"

"Other than the fact I've been told by the police chief to butt out, maybe not." I'd considered it further on my walk. Surely whoever had killed Tarzal wouldn't feel threatened to learn that some amateur was poking her nose in where it supposedly didn't belong. A couple of people had known it already: Justin, of course, and Martha. But neither of them was guilty.

Still, I'd have to be careful. I didn't dare write a letter of clarification or denial, since if I did that would make it clear to anyone in the entire world who didn't know it was me that I was the article's subject.

"Now, how are our sales doing today?" I asked Jeri. It was definitely time to change the subject. Get my mind off that damned article.

Except that, just then my cell phone rang. I'd just stuck my purse behind the counter in its usual drawer and had to go retrieve it.

When I checked the caller ID, I nearly groaned aloud. It was Justin.

I made myself relax just a little before answering. He could be calling about something entirely different from the article. Like, maybe he was about to let me know that the case was solved and the real killer was under arrest.

Right.

I pushed the button to answer, leaning on the counter and crossing my fingers that I wasn't about to get chewed out.

The result would have turned me into a non-believer in superstitions if I'd already decided that they came true.

"Hi, Rory," Justin said. His tone would have warned me if my own thoughts hadn't. "Feel like joining me for lunch in a little while? There's something I want to talk with you about."

"Like the op-ed piece in the latest *Destiny Star*?" I felt my lips curl in anticipation.

"How did you guess?"

———

Believe it or not, I had a wonderful time for the rest of the morning.

At least I did after I turned the ringer on my phone off. Before I did, I received another call, this time from Serina at the Rainbow B&B.

She'd seen the op-ed piece. "That's about you, isn't it?" she asked.

"I'd guess it is," I said as noncommittally as I could.

She gushed over it for a while, then said, "Are you really trying to figure out who killed Tarzal?"

"Parts of the story are exaggerated," was my only answer. Would she want me to help—or was she the killer?

I didn't have an answer.

That's when I turned the ringtone off. I kept the phone in the pocket of my slacks, so when it vibrated I knew when I received calls—a couple more. When I checked to see who they were from, they were local.

Which meant I didn't want to talk to them. Not now, at least. But one was from Arlen. The other was from Carolyn. I figured I'd call her back, since I liked her and thought we might become friends. She might even commiserate with me over the article. Arlen? Not so much.

But while that was going on, I waited on several families visiting Destiny with their dogs—one with a pit bull mix, and another with an outgoing shih tzu who made friends immediately with Pluckie. Both groups seemed to enjoy spending money on dog supplies related to superstitions.

Millie arrived—and Jeri pointed out the article to her, so she read it and gave me a bit of sympathy until Jeri and she took off together for their habitual coffee outing. On their return, I got to work with Jeri in the back room unpacking crates of new inventory that had been ordered specifically for sale at the Lucky Dog.

That was how I finally decided on which amulet to wear. I'd been pondering it ever since I'd learned from Justin that, because this was Destiny, even cops wore some kind of talisman around their necks. He'd shown me his acorn.

As it turned out, my choice was obvious. I'd looked at all the amulets and charms sold at the Lucky Dog Boutique before. They all were attractive and portrayed superstitions relating to animals.

But that was before this latest shipment came in. It contained many charms that looked familiar to me.

It also contained one I hadn't seen before. If I were truly superstitious, I'd have figured I was fated to get this amulet. It was about the size of a silver dollar, but it was made out of hematite—which is a type of iron ore, according to the informative description that had been shipped with it. Also included on that sheet was the statement that people who wore hematite were reputed to be brave, motivated, and creative.

But most important is that the talisman I chose just happened to be in the shape of a dog's head. A black spaniel's head, to be precise. Pluckie's tail and feet were white, but her face was black. The face on the amulet looked exactly like hers.

"See this, Pluckie?" I crowed, holding out the charm so she could sniff it. Of course I bought a chain, too.

"It's perfect!" Jeri confirmed as I put on my new necklace.

"Absolutely," Millie agreed.

I didn't have to say anything. I already knew it was perfect.

Did I feel braver, more motivated or more creative? Who knew?

And had this been part of the inventory received that day because I was looking for the right choice?

I couldn't say it hadn't.

I'd already made a quick trip upstairs to say good morning to Martha . . . and, yes, bring her a paper. I called her before I left to meet Justin and told her about my new acquisition.

"That's wonderful, Rory," she said. "Especially since—well, you know it's bad luck, don't you, to have too much said about you that's complimentary?"

I knew she was referring to the article. "If it truly is complimentary, maybe," I said. "But good compliments are what lots of people like movie stars and politicians want all the time, and they don't suffer bad luck for it." Or did they? Very few stayed at the top of their professions forever, let alone very long.

"Well, just be sure to knock on wood often, especially today," Martha said. "And have fun at lunch."

I figured I'd also squeeze my new talisman.

———

On our way walking toward the Apple-a-Day Café, where Pluckie and I were to meet Justin, I saw Preston Kunningham entering the Broken Mirror Bookstore with a couple of people from the typically crowded sidewalk. Customers?

He saw me, too, and stopped. "Hello, Rory," he said, then slipped away from his customers and walked toward Pluckie and me.

"Hi, Preston." I felt my back stiffen since his expression looked both sympathetic and worried.

My assumption? He, too, had read the *Destiny Star* article.

Which proved to be true. He took me aside on the sidewalk, both of us avoiding a group of young men who could have been basketball players here to enhance their luck. Some were as tall as Tarzal had been. After stooping to greet Pluckie, Preston said solemnly, "I assume you know about the opinion piece in the local newspaper." He was dressed in his obligatory suit, and I thought his face appeared a little less strained than the last time I'd seen him—right after Tarzal's murder.

"Yes, I've seen it," I admitted, waiting for his reaction.

"Are you really trying to determine who killed my poor Tarzal?" He chewed at his bottom lip as if attempting not to cry.

"I'm just trying to help Martha," I said without exactly answering. "I'm sure she's innocent."

"I hope so," he said. "But if she is—well, you need to be careful, Rory. Maybe even make it clear that you're backing off anything that resembles conducting your own investigation. What if it's not Martha but someone else who . . . who . . ." He inhaled deeply, then continued. "Well, you know. But if whoever did that horrible deed gets worried about you—well, you just need to be careful. The best thing would be just to retreat and let the police do their job."

I laughed ironically. "Guess who I'm about to have lunch with now."

"Chief Halbertson?"

Guess my friendship with the police chief wasn't exactly a secret, either, around here.

"That's right. And I think he's going to bawl me out for what's in that story."

"Then you will stop?"

"Don't worry about me, Preston. I won't do anything I shouldn't. And right now, I'm even wearing a new good luck talisman." I showed him my new dog charm. "But thanks for your advice."

————

Justin was waiting for us on the patio at the Apple-a-Day Café. I wasn't sure how long he had been at the busy restaurant, where all the other tables were filled both inside and here, or if he'd again been given special dispensation as the police chief. In any event, we had the most private location possible among the crowd.

"Hi, Rory," he said, rising to pull out my chair at the small corner table. He also bent down to give Pluckie a quick head rub.

I sat. He took his own chair across from me.

Outside, I couldn't look at the artwork on the walls as a diversion. And the seat I took faced only Justin. Everyone else was behind me.

Almost as an impulse, my hand went up to stroke my new dog charm as if for luck.

"Hey," Justin said, noticing it right away. His blue eyes locked on it, and then rose to meet my gaze. "I like it." He pulled his own acorn amulet from beneath his blue button-down shirt and squeezed it slightly. "Now we should both be full of luck for the afternoon."

"Good or bad?" I asked dryly.

"Good, of course."

I wished the look he gave me then wasn't so intense. It was midday, so his face only hinted of the dark beard beneath the skin. He'd have made a wonderful actor playing the role of the handsome, nononsense police chief of some small town, but he was real. Very real. And I braced myself for the conversation I knew was upcoming.

A server came over and took our drink orders. I decided on sparkling water, and Justin asked for coffee. Great. As if he wasn't already wired to give me a hard time, he'd also have more caffeine in his system to make him even edgier.

Heck. I didn't have to be here. I could have refused to meet him.

But since Pluckie and I were here, I decided I would take control of this conversation before Justin did.

I first studied the menu briefly. I wasn't very hungry but decided on a burger and a salad. A good- and bad-for-you meal. Just like this conversation was likely to be both good and bad for me.

What superstitions might apply?

I closed the menu and watched Justin as he concentrated on reading his. When he looked up, his expression tightened, as if he could read what I was thinking on my face. Maybe he could.

"Thanks for—" he began.

"—Nothing," I finished. "I mean, I have an idea what you want to say to me, Justin. I read that article in the *Destiny Star*. I didn't agree to it, nor did I agree with much in it. Although unfortunately a lot of it was probably true. If what you wanted to talk to me about was to tell me to back off, I get it. But will I do it? Honestly, I don't know. What if the killer decides to make sure I don't catch him or her? If I tell you that I'll stop my own stupid little investigation, are you going to tell the murderer so whoever it is will leave me alone?"

His eyes widened—and unfortunately that was when our server came over to take our orders.

At my low-key tirade, Pluckie had sat up at my feet and leaned against my leg, as if to show that she was there for me, no matter what was going on. I snugged her tightly against me, but when Justin and I were alone again—or as alone as we could be on a patio full of diners—I gave her a quick pat and she lay back down.

"Well," Justin finally said. "At least I know your position now. And if you thought I was going to bawl you out for snooping more into the murder investigation, believe me, I thought about it. But I also knew it would do neither of us any good."

He paused, still looking at me.

"Really?" I inquired skeptically.

"No, I won't scold you. And it sounds as if I don't really have to warn you. You're already in a potentially difficult situation. The one thing I want to make sure of here is that you feel free to talk to me. To tell me what's going on, what's on your mind. And let me know if you do run into anything that could lead to the killer." As I opened my mouth to speak—and express my amazement at his attitude—he lifted his hand as if to silence me. "Now, don't take that as my permission for you to keep butting in or snooping around. If I thought you'd listen, I'd tell you—again—to back off. But as much as I'd like to solve the case and bring the suspect into custody, I want even more for you to stay safe."

I felt the hard set to my eyes soften, my head cock slightly as I considered what to say next. "I appreciate that, Justin," I finally said. "And believe me, I want to stay safe, too. If I thought it was the right thing to do, I'd leave now and forget about Destiny and superstitions and their reality. But I ... well, I like it here. I'm beginning to make friends, and I'm having such fun running the Lucky Dog. I'll try to keep things low key from now on. Although—"

"Although?" His smile suggested irony, and it drew a smile from me, too.

"Will you promise you won't arrest Martha?"

He laughed. "For now. At least not until we've got the evidence we'd need to convict her."

"No, it's someone else," I said insistently.

"I really hope you're right," he replied.

TWENTY-FOUR

THE REST OF OUR meal was all good. The food, sure. The company even better, once we got off the topic of the op-ed piece, and me, and what I was doing to potentially get in Justin's way.

And how the story—no, what I was doing that it mentioned—might put me in danger.

We talked instead about how much I was enjoying Destiny. And how much Justin, too, liked the town, and why. Again. But even repeating some of the topics seemed fine.

Partly because I was enjoying his company.

That didn't mean I was flirting. Or stomping on my memories of Warren.

I was just getting on with my life as best I could.

We were there for quite a while. I ordered coffee and a small dessert—a slice of apple pie to share. What better choice could there be at the Apple-a-Day Café? I hoped it would keep the doctor away as the old rhyme foretold, and I didn't see any bubbles in my coffee.

Eventually, it was time to leave. I'd noticed the sounds of conversation ebbing as we ate, but being seated with my back toward the crowd, when we got up to leave I was still somewhat surprised to see that the patio had only half as many customers then as when we'd started out.

Pluckie rose and stretched, then remained at my side as we departed. Justin walked us back to the Rainbow B&B, and it was late enough that it would be Pluckie's last sojourn outside for the evening.

I was glad my dog and I were staying in an active B&B, where people would probably notice if anyone else visited our room. Not that I was ready yet for any kind of relationship with a man, but that gave me another excuse for not inviting Justin upstairs despite how well our evening had gone.

"I'll be in touch," he said as I pulled out my key card to open the front door.

"Good," I started to say, but my word was halved when Justin put his lips on mine in a short but somewhat sexy good night kiss.

I didn't shove him away. In fact, I joined in the kiss.

But I was relieved to turn and open the door and hurry inside with Pluckie.

———

The next morning, Pluckie and I got up early and followed what had become our usual routine, including a walk first thing, followed by my showering and getting dressed for a day of work at the store, and then, on the way out, a quick breakfast of Serina's excellent B&B food.

Usual routine? Heck, we'd only been here for a little over a week.

And … this was actually a day of note—exactly one week after I'd gone to the Destiny Welcome. That night was when Tarzal had been murdered.

Before we left, Serina accompanied us to the lobby. "Are you okay after—well, let's just call it what the *Destiny Star* didn't say about you?"

"Yes, in fact I'm more than okay. I'm not a detective and don't intend to become one, but at least now the whole world knows that I believe in Martha—or at least everyone who can figure out who the nonperson in that article is. And maybe those who do know will come to shop at the Lucky Dog while I'm still in town." I didn't bother to tell her that, yes indeed, I did recognize that I could now be on the killer's radar, too.

When Pluckie and I reached the Lucky Dog a little later, we went upstairs to say hi to Martha. "I've been getting a lot of calls about your notoriety," she said, glaring from where she sat on her couch. "I probably should go downstairs today and run the store, get you out of there at least for the day, just in case."

"But I'm safe," I said. "You don't have any mirrors in the Lucky Dog for someone to break and use to stab me with their own bad luck."

That garnered a small smile from her. "Just be careful, Rory," she said.

"I sure will. And I'll stay lucky, too." I knocked with fervor on one of her antique wooden end tables.

Things remained busy but calm downstairs for the rest of the day. Lots of customers came in, mostly tourists suitably impressed by the superstition-related pet items that we sold, as usual. A few other townsfolk moseyed in to buy food for their pets and casually ask about whether I happened to have seen that dratted article. And, oh yes, if it was me, was there any validity to it?

I wished I could collect all the copies and stuff them into the nearest shredder. Then burn all the shreds.

Unless there was some kind of superstition that doing so would bring the shredding fool bad luck.

Though I'd been kidding a bit with Martha, I knew I needed all the good luck I could get.

I also needed to let everyone in town who had a clue about the identity of the person in that darned op-ed piece know that I was just fine about it.

No one needed to know that I was upset in the slightest—let alone worried about my own longevity.

And so I checked online. Yes, a Destiny Welcome program would be presented that night.

Would I be there? Of course.

Wearing my new hematite black dog amulet for luck and for courage—and putting on as brash a facade in this small but important Destiny world as I could muster.

———

I hadn't shopped for clothes since arriving in Destiny—at least nothing much. I decided to wear the same silvery gray skirt and open-toed shoes that I had worn to the last Destiny Welcome that I'd attended. Instead of my nice blouse, though, I donned the one T-shirt I'd acquired, a red one with the logo of the Lucky Dog Boutique on it.

Serina told me that she, too, was heading for the Welcome. She wouldn't be available to watch Pluckie for me that night. That was fine. My dog, like me, had gotten used to our pleasant room in the B&B. I would just leave her there.

I even walked with Serina to the Break-a-Leg Theater. The crowd seemed even denser there that night than it had a week before. This time, I recognized more people in the crowd, although the townsfolk were undoubtedly way outnumbered by tourists, as it should be.

Serina sat beside me on the aisle, about four rows back. I saw that Carolyn Innes of the button shop and Evonne Albing of Destiny's Luckiest Tours were there, as were many others I'd spoken with.

No woman sat in a wheelchair at the front. Martha had stayed home this night. I assumed that coming here would be too much effort or excitement for her. Maybe both.

In any event, her nephew was present, sitting with his boss, Evonne. Both Jeri and Millie were in attendance, too.

The old Art Deco theater with the newer seating inside looked just as it had last week. But when the curtain was drawn back on the stage I noticed that the platform that apparently had been designated as Tarzal's sole domain wasn't there any more. Interesting.

Once again, Mayor Bevin Dermot, dressed in his leprechaun-like green sport jacket over plaid pants, strode onto the stage. He greeted everyone and, unsurprisingly, welcomed all visitors to wonderful Destiny, where he hoped they would all have the best of luck and a wonderful time.

I was curious who would be the town's featured greeter tonight, with the foremost expert on superstitions no longer available. It wasn't too surprising when Preston Kunningham took the microphone next and talked up the Broken Mirror Bookstore as well as the prized book still being sold there, of course: *The Destiny of Superstitions.* He'd carried one on stage and turned immediately to read the origin of the actors' superstition about telling their fellow cast members to "break a leg" since wishing them good luck would only jinx their performances, especially here, in the Break-a-Leg Theater.

He read a few more, but then someone in the audience stood and said, "Read the one about breaking a mirror being bad luck." It was Derek Vardox, and he waved a camera toward the stage. "And while you're at it, why don't you tell us about your poor partner and what happened to him."

Preston seemed to turn white in his muted plaid suit jacket. "Er ... well, all right." He'd had the other reading marked and had to turn pages in the book to get to why breaking a mirror was deemed to be bad luck, and how it could be countered by touching a five-dollar bill and making the sign of the cross.

"But Tarzal must not have been able to reach the five-dollar bills," called Derek's sister Celia.

"Or maybe Tarzal wasn't the one to break the mirror in the first place." I wasn't sure who that was, but someone else in the audience was speaking. "The killer may have the bad luck now."

I hadn't seen Justin come in, but he spoke up from somewhere behind me. I recognized his voice before I turned to look at him. "I think it might be better to speak of other superstitions, folks." He turned to scan the audience. "I doubt our visitors want to hear any gory details about that sad incident."

I thought he might be wrong, but I didn't particularly want to hear more either—not here and now—since it was unlikely the killer would stand up and admit anything even if he or she happened to be present.

I was still turned, looking toward Justin when I felt eyes on my back and pivoted. Okay, maybe that was an exaggeration. Maybe I realized Celia was staring at me as soon as I turned to face the front again. But she smiled as my gaze caught hers, and then she said, "Mayor Dermot, I'd like to read something from our latest *Destiny Star*. May I come on stage?"

Oh, no. I knew what it was. But why did she want to call attention to me?

Sure enough, she got the mayor's okay and read that damned op-ed piece. I felt my face redden even as my neck grew weak and I stared down at the carpeted floor.

She finished, "And that very special, luck-driven person who found poor Tarzal's body but is doing her very best to find answers and help our poor accused citizen is even here tonight."

She didn't name me. She didn't have to. All the people there who lived in Destiny turned to look at me.

No need for me to feel embarrassed, I told myself. Instead, I should be basking in the attention like a movie star. No, a superstition star.

I stood, drawing myself up into a proud stance, and looked around, nodding slowly as if I was royalty acknowledging the fealty of my subjects.

"This is Destiny," I orated from my seat. "The home of luck. All will be resolved here and the right person convicted of the killing." And then I sat back down and melted.

As if to sweep attention away from me, Carolyn hurried up onto the stage and began a monologue on the superstition of buttons. I just sat there, although I'm not sure I heard anything.

So now all the tourists, too, would know I was sticking my nose in where it wasn't wanted by the police—or by the killer. But I would continue to help Martha, if I could—unless I got so freaked out here that I fled Destiny forever.

Evonne also took the stage a little later and extolled Destiny and its tours. Arlen applauded her even more loudly than the rest of us.

The Welcome seemed to go on forever. When it was finally over, I slipped out of our row and looked at Serina. "That was an ordeal," I admitted to her.

"You handled it well," she assured me. "But—well, Rory, please be careful."

"Of course."

She'd already let me know that she'd planned to get together with some friends after the Welcome, so I watched her leave. When I got into the atrium outside, both Carolyn and Evonne joined me.

"Are you all right?" Carolyn didn't look at me as she asked, but glared venomously toward Derek and Celia, who stood near the door handing out copies of the *Destiny Star* to anyone who'd take one—which included a lot of people.

"Sure," I lied. Then I added, "But I really appreciated how both of you got the attention off me and onto superstitions where all the attention belonged."

We stayed inside the lobby area chatting for a little longer. They asked me to join them for a drink, but I took a rain check.

I needed some privacy after that.

Which I didn't get, since Justin, who'd been speaking with some security people in another area in the lobby and must have been watching me, was suddenly at my side.

"I'll walk you back to your place," he said in a tone that allowed for no argument.

"Fine," I said, actually a little relieved. I didn't really want to walk alone in the dark after I'd been pointed out as attempting to solve Destiny's brutal crime of the century.

And I was glad that I would be in the company of the chief of police—who just happened to be the very nice, very good-looking Justin.

The sidewalks near the theater were crowded but thinned out as we walked down Destiny Boulevard. We talked about this Welcome and who usually spoke at such things—besides the mayor and, before this week, Tarzal. The fact that Evonne and Carolyn did wasn't that unusual.

"Maybe I'll add that to my list of talks as long as I stay in Destiny," I told him, then explained my intention of giving weekly talks on animal superstitions at the Lucky Dog.

Soon, we arrived at my B&B. As before, Justin gave me a quick, sweet kiss on the lips, and I went inside.

I hurried up the steps to my room, figuring that, at this hour, Pluckie would be very eager for her last walk of the night.

I used my key to open the door, but she didn't dash over to me as she always did.

Frowning, I turned on the lights. I didn't see her on the floor, on the bed, in the bathroom ... anywhere.

I used all my self-control to keep myself from shrieking out, calling for my dog.

But Pluckie was gone.

TWENTY-FIVE

OKAY. SHE WAS SMART. She was curious. As careful as I always am, I must somehow have left the door ajar when I went downstairs to leave.

But I couldn't buy that. As I said, I was careful. I hadn't been in a particular hurry. I hadn't been on my phone, and I hadn't left Pluckie alone in that room much before, so the normal caution that I exercised in making sure the door was firmly shut and locked had surely been in play.

Did a member of the cleaning or other support staff come in and let her escape? Serina had been with me, so it couldn't have been her.

Didn't matter. What did matter was finding Pluckie.

I was already back out in the hallway. A lot of the other B&B guests had gone to the Destiny Welcome but not all. I didn't want to wake anyone, but more important to me was finding my dog. Surely someone had seen something. I'd already figured that staying in a busy B&B meant that anything different—such as if I'd considered bringing Justin upstairs—would be noticed.

A roaming dog surely would be, too.

I started off down the dimmed hallway, heading first to the right, slowly passing the row of doors. I still wore the outfit I'd had on for the Welcome, and I tried not to let my shoes make too much noise on the hardwood floor.

On the other hand, a little noise might get Pluckie's attention.

"Pluckie?" I called in little more than a whisper. She was a smart dog. A young enough dog to have full hearing ability.

Had someone taken her inside their room? If she'd gotten out and the person didn't know who she belonged to, that could have happened.

On the other hand, someone smart would have brought her downstairs and used the phone on the registration desk to at least attempt to get hold of the B&B's hostess—who, until the last hour or so, had been with me.

"Pluckie? Where are you, girl?"

I reached the end of the hall and turned, heading back the other way. Still no response from my dog.

There was one more floor upstairs, and I headed there and did the same thing. Nothing.

I headed down to the lobby floor. Had she smelled food in the dining area? The kitchen? I'd fed her before I left, but she was a dog, and she enjoyed eating.

But I didn't see her anywhere.

I hurried outside into the night. Street lights were on near the Rainbow B&B and other nearby buildings. The streetlights here were the ordinary kind found in towns that weren't Destiny.

No sign of Pluckie.

I walked until I reached Destiny Boulevard. At this hour, it was a lot less crowded than during the day but there were still a few people out and about, including several who were walking dogs.

I probably looked like a crazy lady, hurrying up to everyone I saw, especially those with pets of their own, asking if they'd seen a small black and white dog loose anywhere. Or even with someone else, in case someone had seen her loose and gotten hold of her.

But no one had.

She was microchipped, of course. But for that to do much good, she needed to be in the hands of a person who'd take her to a veterinary hospital or shelter that had a scanner that could read the chip and find out my contact information. It contained my phone number, and as always I carried my phone.

I'd have to look up the microchip company's name on a computer and contact them. They might be open twenty-four hours in case of emergency. But I wouldn't have easy access to a computer until tomorrow, when I got to the Lucky Dog.

No, actually, it would be later this morning. It was already after midnight.

What was I going to do? Where was I going to go? I couldn't sleep without knowing Pluckie was safe. Having her with me.

I slowly returned to the B&B—and saw a car pull into the front parking lot.

Serina got out of it. "What are you doing out here at this hour?" she asked. She must have seen my panicked expression. "What's wrong?"

"Pluckie's missing." I told her all the places I'd looked.

"Tell you what," she said. "Just in case, I'll wake up the guests and ask each of them if they've seen Pluckie."

"Okay." That was nice of her, since she might alienate those guests. But I followed her first to the registration desk, where she got a printout of all those currently staying at the B&B. Then I followed her as she knocked on doors and talked to those behind them.

No Pluckie, and no further information about how she'd gotten out or what happened to her.

Serina allowed me to use her computer to check for the microchip company's information. I called and spoke with a real person, but although she said they would stay on alert, so far no one had called to report finding a dog with Pluckie's microchip info. No surprise.

Dejectedly, I thanked Serina and told her goodnight. And then I went back up to my room.

Not that I anticipated sleeping. But at that hour, where else would I go?

I changed from my skirt into slacks but kept on the Lucky Dog T-shirt. I'd be ready to charge from my room if anyone happened to find Pluckie and call the number on the ID tag around her neck.

As I lay there, leaving one lamp on, I couldn't help it. I was in Destiny. What had I done to bring myself some of the worst luck possible—the loss of my beloved, lucky little dog?

————

I barely remained there until sunup. Without showering, I grabbed my purse and hurried back into the hallway. A few hardy souls were also rising then, and several were also heading to the stairs.

"I'm the one who lost the dog," I said, keeping my tone apologetic. "I'm still looking for her…"

The female member of a young couple hurried toward me and took my hand. "I'm so sorry. I hope you find her right away." The man she was with appeared sympathetic, and I felt sure he believed I was out of luck.

Serina was already awake, too, and getting the dining area of the B&B ready to serve breakfast. "Hi, Rory," she said. "I've told my staff to keep an eye out for Pluckie. Oh, and although Destiny doesn't have its own animal rescue facility, you can tell the Humane Society of Ventura County's shelter in Ojai to be on the lookout for her."

"Thanks," I said. I had no appetite, so I decided to take another long walk around the area, and plan to end up at the Lucky Dog.

I also had another thought. Maybe Destiny didn't have its own animal shelter, but it did have its own police force, and I happened to have a contact there.

I called Justin. "Good morning, Rory," he said right away.

"No," I said, trying to keep myself from crying. "It's not so good. Pluckie has disappeared."

"What?" He asked for the particulars, and I gave him what little I knew.

I had just exited the B&B and stood in the parking lot out front, scanning it and the nearby street for a sign of my dog. I was upset enough even to look at the pavement, in case my poor Pluckie had been hit by a car and now lay there hurt or dying.

I didn't see her there, thank heavens. That wasn't proof that she was okay and healthy, but it was better than the alternative.

"I'm on my way to the Lucky Dog," I finished. "But I'm not going there directly. I'll be looking for Pluckie everywhere I can around here."

"I'll meet you there," Justin said. "Killer and I. Maybe Killer can help us find her."

"Thanks." I closed my eyes as I ended our connection. If I ever wanted a romantic relationship again, someone like Justin—no, Justin himself—would be an excellent candidate.

He knew how important Pluckie was to me. And he obviously gave a damn.

I was glad, at least, that I'd be seeing Killer and him soon.

———

Nothing. I opened the door to the Lucky Dog Boutique and dragged myself inside.

There'd been no sign of Pluckie.

As I entered, I couldn't help remembering the first time I'd come through this entrance, pulled along by my intrepid little dog who knew something was wrong inside.

Who wound up helping to save Martha's life.

Martha. Should I tell her what was happening? It was barely eight o'clock in the morning. It could wait.

One thing I was fairly sure of was that Pluckie couldn't be with her. How would he have found his way here, into the closed shop and upstairs?

Although ...

No. I was grasping at straws.

Even so, I did make my way to the stairway and call softly, "Pluckie, are you there?"

Unsurprisingly, there was no response, canine or otherwise.

I sighed and turned back.

I liked the Lucky Dog. But I liked it a whole lot better when my own lucky dog was here with me.

I thought about what to do now. Wander Destiny some more? Maybe. But I'd wait for Justin and hear if he had any ideas. Hopefully he'd alert all of his cops and have them keep on the lookout for Pluckie, too.

Which would be a good thing. Getting the entire town involved in looking would be even better.

Derek and Celia Vardox owed me, or at least that was my opinion since my current notoriety was their doing. Maybe they could put something in the *Destiny Star* about Pluckie. But since the latest edition just came out, I didn't want to wait a week before everyone learned that she was missing. They could surely add it to their website now. They had already told me it was updated daily.

Plus, when I had looked up the Destiny Welcome on the town's website, I'd previously seen updates on how Martha was doing. I'd also seen other notices on the home page about things that were happening—mostly superstition related. Pluckie was definitely involved with the town's superstitions. I'd go on line now and also request that a notice of her disappearance be posted there.

I hurried to the front counter of the store and removed the laptop computer from its locked drawer. I placed it beside the cash register and booted it up.

Fortunately, Martha's upstairs WiFi worked down here, too, so I had no trouble getting onto the Internet.

As I Googled the *Destiny Star*'s website, I heard a noise behind me. Pluckie! But when I turned, it was Martha, who'd come down-stairs.

"I thought I heard someone down here. It's awfully early, so I thought I'd better check things out to make sure we weren't being robbed."

She was looking much better now than I'd seen her since arriving in town, and apparently she wasn't having a lot of trouble navigating the steps.

Or at least she wasn't flaunting her difficulty now…

Okay, one issue at a time. I still didn't think she was guilty in Tarzal's murder. And at the moment, I really didn't care who was.

My first priority was Pluckie.

I told Martha quickly what had happened, turning away from her and getting back on the computer.

I saw that, to get something posted on the city's website, there was a link to click, which I did. I quickly composed something about Pluckie's disappearance and how there'd be a reward for anyone who found her. I wasn't sure how much, but she was worth a lot more than money to me.

When I got onto the *Destiny Star*'s site, I learned that the best way to contact them was via email, so I signed onto my account. I glanced at my messages there before preparing to send one to the *Star*—and stopped.

One right at the top was labeled, "Finding Pluckie."

The user who sent it was Destiny Resident, whoever that was. I opened it immediately.

And drew in my breath.

It said, "Too bad you haven't spent more time making sure that justice is served in Tarzal's murder, since Martha Jallopia is the guilty party. If you'd let the police arrest her and not made a fool of yourself, your dog would not have run away. She is near where the founders of Destiny should have built the town, and she could get hurt pretty bad there—or worse. Here is where you can retrieve her if you find her in time."

TWENTY-SIX

DIRECTIONS WERE INCLUDED WITH the email. They indicated Pluckie was up in the mountains featured in the tour of Destiny.

"What's wrong, Rory?" That was Martha, beside me. I'd forgotten she was here.

"I've got to go find Pluckie," I said, realizing that tears were running down my face. "I need to print this."

"Sure." She stepped forward and pushed a few buttons. I heard something mechanical in the back room. I hadn't even thought of looking for a printer there.

I hurried into the storeroom and looked around. There, on a shelf near the door, was what I needed. I grabbed the page and ran back into the shop.

When I got back inside, Justin was there, and so was Killer. "Martha said you got an email about Pluckie." He was at the counter and bent down to look at it.

"I did. I have to go. She's up by the end of the second rainbow."

"You mean where the town's founders went?" Martha asked.

I was already at the door. "That's right. I've got to go get my car." I turned, ready to run to the B&B.

"Hey," Justin said. "I'll drive. I've got wheels right here. We're coming with you anyway."

———

Once we were in his official-looking black sedan with the engine running, Justin got on his radio and reported to the police dispatcher where he was going and why. "Send some officers up there to meet us." When he got off the radio, he turned toward me and said, "No, they'll meet *me*. On second thought, I want you to stay here, Rory. We don't know what we'll find there. Better get back out of the car."

He looked at me, one of his most intense glances with those brilliant blue eyes as if just by staring he could make sure I followed his orders.

Not going to happen.

"I'm coming with you," I said firmly. "And if you don't start off now, I'll get out of here and grab my own car after all." I didn't like the way my voice quivered with emotion, but at least that should convince him of my determination.

"Rory…" His tone was the most ominous I'd ever heard from him, but I glared right back as I reached for the car door's handle.

"Justin…" I imitated that tone, ready to leap from the vehicle and start running. But first I pleaded with him. "Look, please get going. The more we stall here, the worse it could be… could be… for Pluckie." To my horror, my voice cracked and I nearly started sobbing.

I yanked the car door open but felt Justin's strong arm and chest span across me to slam it shut again.

"Damn it, Rory." He immediately pulled back, put the car in gear and sped off. He even turned on the red rotating light on his dashboard that identified this as a police car.

Only then did I glance behind me toward the back seat. Killer lay there with his head up, pointed ears alert, as if this was not his first big adventure with his human dad. Maybe it wasn't, but that was a conversation I'd save until later.

Right now— "Do you know much about the terrain up there?" I asked Justin. "I mean, this little map is a printout of one of those online satellite photo sites like Google Earth. It looks pretty rough." I swallowed. Even with this, how would we ever find Pluckie?

"I've done a bit of climbing around here as part of my ongoing training. But, no, I'm not entirely familiar with it."

And the information I'd received could be false. The whole thing might be a trap. Pluckie might already even be ...

No. I wasn't going to think like that.

It might even be bad luck to consider it. Although luck wasn't the reason for any of this. Some horrible person was—and I'd no idea who, or why, except that it could be Tarzal's real murderer.

That person must have dognapped Pluckie from our room at the B&B while nearly everyone was at the Welcome. No one had seen it happen. But if it had been someone I knew, when had it occurred? I started wracking my brain for people I'd met who hadn't been at the Welcome but couldn't come up with many. Of them, the one I'd had most contact with was Martha. And even if she'd improved a lot, I didn't see her as willing, let alone able to do this.

No, it had to be someone else—but I'd still no idea who.

With the police lights on, Justin swerved around cars on the town's streets. He may have fully ignored the curious and even angry faces on those we passed, but I noticed some of them, yet gestured no apologies their way. What we did was vital.

We even zigzagged around tour vans as we got on the sloped road up the mountain. The route was familiar. It was narrow and treacherous, even with guard rails on the other side. I trusted Justin's driving. I had to. He was a cop, so this was probably no big deal to him. And even if it was, it didn't matter.

Even so, I was slightly relieved that most of our climb, except when passing other vehicles, was on the side closest to the craggy mountain.

After we passed another tour van, I glanced back. We were high enough up that I could look down on part of the road we'd already driven on—and saw two cop cars following. Good. We'd have backup. Well, Justin would. I wasn't an official anything—just a distraught pet mama who wanted her baby back safely.

And then there we were, in the flat parking lot already occupied by a couple of tour vans. This was where Arlen had given his spiel about the founders of Destiny believing that they should found a town at the end of the next rainbow they saw, after the first that had yielded them their fortune in gold. A place of good luck? Maybe. If any of that tale was real. And for me, and Pluckie, as well as for those Forty-Niners?

That remained to be seen.

I naturally suspected Arlen for this but tried to keep an open mind. Surely most townsfolk had visited this area, too.

I quickly exited the car. So did Justin. A lot of people were milling around, presumably having exited the vans. Most were near the vista side of the parking lot, which was fine. I needed to go the other way up the mountainside.

"Show me that print-out," Justin ordered. I stared at it even as I handed it to him.

Best I could tell, there was some kind of path at the far end of the parking lot. One that appeared narrow, for foot-traffic only, steep and along the edge of the mountain.

And that was supposed to lead to Pluckie.

If it didn't? Well, I had to go check it out, no matter what. I began hurrying in that direction.

"Hey, wait, Rory." Justin was suddenly at my side. He grabbed my arm. "Look, you stay here. I'll go up there and—"

"No, I'll go."

"We'll both go, then." The frown he shot me might have intimidated me some other time, but not now. "I'll bring Killer, too." I wasn't sure that was a good idea since the path looked treacherous, but on the other hand the Doberman might be of huge assistance sniffing out my little spaniel.

When we got to the edge of the parking lot farthest from the road leading up the mountain there was, in fact, a narrow, well-worn but unpaved path leading from it. I couldn't see very far along it since it hugged the curving mountainside and some fluffy plant life grew around it—mostly a few sparse white flowers, as well as green vines of some kind.

The path was wide enough for maybe a person and a half, but too narrow for us to attempt anything but single file. I started to dash onto it, even ahead of Killer on his leash, but Justin pulled me back by my arm. "We'll go first."

I heard a noise behind us and turned. Some uniformed cops were joining us. "What's going on here?" said the first, a muscular-looking guy.

"The person who dognapped my dog sent a map," I summarized quickly, then followed Killer and Justin as they started to scale the path. Since he'd presumably been on his way to the station, Justin was wearing his typical nice-looking clothes, a blue button-down shirt and dark trousers. His black slip-on shoes appeared more dressy than utilitarian, I wondered how his traction would be on the slope.

I still wore my red Lucky Dog T-shirt, and the jeans I'd slipped on last night after taking off my dressy skirt. I also wore my work shoes, which was a good thing because of their nonslip soles—although that feature would be better on floors and paving than a mountain path.

I quickly caught up with Justin's back as he followed Killer around a corner on the narrow path. I wished I could feel safe walking beside Justin and hold his hand for reassurance—though there wasn't much he could assure me about right now. Instead, I remained behind him. If we ran into anyone coming down, that would work better, too.

Up and around we went. I breathed heavily, and the thinning mountain air didn't help. Was this all for nothing?

Where was Pluckie? Would we find her?

Of course we would. We had to.

I heard men's voices behind us as well as other noises like footsteps on leaves that suggested we weren't alone on the path. Justin's team of cops was keeping up with us. Would they be of any help?

It didn't provide me with any more of the reassurance I was asking for.

And then—there was another noise. Louder, cracking and thumping and frightening, from somewhere above us. I looked up—in time to see a large rock catapulting down the mountainside.

"Justin!" I screamed. It was going to hit him! I leaped forward and pushed him ahead since sideways would potentially cast him down the mountainside. Killer had turned back to face us and barked.

I acted just in time. The rock would have struck Justin right in the face if he'd proceeded at the same pace as before. This way, it still hit him, but in the shoulder. It came close to my head, but I hadn't thought of that as I'd tried to shove him away. It wouldn't have stopped me anyway.

"Ow!" he hollered. Then, "damn" and some other swear words, most known to me but a few not. He slid onto his knees, holding his shoulder. Killer edged up and began nuzzling him.

"Is it bleeding?" I demanded. "Are you okay?"

I was summarily pulled aside by strong hands that weren't Justin's, presumably the cops who'd been following us. "Chief, are you okay?" the officer repeated.

"Fine." But the way he spoke through gritted teeth and clutched his shoulder with the other hand shouted otherwise.

"Let's get you back down the hill," said the cop—Officer Bledsoe, according to the nametag on his uniform. "One of the other guys'll get you down and I'll go ahead."

"Me, too," I insisted. Justin might be hurt, but he was clearly going to survive, thank heavens. And I still needed to find Pluckie. If any of the other cops wanted to follow, then so be it. But I couldn't stay there.

It took a little maneuvering to get beyond Justin and Killer on the narrow path, especially since Justin was also being manhandled by his cops while hollering at me to stay with him, that his men would find Pluckie. I considered briefly whether to take Killer with me but figured the dog would rather stay with his man. And not knowing what the terrain would be, or how I'd get Pluckie down, I didn't want the additional encumbrance.

Instead, I plunged forward, wishing I could breathe more easily and that there was some kind of rail to hold onto for steadiness. But there wasn't. And now I was plagued with a new fear. Did whoever had stolen Pluckie shove that rock toward us? Was I just heading into more trouble, more danger, with my only backup behind me?

Probably. But I'd come this far, and I was determined to see this through.

And besides, when I turned briefly to glance around, I saw that at least three cops remained behind me. I surely would be safe.

I kept hiking upward. I wasn't sure how much time had passed, but it felt like hours. Probably no more than another fifteen minutes, though. Longer?

And then I saw it. And heard it. The set-up. The reason whoever had stolen Pluckie had sent that email that resulted in my being here.

In front of me was a leaning ladder. Its top had been roped to some overhanging plants. It covered nearly the entire path.

Walking outside it would mean being very close to the edge of the mountain on this narrow path. Too dangerously close.

Continuing forward would mean walking under the ladder.

Whoever did this must have seen the *Destiny Star* op-ed piece and known my mixed emotions about this superstition in particular.

And why wouldn't I just turn around, not take a chance on the bad luck of walking under a ladder?

Because, beyond it, there was Pluckie. My little dog was leashed to a bush, lunging and barking. If the leash came loose, her lunge could send her tumbling down the mountainside.

I'd stopped, and one of the cops was now sideways beside me. "Shit," he said, looking toward the ladder.

The others caught up with us. "You gonna go get that dog, Bledsoe?" one asked the guy who'd followed me and now was closest.

"Walk under a ladder? Hell, no."

The others didn't sound any more eager. Clearly, they were all Destiny residents and believers in superstitions. And would I trust them anyway?

As Bledsoe had said, *hell, no.*

I looked forward, priming myself to hurry toward my dog, no matter what stood in my path.

That's when I noticed that there was a black cat near Pluckie, beyond where she could reach with her leash, and it appeared to be taunting her.

It would probably cross my path when I went forward. But I couldn't let that stop me. Bad luck? This whole situation was bad luck.

You're a superstition agnostic, I reminded myself. I started walking again toward that ladder.

And then I heard the howl of a dog, as I had on the night Tarzal was killed ...

I halted only for a second near a pine tree and knocked on its wooden bark-covered trunk. Then I plunged ahead, right under that damned ladder. The cat did cross my path—and just then some more rocks started sliding down the mountainside toward me. They were smaller, at least, than the one that had hit Justin. But one struck my arm as I emerged at the far side of the ladder.

The path here was a little wider. I knelt briefly to give Pluckie a reassuring hug, ignoring the slight pain in my right arm. When I rose I pulled at her leash—which was as loose as I'd feared. She could have yanked it off the branch with her lunges and fallen ... and died.

No time to think about that now. I needed the leash so I'd feel safe with one of us leading the other back down the mountain. Carefully, I picked Pluckie up and tucked her under my left arm after unhooking the leash from her collar, aiming my back toward the hillside where a few rocks still slid toward us. I used my right hand to finish undoing the loose knot in the leash. My fingers got it free even as another stone slapped my butt.

Oh, well. Though it hurt like the other injury, that area was better padded than my arm.

I reattached Pluckie's leash to her collar as she snuggled against me. Then, still holding her, I strode back under the ladder.

Twice. Two times I had walked under that ladder. Did the second cancel out the first, so I wouldn't have bad luck? Or would I receive twice the amount of bad luck? Had knocking on wood helped at all? But was any good luck that may have been garnered canceled by the black cat?

Was this walk under a ladder similar enough to what had happened to my Warren that I was about to die, too? Or was that superstition simply a sham?

I had no idea. But the three cops were waiting on the path where I'd left them.

"Are you all right, Miss?" asked Bledsoe.

"I guess that remains to be seen," I said.

That was when I saw Justin. He was making his way up the hill behind those cops, clutching his shoulder. I saw some blood on his shirt near his fingers. At least he didn't have Killer with him. Maybe his dog, at least, had been taken back down to the parking lot.

On the other hand, it might have been a good thing to have him here, sniffing the ladder for a familiar scent or whatever. But as far as I knew he wasn't trained as any kind of K9 with special sniffing skills.

"What are you doing here, Justin?" I demanded. "You're supposed to be getting first aid."

"Yeah? And you're not supposed to be dealing with this by yourself, let alone walking under a ladder." He aimed glares at his subordinate cops, who let him get by them. "Are you okay, Rory?"

"Better that you ask that about Pluckie."

"Are you both okay, then?"

I didn't tell him then about the two rocks hitting me, or the howling dog or black cat. Or even knocking on wood. It was enough that he knew about the ladder ... for now. Once we got back down the mountain would be enough time for me to let him in on the rest.

"Yes," I said. "We're fine."

I raised my voice at that, as well as my eyes. I hadn't seen any motion on the mountaintop, but there were enough plants and overhanging cliffs to obscure anyone who might be there. Like everything else that had happened, I didn't believe the rocks had begun to tumble on their own any more than Pluckie had come up here by herself, set up the ladder, and tied her own leash to those plants.

And whoever had done this to my dog was going to pay.

TWENTY-SEVEN

JUSTIN WAS GOING TO be okay. As it turned out, I was worse off than him.

Not my injuries from falling stones. They were minor. And Justin did require some bandaging, antibiotics, and low-key painkillers.

But my psyche—that was what really hurt. Someone had tried to injure me, yes. Worse, though, was that they'd taken Pluckie and put her into a precarious position.

What if I hadn't found her there … or I didn't until it was too late?

What if they tried it again?

One of the officers who'd joined us drove us back to town in Justin's car, which meant the chief sat in the front passenger's seat, and I got the backseat with both dogs.

Yes, one of those superstitious officers, who hadn't volunteered to go get Pluckie when it meant he'd have had to walk under a ladder, was driving.

Never mind that I would have gone anyway, even if one of the cops had stepped up and volunteered.

And yet I was alive, and my poor Warren wasn't. Why?

We were driven first to Justin's doctor, whose office was near the hospital where Martha had been treated. As they checked Justin, I stayed outside with the dogs.

While I walked Pluckie and Killer in the remote neighborhood that looked like it could have been in a town besides Destiny, I thought again about Martha and almost smiled. Surely even Justin would be able to see that, though her health was improving, she wasn't in good enough condition to have set this up to harm Pluckie and me way up on that mountain. I still believed the person who'd killed Tarzal was guilty of this, too, as a distraction and a warning. That meant Martha was also innocent of Tarzal's murder.

Unless, of course, I was wrong and there'd been some other reason for this horrible situation besides trying to get me to back off from my now-public nosiness in locating the killer. But what would it be?

And also unless Martha had an ally who'd taken care of this nastiness. And who would that be? Arlen? I'd already thought he could be involved, since I knew his awareness of that mountain area. Even though the two family members didn't see eye-to-eye on everything, maybe he cared enough about his aunt to try to clear her of being a murder suspect by doing something wild to implicate someone else.

Yet that email I'd received claimed that Martha was, in fact, guilty, and I was getting in the way of her arrest.

So who could have stolen Pluckie and gotten up the mountain in time to set up the ladder, too?

Nearly anyone. Even someone who'd been at the Destiny Welcome, if they knew the site and had left early or had someone helping them.

Those disjointed and dispiriting thoughts made me eager to go in for my own medical exam—which meant they really grated on my mind, since I wasn't overly fond of doctors.

And I was sure there had to be a lot of superstitions dealing with health and physical exams and all other related stuff.

As soon as Justin came outside and took over canine patrol, I got my examination, too. Nothing major was found, so I was quickly released.

Both of us were done. Even though it wasn't a long walk back into the downtown area, I waited with Justin for his driver to pick him up and chauffeur him back to the police station. Soon, we both stood in the filled parking lot among both civilian and cop cars, each of us holding a dog leash. The canines on the other end didn't seem to mind but sniffed the ground around them.

"I've already got one of my best detectives looking into what happened, Rory," Justin assured me as Pluckie and I prepared to walk back to the Lucky Dog.

His best detective, like Alice Numa? Or someone else who hadn't yet solved Tarzal's killing but zeroed in on an ill senior lady as top suspect?

That didn't exactly reassure me that even this less critical situation than a murder would be solved soon.

But all I said was, "Thanks."

I'm sure he recognized my skeptical, sad, and angry state of mind since he reached out and grabbed my arm. The gesture must have caused him pain, because a wince darkened his face, making me want to touch his cheek in sympathy. But I didn't. I just looked at him.

As his eyes sought mine, I saw sympathy radiating from them. "Rory, I'm pretty sure this all was related to Tarzal's murder, and the fact that it's now known to the Destiny world and even beyond that you've gotten involved. I won't remind you that I told you to back off." But of course he had just done it by saying that. "I'm sorry about what happened to Pluckie, but I'm glad she's okay." It looked painful, but he bent from the waist and patted my dog's head. "And now, though you don't want to hear it, maybe you'll understand the reason better now. Civilians, even with the best of intentions, should not get involved in a police investigation, especially one as important as attempting to nail a murder suspect."

"Okay." I stared straight at him. "Suppose I've learned my lesson and have every intention of backing off."

"Do you?"

I didn't respond directly. "The thing is, now, I've been given one warning, but that doesn't necessarily mean that warnings or worse are ended, even if I figured out how to announce to the world, or even just all of Destiny, that I got it and don't give a damn who killed Tarzal. Especially now, when I'm sure you've figured it can't be Martha—"

"Now, look, Rory," he interrupted.

But I didn't stop. "Okay, maybe you do still think it could be Martha—or are using your publicized suspicion of her to throw the real killer off track." He blinked and stared as if I'd read his mind, but when he opened his mouth to respond I kept going. "Do you really think the murderer would buy into any protestations I might make now, figure I'm out of it and leave me alone? Maybe, but a person who's a murderer isn't all of a sudden going to trust someone he or she must somehow be afraid of."

"Then you're not going to back off even now?" His voice sounded ominous, and I took a step back, which made Pluckie scoot around my legs.

I recalled Serina's suspicion that Justin could be the killer. Interesting, especially now. My suspicions flipped a bit. Could he have set this all up about Pluckie and allowed himself to get injured to make it look like it was as impossible for him to be a murderer as it was for Martha?

Of course not. Right?

At the moment, I felt stymied.

Who was the murderer?

Who had dognapped and endangered Pluckie—and me? And Justin.

And was I really going to stop looking, even knowing that the killer wouldn't necessarily believe it and leave us alone?

"I hope you feel better, Justin," was all I said. I patted Killer's head, then Pluckie and I left.

Martha was still downstairs at the Lucky Dog Boutique when my lucky, rescued, lovable dog and I returned there. So were Millie and Jeri.

And Arlen. Interesting. I recalled my wonderment whether the two family members were, in fact, in collusion about some things, even if they didn't agree on everything.

But since my form of investigation had been undertaken to help Martha, why would they attempt, in such an odd and menacing manner, to scare me off? And why claim in that email that Martha was the killer?

Unless it had just been Arlen...He'd have had time to get back here while Justin and I were at the doctor.

"You found her!" Martha exclaimed immediately as Arlen bent to pat Pluckie's head and smile up at me.

From different areas of the store, Millie and Jeri waved and grinned, too, so they must have known about Pluckie being missing, but they were waiting on customers and didn't join us.

"I'm so glad, Rory," Martha continued, then tilted her head and looked at me. "I guess this is a silly question, but what's wrong?"

I supposed my anger and pain were apparent in my expression and perhaps looked out of place since Pluckie was with me. I'd found my dog. I should be relieved. Happy. Ready to get back to what my life had become here, a store manager in Destiny. Or maybe I could just head for home.

But it wasn't as easy as that. I'd found no answers, only a lot more questions.

"It was an awful experience." I described it, moving my glance from her to Arlen and back to watch their reactions, especially when I mentioned having had to walk under a ladder to save Pluckie. Twice. But their only reactions seemed to be sympathy for me. They were both either innocent or good actors—or maybe both. Or one of each, if only Arlen was involved.

"I'm so glad you're okay," Martha said when I'd finished my story. She walked unsteadily toward me and gave me a hug. When she stepped back, her sympathetic expression filled her face with even more wrinkles. I just couldn't believe she was involved at all in what had been done to Pluckie and me, let alone that she'd murdered Tarzal.

Of course that could still be wishful thinking.

And the sooner she took back full control of her shop, the sooner Pluckie and I could flee this town.

At the moment, that thought was more than welcome, even though before Pluckie had been dognapped I'd almost felt like I was settling in here for the long haul.

For the rest of the day, I kept Pluckie close as I helped at the shop, especially after Millie left for the day. Though Martha remained downstairs, she was clearly tired so Jeri and I ran things. Arlen tried to help at first but Martha seemed to resent that. He didn't stay much longer. His goodbye gaze at his aunt wasn't exactly warm and loving. But frame her for murder? Well, I still didn't know.

I was glad that we stayed busy. As long as Pluckie remained close to me, I didn't dwell—much—on what had happened. But when late afternoon arrived and things started to slow down, I forced myself to go into the back room and review our inventory. By then, I'd helped Martha back upstairs. And I preferred concentrating on how many stuffed black cats and toy rabbits' feet and bags and cans of Lucky Dog Food or Lucky Cat Food we had in stock than what my mind kept gravitating toward: Pluckie's ordeal, as well as Justin's and mine ... and Tarzal's murder.

I got an idea then. A smart one? No. I was certain Justin wouldn't think so. But maybe it would result in bringing everything to a conclusion.

To be fair—and maybe because I was a little scared by my own idea—I called Justin. I planned to invite him to meet me for dinner, and I'd tell him what I was about to do. Give him the opportunity to try to talk me out of it. And if he wasn't successful in that, maybe he could help figure out the best way for me to provide myself and Pluckie with protection.

But when I called his cell phone, it immediately went into voice mail. I left a message, then hung up. Maybe he'd gone home to rest after his injuries and turned it off. When I tried calling him at the police station I was told he wasn't there, with no details about where he had gone, but I believed I'd figured that out.

Well, that was fine. And I didn't have to do what I'd intended immediately. I could ponder it overnight.

Only, it didn't work out that way. After Jeri left and I'd called Martha to let her know I was locking up for the night, I went outside with Pluckie to follow through—and saw Celia Vardox hurrying toward me from down Destiny Boulevard.

"Hey, Rory," she said. "I just heard about what happened to your dog and all. I'd like to interview you about it for the *Star*."

I stood there for a moment, staring at her. And then, as she reached Pluckie and me, I said, "Well … let's talk about that."

"Over drinks?" she asked. "I'll buy."

"All right," I agreed, and the three of us started back down Destiny Boulevard. On the way, I refused to answer Celia's questions but just talked about how busy the streets were, as usual, and how great it was that Destiny was such a busy tourist town.

But my mind was reeling.

Coincidence, or fate, or some superstition I didn't know about coming true? Was there one that said that if you ponder something for a while and it's something that should be done, it'll come true whether or not you intentionally follow through?

Or was it the opposite—if it was something that shouldn't be done, it will come up anyway and bite you in the backside?

For the idea I'd been pondering was to follow up on that op-ed piece in the *Destiny Star* by writing my own response letter that, yes, I was acknowledging that the subject of that story was me. And that, if the dognapping of Pluckie was the result—the attempted revenge of whoever was worried that my snooping would reveal they'd murdered Tarzal—then they'd be sorry. I might have stopped looking if they hadn't threatened my dog, but now I was determined to get my own revenge.

And, yes, I realized on some level that a challenge like that could push all the wrong buttons of the killer. That was why I'd thought about telling Justin first.

But I'd talk to him tomorrow.

And I'd be cautious.

At the moment, though, I was choosing to look at Celia's request as some big, fat, superstitious omen that my idea had to come true.

TWENTY-EIGHT

Celia suggested that we head for the Clinking Glass Saloon. I'd noticed the place when I'd visited the *Star*, since the bar was nearly across Destiny Boulevard from the newspaper's offices.

"Sounds fine to me," I said. "As long as they don't mind that I've got my dog with me." I'd enjoy a drink or two, but for now—and undoubtedly for a very long time—I didn't want to let Pluckie out of my sight.

"They've got an outside patio like a lot of dog-friendly places in town," Celia assured me. "It'll be fine."

A slight breeze was blowing and it ruffled my companion's wavy brown hair as well as my own longer blond locks. I'd mostly seen Celia before in sweaters and nice slacks, but tonight she had on a short black skirt and lacy gray blouse. One thing that was still the same about her attire was its accessories. She had a large *Destiny Star* tote bag over her shoulder, and I figured it must contain her tablet computer, notepad, pen, and whatever else she needed to take notes. Which had seemed a bit strange to me before.

I wondered if I'd feel a little underdressed in my Lucky Dog T-shirt and slacks, although I'd never been to the bar and didn't know how dressy its patrons got.

On the way, rather than talk about her article or what she wanted to include in it, I asked if she knew what superstition was related to clinking glasses.

"The touching of glasses and the sound that it makes is supposed to ward off evil spirits that a person might swallow along with her drink," she said authoritatively.

Then I would definitely clink glasses with my companion this night. No sense tempting demons or fate, just in case that superstition happened to be true. And, yes, I still hadn't made up my mind about any of them.

Especially the one about walking under a ladder, now that I'd done it myself but with differences from how Warren had. Were they like the differences between tripping while walking downstairs versus upstairs?

The outside of the saloon was unobtrusive, except for its neon sign that showed two large wine glasses touching one another, with stems crossed. The windows were darkened, and even outside I could hear loud music. I didn't see a patio from here but followed Celia to the door with Pluckie still leashed beside me.

"Hello, ladies," said a tall man dressed all in black. "You can come through here with your dog, and I'll show you the way to our outside area."

The bar, nearly as dark inside as our host's clothes, was crowded and noisy, with conversation even louder than the music blaring in the background. That was another reason to be on the patio, even if Pluckie weren't with us—assuming it was quieter.

The air here seemed warmer than on our walk. Maybe it was because of the number of people who also occupied the patio. There weren't any heaters around, which was good.

We were shown to a table for two near the outside rail. The table was of polished wood, and the chairs matched it. Menus stood up from a stand in the table's middle, and the guy seating us grabbed them and handed us each one.

Pluckie sat on the concrete floor beside me, looking up as if she wanted me to order her a drink, too. Which of course I would—one appropriate for her.

"Happy drinking," our host wished us. "And don't forget to do what our name says and clink glasses for good luck."

We examined the selections, and when our female server, also dressed in black, took our orders, we each asked for a glass of wine—mine Cabernet and Celia's Chablis. And, for Pluckie, a bowl of water.

Celia reached into the tote bag whose strap she had hung over the back of her chair and pulled out her tablet computer.

"Okay," she said, loud enough to be heard over nearby conversations, "this'll both record you and let me write my own comments. I don't want you to speak too loud so you'll be overheard by other people, but I'll still need to be able to understand you when I download this."

That made me nervous. Yes, this was my choice, yet the idea of my every word being recorded and analyzed and, perhaps, quoted, nearly caused me to shudder. But, gamely, I said, "Okay."

Our wine was served before we began. We both grinned as we clinked glasses. "To learning truths," Celia said.

"And staying safe doing it," I added while scratching gently behind Pluckie's long black ears.

Then, knowing I was on camera and being recorded, I responded to Celia's questions. I described, while trying not to shudder, how I'd realized that Pluckie was missing, looked for her, and found instead that terrible correspondence on the computer. How I'd followed the instructions to visit the area at the end of the town fathers' second rainbow, way up in the mountains. Saw Pluckie beyond the ladder I'd have to walk under to get to her. The falling rocks that hit the police chief. My brazen move beneath the ladder, getting hit with rocks myself, then, at last, rescuing my dog.

And then I scowled so harshly that I knew my face would be filled with creases on camera, but I didn't give a damn. "Whoever did this should know I won't forget—and I will find them."

I almost smiled at Celia's horrified expression. She reached over and turned off the equipment. "You realize that you might only be angering whoever it is even more. Or at least presenting enough of a challenge that they might come after you again."

"They have to pay," I said simply—although I did reach into the neck of my T-shirt and pull out my amulet, which was now part of my standard wardrobe no matter what I was wearing. I stroked it with my fingers for luck. Could it also have ramped up my luck in saving Pluckie? "And if I just act scared—which I am, of course—they may just come after us again."

"Maybe not, if you stop chasing Tarzal's murderer," Celia reminded me. Her words and apparent concern made me cross her off my mental suspect list—even though she could just be a good actor like others I'd considered. And were her words a warning instead of an observation?

"Whoever it is probably wouldn't believe it even if you start filming me again and I act all scared and contrite and promise not to do it. So ... maybe I'm tempting fate and luck and doing all the stuff you're supposed to not do, especially in Destiny, but go ahead with your interview."

Which she did. I admitted I was the person featured in the *Star's* op-ed piece, and that although I recognized it wasn't my business I was trying to help a new friend, Martha, by figuring out what legitimate suspects there were besides her for the killing of her business neighbor Kenneth Tarzal.

"My intent is to let the authorities know whatever I find," I said. "Especially if I learn who endangered my dog." I bent down and hugged Pluckie on camera. Then I sat up again. "I don't like doing this. Not at all. I'd prefer just putting it all behind me. But I don't see that happening till the killer—and dognapper—is caught. So, please, whoever you are, why don't you just turn yourself in—for your own sake, not just mine. I'm a small cog in all this, but the police are after you. You're going to get caught, probably not by me but by the authorities."

Yet I knew the damage had been done, and I'd remain in danger. Would whoever it was come after Pluckie or me again? I would remain vigilant.

And I'd also talk to Justin about it as soon as I could.

———

Which turned out to be faster than I'd imagined. No, Celia didn't post my interview on the *Destiny Star* website as we spoke, but I knew she would soon.

She insisted on paying for our drinks, which was okay with me since we nursed those couple of glasses of wine—and the bill amounted to thirteen dollars plus a few cents. The number thirteen and I had always gotten along well before, but I knew it had unlucky connotations so I was just as glad not to mess with it that night.

Celia was nice enough to walk me back to the Rainbow B&B so Pluckie and I wouldn't be alone even now, before my challenge went public. And I wouldn't have to take Pluckie outside again that night, not after our pleasant walk back. Celia left as I unlocked the front door.

Serina was in the lobby. Even though I didn't completely trust her, since she'd been Tarzal's girlfriend, I did give her a quick recap of what I'd done. I watched her reaction: horrified. "Are you asking for more trouble for both you and Pluckie?" she demanded.

I picked up my dog and hugged her. "No, what I want is for all this ugliness to be over."

"It will if both of you get killed," she reminded me, but then she came over and joined our hug-fest. "I'll double check that all the outside doors are locked tonight, but I don't know if all the guests are in. Just make sure your own room is locked, okay? And I still have no idea who stole Pluckie from your room or how they did it, so we have to be careful."

Another person I now believed to be innocent. Not that I'd let down my guard around Celia or her.

I did double check to make sure my room door was locked behind Pluckie and me. I even moved a small chair from the desk area in front of it so I'd at least get some warning noise if someone entered.

"I know you'll bark, too, Pluckie," I said, patting my dog.

I'd keep my cell phone close in case I had to call for help. And was startled when, a little later, that phone rang as I got ready for bed. I checked the number. Justin's.

"Hi," I said. "Are you all right?"

"Yes, but I was going to ask you the same thing. Getting slugged by rocks tired me out, so I just went home early. I slept all this time so I just got your message. I know it's late and I apologize, but after all that went on today..."

"I'm glad you did." I planted my butt, now clad in pajama bottoms, on the coverlet on top of the bed. "You're not going to like what I just did, but I couldn't just sit back and wait to see if Pluckie was stolen again, or I was attacked, or whatever."

The friendliness in his tone turned cop-professional icy. "What do you mean?"

"Well, I just issued a challenge to the killer and dognapper. And I think they've got to be the same person."

"What did you do, Rory?"

I told him.

"Damn it!" His words were punctuated with a crash that suggested he'd punched something that fell over. "Don't you realize that someone who killed at least once won't have any compunction about doing it again to save himself—or herself?"

"Of course I realize it," I said. "That's one reason I called you. I don't really have a lot of money to spare but I want to know of a good security company around here that I could hire for a short while till we see what happens."

"The hell with a security company. The Destiny police force is going to be sitting on your back, Rory. Especially me."

I didn't argue, even though a part of me sizzled with resentment. I didn't like being watched or told what to do.

But I did like the idea of being protected. By the cops. And, yes, by the chief of police in particular.

Sure, I'd considered him a possible suspect—but not seriously. And certainly not after what he'd suffered to help save Pluckie.

Justin said he would pick me up after breakfast the next morning. He'd be sending extra patrols to the area even tonight, before the *Star* interview was likely to be made public. I was to be careful. I was to call him as soon as I woke up. I had the sense that he didn't want me to be alone except for bathroom visits—but fortunately that wasn't among his edicts.

"Isn't all of this bad luck?" I demanded.

"You've made your own bad luck," he said, then amended more softly, "or at least you're adding to whatever the killer may already have sent your way."

"Yes, but it's good luck for me that you now know about it. I'll play by the rules somewhat now, Justin, and at least keep you informed if I hear or learn anything, okay?"

"Of course that's okay," he exploded again. Then, "of course," he repeated more softly. "What's not okay is that you've upped the ante and made yourself more vulnerable. But now we'll just deal with it. And keep you, despite yourself, out of harm's way."

"Thank you, Justin," I said.

I only hoped he was right.

I hoped so even more later. In the middle of the night.

Pluckie woke me by stirring beside me—similarly to the way she had on the night Tarzal was murdered.

"What's wrong, girl?" I asked, feeling myself start to shake. Had Celia posted the interview already?

Was someone about to burst into the room and kill me? Did my dog hear or smell someone approaching?

And then I heard it—as I had before.

A dog howled in the distance.

This time, did it also mean death?

TWENTY-NINE

LIKE LAST TIME, MANY of the guests at the B&B mentioned hearing the dog's howl the next morning downstairs in the crowded breakfast room. They spoke largely in hushed tones, asking Serina, who was in charge as always, if it truly meant someone was going to die, as the superstition said.

I half expected her to make light of it. After all, she was the front gate to Destiny for a lot of these tourists and the ones before and after them. She could scare them all away if she said yes and informed any of them who didn't know that the last time howling like that had occurred in town, a citizen had been found murdered the next day.

Was it real? A projected noise? Where had it come from?

Hey, I thought as I took Pluckie outside. That part of it could be a good thing for me, at least. Tarzal might already have been dead by the time everyone heard the howling then, and here I was, still alive and walking my dog.

Deep inside, I attempted to shrug the whole thing off—but I recognized that I was scared. Even shaking. A real howl or not, it could presage harm to someone ... maybe me.

I saw a marked police car across the street and silently thanked Justin. No, I hadn't called him when I woke up. I hadn't considered it necessary. I intended to be cautious.

But I had exited the B&B warily, recognizing that it was absolutely necessary for Pluckie to come out first thing like this to relieve herself.

She wasn't self-conscious at all, and having an officer of the law observing her—and, for safety, me—was definitely a good thing. As soon as she was finished and I'd cleaned up after her, I hurried back inside the B&B. Time to get ready to head to the store.

It was still pretty early, though, so I decided to take my time. No sense walking on the streets until they became crowded with tourists. Safety in numbers? As long as I remained wary and aware of who was near me.

I grabbed some food to take upstairs with us, then fed both Pluckie and myself in our room. Then I looked on my smartphone to check the *Destiny Star* website.

Yes, the interview was already there. The posted time said it had been there since one o'clock that morning.

I listened to part of it. I sounded like ... well, me. But an angry me. A determined me.

A scared me? For those who know me, that might have been obvious, too.

Word had already gotten out. Apparently, a lot of Destiny's citizens didn't sleep, or got up early, and had listened to the interview.

Maybe they informed each other by phone or superstitious mind games, who knew?

One way or another, there were a lot of comments already on the website. Even Mayor Bevin Dermot weighed in, scolding a visitor to his town who dared fate and superstitions to harm her. He claimed he wished me well, and I had a sense he also wished me gone from Destiny.

Or was that just a ruse? Was he guilty of killing Tarzal to stop him from criticizing superstitions and the people who believed in them? I didn't recall seeing him at the end of the Destiny Welcome. He'd also have had enough contacts to set up what had happened to Pluckie yesterday, even if he decided not to do it himself.

I was beginning to like Carolyn Innes of Buttons of Fortune a lot. Yes, she scolded me a bit online, too, but in a way that made it clear she worried that I was jeopardizing my safety even more by going public.

Her concern was echoed by Preston Kunningham, whose comments incorporated the sorrow of what had happened to his business partner. He didn't want to see that occur in Destiny again.

Evonne Albing of Destiny's Luckiest Tours had weighed in, too. She made it clear that the area to which Pluckie had been taken was on their tour route, as was the Broken Mirror Bookstore and more, for anyone who wanted to see where some of what I mentioned had taken place.

Could she have set it up? Murdered Tarzal?

Her manager Mike Eberhart, whom I'd also met at Wishbones-to-Go, commented on Evonne's comment, as if to second it—and also mentioned that their tours might not feature the Lucky Dog Boutique that I managed, but it was right next door to one of their featured places, the Broken Mirror Bookstore. He was in essence telling people who might not know where I could be found in case they wanted to harm me. That didn't really matter, since whoever had stolen Pluckie knew at least where I was staying—right here. I didn't know Mike very well—but who said I had to know the person who'd killed Tarzal and set up Pluckie for him to be guilty?

And what about their tour-guide employee and more, Arlen Jalopia?

Enough. It was time for me to stop reading this and head to the Lucky Dog.

Maybe it would be a lucky place for me that day. I certainly hoped so.

———

I'd only gotten out to the sidewalk in front of the Rainbow B&B when a black car nearly screeched to a halt beside me, at the curb. I startled, nearly dropping Pluckie's leash—but I'd have thrown myself carefully on my dog to protect her if that had been necessary.

It wasn't. The car was Justin's.

His window rolled down and he leaned toward me from the driver's seat. "You didn't call me. But if you think you're walking to the store this morning, after the challenge you issued to our suspect, you're wrong. Get in, Rory."

I've mentioned before that I don't particularly like to obey orders. But as a sales associate, and then an assistant manager at a Mega-Pets, I'd learned to adapt.

This order I realized was for my own protection. That part I liked.

But the fact that it was snapped at me, as if I had no choice but to do as Justin demanded? That earned him an angry stare through the window and my not reaching for the door handle.

"If you'd care to walk with us today, that would be okay as long as Pluckie doesn't object." I bent, and Pluckie wriggled her furry little body in my direction. "What do you think, girl? I guess you don't mind taking orders from me, or at least you've pretty much always listened. This man told us what to do. Would you mind his company?"

By then, Justin had parked his car and gotten out. Today he wore his standard blue oxford shirt and dark slacks. "Oh, come on, Rory. What do you think you're doing?"

Pluckie hurried over to Justin and jumped up, her paws on his legs, her tail wagging eagerly.

"I guess it's okay for you to join us," I told Justin coolly. "At least Pluckie doesn't mind."

His glare might have intimidated me if I wasn't already so irritated. As it was, I just nodded at him and began walking down Fate Street toward Destiny Boulevard.

My spine was straight, my brow frowning, my mouth pursed. I thought about Warren then, and whether he would ever have issued me edicts the way Justin did.

No, my sweet, lost geek wouldn't have. But I also realized that I was equating the authoritative policeman with the love I'd lost.

Would I ever be ready to care for another man? Maybe. Someday.

But someone as officious as Justin?

Well, that I didn't know—but I admitted very briefly to myself that I did appreciate the fact that, irritating as Justin was, I liked that he was concerned for my safety, and Pluckie's. Especially the day after he had been injured while trying to come to my dog's aid.

We reached the shop. It was still only eight o'clock, a couple of hours before I'd open. Jeri was to be my first helper of the day, and she wouldn't arrive until around nine thirty.

I could possibly wake Martha, but no sense worrying her, at least not before the day officially began.

And I felt sure that Justin wasn't going to stay here.

He waited while I unlocked the shop's front door, then walked inside ahead of me. I expected him to do the cop thing I saw all the time on TV: whip his gun from his pocket, hold it straight out in front of him with both hands at eye level, and start yelling "Police" as he checked to make sure no one was there. He didn't—but he did look around in the shop, the back room, the alley behind it, and up the stairway toward Martha's.

"There'll be a lot of patrols go by today," he said, "so if you need anything, or something bothers you, be sure to check outside or call." He looked down at me, and this time there was concern and warmth in his blue eyes. "I'm worried about you, Rory. I know you're trying to help Martha and also help me, but I can't agree with how you're doing it. There are other ways besides putting yourself in danger."

"I was already—" I began, but then his lips lowered toward mine.

Did I want this? Well, yes. For luck and reassurance and—well, I just wanted it.

Our kiss was brief but warm.

"I have to get to the station now," he said somewhat breathlessly as he pulled away. "But I'll be back to check on you later. I'll call you now and then, so please don't turn off the ringer on your phone. And call me any time you feel even a little concerned. Okay?"

"Okay," I said, standing on my toes to give him a quick farewell kiss.

And then it was just Pluckie and me in the shop.

Or so I thought. But when I turned, I saw a black cat dart from near the counter into the back room.

THIRTY

It was no surprise that Pluckie saw it, too. She barked and ran after it. The cat slipped into the back room and disappeared before my dog caught up with it.

A good thing. The small feline hadn't exactly crossed my path or Pluckie's. Surely it didn't portend bad luck.

Was it the same one I'd seen after Tarzal's murder? And/or up on the mountain with Pluckie? Not necessarily. I'd noticed that all cats were welcomed in Destiny, and black cats had a special place in this town's hierarchy. Of course I'd heard there were caring animal lovers who caught all kinds and colors of strays and had them fixed so there wasn't an overabundance around—but I felt sure that black cats could get away with a lot more than the rest.

I picked Pluckie up and we both returned to the store's showroom. Lowering her to the floor, I pulled my phone from my pocket to check the time.

Was it only 8:15 in the morning? So much had happened already—including all those responses to the *Star*'s online interview of me. And here I was, all alone except for Pluckie after seeing a black cat. Maybe it didn't mean bad luck, but I shivered a little as I tried to shrug off my unease.

Jeri wouldn't arrive for another hour. I decided to do a quick check of our displays to see if anything needed to be refilled before we opened for business. That was something that the assistants generally did on their arrival before ten a.m. I needed something to work on that didn't require a lot of brainpower but would distract me from the rest of my thoughts.

"Are you okay, girl?" I asked Pluckie. She stood where I'd placed her and sniffed the air. "Do you still smell that cat?" I wished I could ask my dog if she could tell how that cat had gotten into the shop and understand her response. From Martha's, upstairs? From outside? I supposed it didn't matter. Having a cat inside a pet store wasn't unusual or outrageous, even here in Destiny.

I considered calling Martha but decided to wait till later. She might be up early today, as she was on some days, but in case she wasn't there was no need to disturb her rest.

But this was a good time to check our shelves.

I went first to my favorites—where the stuffed superstition-related toys for dogs and cats were kept. There were quite a few faux black cats there, along with the other items including rabbits' feet. On lower shelves, the items for cats such as wands to which representations of crossed fingers and horseshoes were attached were not as plentiful, so I started a list of things to check for in the back room.

The store's phone rang. A bit early for that, I thought, but hurried to answer. "Hello, Lucky Dog Boutique," I said into the receiver.

"Rory? Is that you? Oh, I hope it's you. Could you come over? I need your help."

It was a male voice—a frantic-sounding one. It wasn't Justin, but it sounded older than Arlen. Rather than guess, I asked, "Who is this?"

"Preston. Next door. I never thought—not me. But I need help. A demon is after me. I spilled salt, and—please help."

I knew the superstition of needing to throw a pinch of spilled salt over one's shoulder to prevent being attacked by a demon, but that was one I never imagined anyone would think could come true. On the other hand, a lot of people tossed spilled salt over their shoulders even without knowing what might theoretically happen to them if they didn't, simply by superstitious habit.

But Preston? Yes, he was a believer—or at least he made his living off the town's superstitions, especially those memorialized in his dead partner's book.

Did this have something to do with Tarzal? His loss? His murder? Was the killer now threatening Tarzal's partner?

I recalled Preston's posting to the *Star* article: worry about me. He probably wasn't a threat—was he?

I had to find out if he was okay, without being foolish about it. "I'll be there in a minute," I told Preston. I leashed Pluckie, not wanting to leave her alone here. And as we went outside and I locked the shop door behind us, I looked along the street. People were starting to fill the sidewalks again. A few cars were parked at the curb, mostly across the street.

I didn't see any obvious cop car either stopped or patrolling, but I knew I was under observation. Someone was probably watching me as I headed toward the closest neighboring shop. I wanted to show them where I was going.

Also, just in case, I popped a quick text message to Justin. "Going next door to bookstore for a few minutes. Preston needs help with something." There. He wouldn't be able to complain that I wasn't keeping him informed.

On the sidewalk right in front of the bookstore was a heads-up penny. The few people around us apparently hadn't seen it. I stooped, picked it up and thrust it into my pocket as Pluckie pranced beside me. "Hey, it won't hurt to try for a little more good luck," I told her.

The door to the Broken Mirror Bookstore was unlocked, so Pluckie and I walked right in.

The place looked much as it always had to me—a table covered with copies of Tarzal's *The Destiny of Superstitions* right in the prime center position, surrounded by an uneven myriad of filled wooden bookcases that formed a maze in the shop.

But I didn't see the man who'd called me, or anyone else, for that matter.

I watched Pluckie to see if she appeared excited or nervous or interested in a scent, but at first she had her nose to the floor. Then she put her head up, pulled on her leash, and barked.

"Preston," I called. "It's Rory. Are you here?"

I followed Pluckie around some shelves as she kept pulling me forward.

When we passed the last tall bookshelves near the jutting wall of the interior office, that's when I saw that the new mirror that had been hung to replace the one involved in Tarzal's murder had also been broken. Large shards were on the floor. Framed five-dollar bills remained mounted beside where the mirror had been.

This time, there was no dead body. No odor of death.

Even so, I picked Pluckie up to protect her paws again and, shaking, I pulled my phone out of my pocket as I turned to leave the shop.

"Oh, there you are, Rory." Preston sped toward me through the door that led to his storeroom. As always, he was dressed nattily in a suit, this time a charcoal tweed. His eyes were huge, and his silver hair looked uncombed in a manner I hadn't seen on him before. "Thank heavens you've come. I'm so afraid— It was like this when I came in this morning. I had breakfast in the back room first, and that's where I spilled the salt. A lot of it. I tossed a pinch over my shoulder but I was so worried anyway, and when I came in here and saw this—it's horrible!"

"What happened here?" I asked. "Chief Halbertson is already on the way here, but I'm going to call him again and let him know that another mirror is broken here."

"Let me show you something else first." Preston gestured for me to follow, and I hurried in that direction.

Which was when he grabbed me, yanked my phone out of my hand, and shoved me into the back room—after also yanking Pluckie's leash from me and slamming the door in my dog's face.

"What are you doing?" I demanded.

But I had a bad feeling that I knew: My snooping had, in fact, led me to the person who'd killed Tarzal and dognapped Pluckie.

Or not. Maybe there was another explanation.

"I need to show you what else I found this morning," he said. He was almost crouched at my side, no longer touching me. But he still had my phone.

"Not till I get my phone back," I said. "I don't know what's going on here, but—"

"But I know how fond you are of Martha. And she came in here this morning. She's the one who broke the mirror, who killed my poor partner. I was able to subdue her, but finding her here was what led me to spill that salt."

He wasn't acting consistent with what he'd said before. He also wasn't making any sense. In fact, he acted as if he'd been drugged.

Had Martha drugged him? She still was on some pretty heavy-duty meds at times. What if—

Preston hurried ahead of me and around some large piles of boxes labeled with book titles, including one tall stack of Tarzal's. And there was, in fact, what appeared to be a whole container of salt spilled on the floor near them.

"Look," he said.

I followed, avoiding the salt, and did as he said.

Martha was there, lying on the floor on her back at the far side of the boxes. She was unconscious, her hands bound with string in front of her.

I quickly knelt and touched her neck. She had a pulse, at least. I turned to stand and confront Preston.

Too late. He'd maneuvered his way behind me and threw his arm around my throat. I saw gloves on his hands. I started to gag. Could I go limp and make him let me go? I tried—but he shoved me onto the floor.

When I turned back toward him, he was aiming a gun at me.

"I don't want to shoot you, Rory. That would lead to all sorts of questions I won't have answers for. But, you see, Martha will have called you to meet her here—and she'll stab you with part of the latest broken mirror. Since you were not only still snooping but bragging to the world about it thanks to the *Destiny Star*, she had to stop you. She figured that killing you the same way she did Tarzal wouldn't point to her but to me once she got back to her shop and hid out upstairs. But I'll have come in here, just a little too late. I couldn't stop her from killing you, but I was able to subdue her. And, poor thing, she spilled salt so she was subject to a lot of bad luck." He grinned nastily. "She's such a druggy now that putting this all together wasn't all that hard."

"If she's such a druggy, then why couldn't I stop her?" I demanded, knowing how strange the question was. But talking was better than any action right now...

"Good question. Well, she caught you by surprise so it was too late for you, but I saw what she did and was able to grab and bind her." His voice was hard now, not at all the airy, frightened, strange tones he'd used before to lure me here. Nor was he still grinning.

"Like I said, the cops are on their way," I reiterated as strongly as my shaky voice would allow. I hoped it was true.

"What a shame. They'll be too late to save you from Martha." He kept the gun trained on me as he edged sideways. He picked up a large, wicked looking glass shard from the top of a nearby box—part of the mirror—and held at an angle. I had no doubt that he was serious.

What I didn't know was why.

I had to ask. For one thing, it might buy a little more time. Maybe I could figure out another way to distract this madman.

What superstitions were there that involved insanity?

"I don't understand, Preston," I said as calmly as I could despite the tremor in my voice.

"You should," he said coldly. "Like everything else, this is about money."

Not superstitions? Or was it about superstitions involving money?

"I get it. You wanted more."

He nodded, his gun still aimed at me.

I had to ask. "Why would you kill your own partner to get more money? I mean, he was the reason for the bookshop and its success, wasn't he?"

"Yes, but we could have made a lot more money around here, thanks to him. Instead, he was going mad."

Interesting, coming from this man.

"He didn't even stop his stupidity when he spilled milk and tripped on it and got hurt—obviously suffering bad luck," Preston continued. "A situation I planned, of course. He might even have figured that out. He was on top of the world of superstitions. The world-proclaimed expert. He knew they were real—or at least he should have known better than to question them. They were making us rich, at least till he changed. But he was even considering writing a second book, a tell-all about the gullibility of people rather than the reality of superstitions."

"Did he have reason to question them?" Maybe, on my possible deathbed, I'd find my answers about Warren and walking just once under a ladder.

Not that I intended to die here…

"He thought so," Preston sniffed. "He saw that things considered lucky didn't always work, and the same about supposedly unlucky things. But for either to be valid, you have to believe in them."

A rather circular argument, I thought, even if it was true.

The thing was, I'd started to believe more in luck since I'd gotten here. And in the validity of superstitions—at least some of them.

And now—well, I had walked under a ladder twice yesterday to save Pluckie. I had no regrets about rescuing my dog—even if it had resulted in the bad luck that brought me here, with a gun held by a madman pointed at me. But I hadn't died immediately.

Neither had Warren, though his death had happened fairly soon. But I now thought that the superstition of walking under a ladder, no matter how many times you did it, could be one of those that was real. Or not—if I managed to survive, which I intended to do.

It would help to keep Preston talking. And maybe I'd get more answers.

I was really uncomfortable lying there on the floor, so I shifted a little. I wasn't far from where Martha lay. There were stacks of boxes containing books nearby, but I didn't see anything I could use as a weapon or even a distraction.

I glanced toward Martha. "Why did you decide to frame Martha in Tarzal's death?"

"The killing of two birds with one stone." His brutal smile caused a shiver of fear to creep up my back. "Although that's a saying, not a superstition."

"What do you mean?"

"You know that thing Martha said about your black and white dog being an omen about a good business meeting?"

"Yes." I wondered if he'd gone off on some incomprehensible tangent.

"Well, Tarzal and I actually had planned to meet with her. We—especially I—wanted her to sell to us the property that damned pet store sits on. I'm trying to buy up a lot more property in Destiny, lease it to the right kinds of businesses that'll attract more tourists and pay more rent. That site's a good one. I also intend to buy the property along Fate Street behind this store, but Destiny Boulevard is really this town's prime location. Martha didn't want to sell. Tarzal was wishy-washy about buying. So, getting rid of both of them would help with my goal."

"So how did you set Martha up?" I had to keep him talking...

"I didn't know at first if I could," he said with a shrug. "But when I got to our shop early that morning I peeked in at the Lucky Dog and there she was, downstairs. She looked reasonably steady, though I saw her chug some pills down with water. The timing was perfect."

"So you killed your own partner." I was disgusted and worried. I carefully stuck my hand in my pocket and manipulated that supposedly lucky penny.

"Of course, before he spoiled everything." Preston yanked my hand from my pocket. Seeing that it was empty he patted my pockets on both sides, then backed off. I guessed he wasn't concerned whether any change in my pockets included a lucky penny. But had his nearness, his touching it vicariously, negated any potential good luck?

"And now that he's gone, things are better?" I tried to keep the disgust out of my voice.

"Sure. I'm even selling a lot more copies of his book now that he's an apparent martyr to superstitions. I'm winning all the way." He glared at me. "But I don't need any nosy amateur detective to ruin it."

I half expected him to pull the trigger then. "Didn't you hear that the coroner saw your face in Tarzal's dead eyes?" I asked, half in desperation. "They know it was you who killed him. And if you hurt me, you'll be their main suspect."

"Good try, bitch." He brought the gun up and aimed it.

But suddenly I heard the loud howl of a dog. It seemed to come from behind me, from the alley behind the stores, and reverberated through the room.

"What is that? I didn't set that one up." Preston's eyes bulged. "I fed superstitions by playing the sound of a howling dog over a loud-speaker the night Tarzal died, and on the mountain for effect, and last night, too, since I intend to kill you—and possibly Martha—today. But I didn't do that one."

He looked horrified. He was facing in that direction while holding the gun on me.

He gasped, and only then did I realize that the back door had opened.

Pluckie dashed in.

"No!" Preston shouted. He moved the gun to point at my dog. "You should have died on the mountain, mutt."

"You set that up?" I demanded, fury suddenly overpowering my fear. He'd nearly admitted it by mentioning the howling there, but … "You dognapped my Pluckie?"

His grin toward me was evil—and thankfully, for the moment, got his attention off Pluckie. "It was easy. Tarzal was Serina's guy. He'd told me where to find the master key for the rooms in case we ever needed to demonstrate a superstition to a guest. Nearly everyone was at the Welcome that night. I left early and sneaked into the B&B. No one saw me there when I grabbed your damned dog." He swung his gun back toward Pluckie. "I wanted you gone from Destiny one way or another. I thought tying her loose on that mountain and setting up that ladder would mean the death of both of you. I set up rocks to fall on the path, too, as a backup just in case. I was wrong—but I'll fix that now."

This time I was the one to yell "No!" I was immediately on my feet and shoving him, even as I grabbed his hand, fighting for the gun. He wasn't going to hurt Pluckie, not yesterday, not today, not ever.

The gun fired, but I'd gotten hold of his wrist so the shot was high, entering the wall.

"You bitch," he shouted, fighting with me. "Your own dog just howled to foretell your death."

"Don't count on it, Preston," I hissed, still trying to get control of the firearm.

Then— "Freeze," came a shout from the back doorway, behind Pluckie, who'd run over to lick Martha's face.

And Justin barged in, holding his gun in the way I'd figured he had intended this morning when he'd seen me into the Lucky Dog.

In moments, he aimed it toward Preston, even as I let go and backed away.

THIRTY-ONE

JUSTIN KEPT HIS GUN pointed at Preston until uniformed officers burst into the room behind him and grabbed the man who'd tried to kill me. They took his weapon and made him put his hands behind his head.

"Come out of here, Rory," Justin said, ushering me toward the door into the bookshop. "We'll let my officers handle this."

That was fine with me. "Did you call 911 to get some EMTs here? Martha needs help." I bent, picked up Pluckie who was now by my feet again, and hurried ahead of Justin out of the room—all the while recalling the last time Pluckie, and EMTs, had helped to save Martha's life, at the back of the Lucky Dog Boutique, though, and not the Broken Mirror Bookstore.

"They're on their way," Justin said.

Pluckie started squirming in my arms. "What's wrong, girl?" I asked—and then heard a crash followed by shouts from the back room.

"Damn!" Justin again grabbed his weapon, told me to stay there, and, holding the gun in front of him, hurried through the door into the storeroom.

Hugging Pluckie close to my face, I shivered at the amount of activity I heard—and the idea of what might have happened. Was someone hurt? Had Preston somehow been able to fulfill his intention of killing Martha? He'd missed out on me, but—

A knock sounded on the shop's front door. "Emergency Medical," shouted a female voice.

Still holding my dog, I got to the door as quickly as I could and opened it. "Come in," I said to the first of the two uniformed medics who stood there holding large bags. "But you may have to wait. The patient is in the back room, but so are cops—and something's going on back there."

I preceded them to the closed door. My turn to knock. I called tentatively, "Justin, the EMTs are here. Can I let them in?"

The door opened almost immediately. Justin's face was pale, his blue eyes almost haunted-looking. "Good timing. Come in. There are two people you'll need to check out."

As the pair of paramedics edged by Justin, I reached out to touch his arm. "Two?" Had Preston somehow shot one of the cops?

Justin closed his eyes and inhaled deeply. "The other one's Preston. Believe it or not, he tried to run from the cop who was leading him through the room and wound up skidding on a pile of salt that was on the floor. He slid against one of the tall stacks of boxes—boxes of Tarzal's books—and the stack fell against him. He fell down at an odd angle, and appears to have broken his neck. I think…I believe he's dead. But first he managed to say, 'Dog howled. Someone had to die.'"

Really? Salt? Time for me to close my eyes and bite my lower lip. "Oh, geez. He truly was—is—a believer in superstitions."

I couldn't just assume Preston was dead. And the irony that he might be gone, thanks to a superstition—and the books of the partner he'd murdered? Much too coincidental. And eerie. Yet was a demon involved with that spilled salt?

And was that demon Tarzal?

This was Destiny. And Preston was, in fact, dead. We learned that a few minutes later—yet not before a black cat, probably the same one, darted from the bookstore's back room into the shop, eluded the barking Pluckie after I put her down on the floor, then managed to get out the partially ajar front door.

———

Martha, however, although overdosed on her regular drugs, would be fine. We confirmed that a short while later, at the hospital. Justin stood at her bedside beside me.

He held my hand, and I grasped his, too. For friendliness and reassurance, nothing more. Although I really appreciated his presence now. And definitely before, when he'd saved me.

Martha was conscious by then. I wasn't sure if they'd given her an antidote, or she was so used to the drugs that her body somehow dealt with them, but even though she still lay there, looking weak, she opened her eyes.

Though I hated not having Pluckie with me, I'd left her with Millie and Jeri at the shop. I trusted the assistants more than I did most people in this town and had never considered them genuine suspects even before I knew who the killer actually was.

That doesn't mean I didn't give them explicit instructions and dire warnings if Pluckie so much as got into an extra container of treats while I was gone.

"How are you feeling?" I asked Martha now, my voice soft.

"Okay. No, better than okay. I'm no longer a suspect in Tarzal's murder." Her smile was weak but it lit up her whole aging face.

"Then you know what happened?" I'd hoped that the one benefit to her being drugged was that she'd have slept through the confrontation at the rear of the bookstore.

"Pretty much." She closed her eyes, and when she opened them again they were moist. "I kept my eyes closed, but I could hear Preston." She shook her head. "I really liked my next door neighbors. Both of them. That doesn't mean I wanted to sell my property to them. I liked the location and my apartment upstairs. They kind of indicated I could rent it back from them, but I didn't know for how long. And it's *mine*."

I nodded. "It's yours," I repeated.

She wriggled a bit, then used her hand to grasp a button that she pressed. The bed beneath her head rose just a little.

"You're a good guy, Chief Halbertson," she said, looking at him. Justin just smiled.

"He is," I agreed.

Martha looked at me. "I know you're a bit confused about my relationship with my nephew, Rory. Arlen's basically a good guy, too, but greedy. And interfering. I had him work in the shop for me when he first came to town. He kept telling me about things to change, more items to sell, how, if he was in charge, he'd make sure the Lucky Dog was the most popular store in Destiny."

316

That little speech seemed to exhaust her. She closed her eyes again.

"There's nothing wrong with that," I said. In fact, I liked that idea. I hadn't even started my planned weekly talk about pet superstitions that I intended to present tomorrow—Friday—night, and I'd had other ideas, too, for popularizing the store.

But I also respected Martha and presented suggestions to her in a way that I thought was helpful, not critical of what she'd already accomplished—and I had the sense that Arlen's approach had been way different.

"Of course there's nothing wrong with it!" The vehemence of Martha's exclamation startled me. "I want my store to be the most popular in all of Destiny. Everyone loves pets—and everyone should love the Lucky Dog Boutique, especially with your wonderful lucky dog around." Her voice remained loud but started to get hoarse, and I leaned down toward her.

So did Justin. "Sssh, Martha," he said quietly. "Just relax for now."

"I will," she said, settling back against her pillows once more, "if Rory promises she'll stay here and continue to run the store."

That startled me, or at least the timing did. Was she trying to use my sympathy against me?

"For a while," I said to calm her. "Until you're well enough to take it back yourself."

"That would be tomorrow or the next day," she said, "now that I'm not a murder suspect. But that's not what I mean. I want you to stay here permanently, Rory. Run the Lucky Dog Boutique and use your great ideas to build it up more. Those ideas of yours sound good, very creative and potentially useful. You know the kinds of things Arlen suggested?"

"No," I said.

"How about selling hair dye so anyone could dye their dog black and white for good luck? Or figuring out a way to bottle dog saliva as a salve against sores on the skin. Or other bottles of stuff that we'd market as pseudo–dog fat to fight rheumatism. Ugh."

I grimaced in response. "Ugh," I repeated.

A nurse came in just then to check Martha. "It's time for us to go, but we'll be back later," I promised her.

Justin and I ducked into the wide, sterile-looking hallway. Visitors and staff walked by, but it was a lot less crowded in here than outside, on Destiny's sidewalks. We joined them, walking toward the elevator.

We were the only ones inside the car down to the ground floor.

"Are you considering what Martha asked?" Justin's gaze, looking down from beside me, was intense, but did I also catch a hint of hopefulness there?

We reached the lobby then, so I used the opportunity to avoid answering.

"I'll walk you back to the Lucky Dog," Justin said, his expression still inquisitive.

Even as we started our stroll back to the shop, I didn't respond to his question. Not yet.

Instead, I finally asked what I'd wanted to learn from him for the hours since he'd shown up at the Broken Mirror at the most opportune time. Luck? If so, it was certainly good luck, on my part. Because of the heads-up penny?

"Why did you arrive at the Broken Mirror when you did?" I asked him.

His glance looked a bit frustrated, but he answered nevertheless. "I got your text, for one thing. And you know I had patrols going by the Lucky Dog to make sure you were okay." His tone indicated he recognized the irony in what he said.

We were still on the street where the hospital and doctors' offices were situated, so there weren't many other people around. But we soon turned down a narrow street that led us to Destiny Boulevard—not far from the Apple-a-Day Café. And a lot of people, as always, strolled along the sidewalk.

Justin explained that he had gotten a call from the cop in the latest car to come by because the officers inside had seen a black and white dog slip out of the Broken Mirror Bookshop's front door and hurry around back. I hadn't thought about it, but supposed I hadn't made sure it was closed when I'd gone inside with Pluckie —which turned out to be a good thing.

"They'd been with us up on the mountain yesterday," Justin continued, "and had been involved in saving Pluckie. They were pretty sure it was her. They told me they were going to check things out. I wasn't far away so I told them I'd be there, too. Soon as I arrived to look for Pluckie I heard her howl and followed the sound. That's when I found her, outside the back door. And when I listened and heard what was going on inside ... well, you know the rest."

"I do," I said softly. "Thank you, Justin."

"Just doing my job," he said almost gruffly, his side gently bumping mine in the crowd, but then he smiled. "Well, not exactly. I know your proclivity for getting into trouble, and I was damned worried about you, Rory. In case you can't tell, I care about you." I opened my mouth to respond, but he raised one hand. "I understand that you're not ready to hear anything and may never be, but that doesn't change anything. Except …"

"Except what?" I asked. My gut was doing flip flops inside me. On the one hand, I really liked this guy. On the other, he was definitely right. Too soon for me to get really attracted to anyone.

"Except I would love to hear your answer to Martha. Will you stay and run the Lucky Dog Boutique permanently?"

He stopped and turned toward me. He reached out and grasped both of my hands in his. I looked down at my Lucky Dog T-shirt and slacks. I was surprisingly committed to the place. I liked it here, and thought that since Martha was open to further ideas to boost business I could do a lot more here than in my assistant manager's position at my MegaPets store.

"Nothing is permanent, Justin," I told him, and nearly reached out to stroke his cheek when his expression became sad. "But I'm willing to stay and run the Lucky Dog for the foreseeable future."

And if it worked out—well, who knew what the unforeseeable future might bring? I'd been saving up some money while working at the stores. Maybe, if all went well, Martha would be willing to sell the Lucky Dog someday—and I might be willing to buy it.

Depending, of course, on whether I ever discovered the truth about superstitions, especially walking under a ladder. *Is that okay with you, Warren?* my mind asked. But like before, there was no immediate answer.

Or was there? I suddenly had a sense that my life was on the right track, at least for now. That I'd somehow received his go-ahead. That, if nothing else, his walking under a ladder had had some positive aspects along with the negative.

Justin apparently liked my response. He grinned—just as we reached the front door of the Lucky Dog Boutique.

I opened it to peer inside. The place was busy. Even so, Jeri noticed me and let loose of Pluckie's leash. My dog ran toward us, and I caught her, then grasped the end of her leash. "Hi, girl," I said.

"Are you free to join me for dinner tonight?" Justin asked. "I'll be able to tell you more then about our investigation into what happened with Preston and how he killed Tarzal."

"Do Tarzal or he have relatives?" I asked. "Who's going to run the Broken Mirror Bookstore now?"

"I don't know, but maybe I'll have answers for that, too."

"You've got all the answers, then," I joked.

"Yes," he said. "I do." His grin, as he lowered his face toward mine, was contagious, and I returned it.

And yes, I also returned his quick, though clearly heartfelt, kiss.

Even as I wondered if there was any superstition that involved two people kissing in front of a pet store that one of them now intended to manage for a long time to come.

© Christine Rose Elle

ABOUT THE AUTHOR

Linda O. Johnston (Los Angeles, CA) has published thirty-seven romance and mystery novels, including the Pet Rescue Mystery series and the Pet-Sitter Mystery series for Berkley Prime Crime.